# Have you ever seen a Moose taking a bath?

Story by Jamie McClaine
Art by April Goodman Willy

First Edition 2001

Library of Congress Cataloging-in-Publication Data
McClaine, Jamie
Have you ever seen a moose taking a bath/Jamie McClaine: illustrated by April Goodman Willy

p. cm.

Summary: Join the antics of a bathing moose who belly flops and sings his way to being a clean moose while reassuring children that bath time is fun
(1. Moose-Fiction.  2. Bathing-Fiction.  3. Nature-Fiction.
4. Stories in rhyme-Fiction.)   I. Willy, April Goodman, ill.  II. Title.
LCCN: 2001095024
ISBN 0-9709533-1-3 (Hardcover)
ISBN 0-9709533-0-5 (Softbound)

Printed in China

The Illustrations in this book were executed in acrylic on sandpaper
The text type was set in Americana
Book design by Scott Willy
Printed by Everbest Printing Company through Four Colour Imports, LTD., in Louisville, KY

For Fred, Maci and Graysen.
Dreams do come true!
I love you!

For Scott, Adrienne and Nicholas.
Your loving support
continues to inspire me!

Have you ever seen a Moose taking a bath?
You will giggle and snicker and out-'n-out laugh.
It's an absolute stitch; a sight to behold.
It's the same one and all from the young to the old.

On go the goggles
and nose plug pinched tightly
    this bathing bonanza
is not taken lightly.
    His scrubby-dub brush
and Mr. Moose Bubbles
    his ducky Bill Webber
and towelsies in doubles.

    He's ready, he's set
from tip top to tip toes
    bathtime's upon us,
get ready, set GO!

A run and a leap then into the air
with all fours spread wide and the wind in his hair.
He tips to the left and he dips to the right

then, OH NO look out!  It's a crash in mid-flight!
Oh what a shame, he was looking quite regal
'til colliding mid-air with Ernest the Eagle.

Hooves over antlers, oh what a crash
I opened my eyes to a belly-flop splash.
Confused, a bit dazed, but a shake of his snout,
brought quick back to mind what his bathtime's about.

Have you ever seen a Moose go rubby-dub-dub?
He has lots of fur inches that need a good scrub.
He dives and he dives and he rolls and he rolls
'til he's soppingly drenched from antlers to soles.

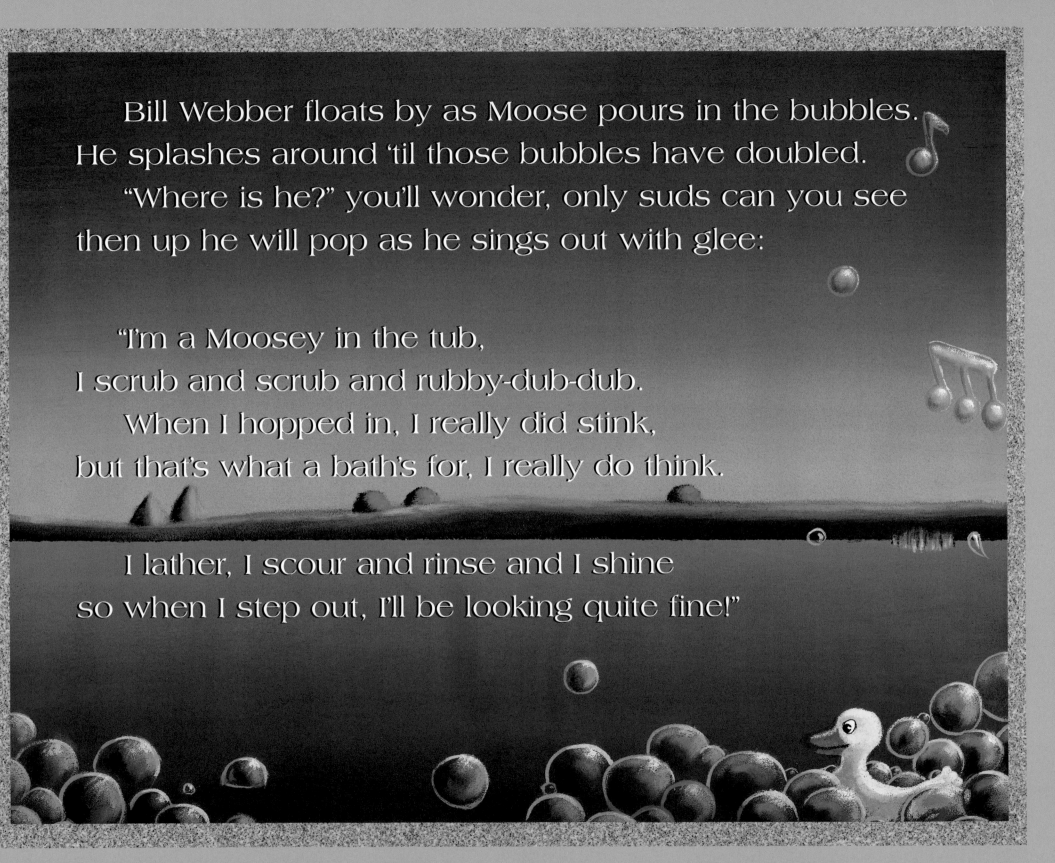

Bill Webber floats by as Moose pours in the bubbles.
He splashes around 'til those bubbles have doubled.
  "Where is he?" you'll wonder, only suds can you see
then up he will pop as he sings out with glee:

  "I'm a Moosey in the tub,
I scrub and scrub and rubby-dub-dub.
  When I hopped in, I really did stink,
but that's what a bath's for, I really do think.

  I lather, I scour and rinse and I shine
so when I step out, I'll be looking quite fine!"

You'll be laughing so hard as this act is unfolding you'll be roaring out loud while your sides you'll be holding.

His scrubby-dub brush
every spot it will hit
    from the crest of his head
to his hairy armpit.
    He'll buff on his chest
and belly and hiney
    then legs one through four
and hooves 'til they're shiny.

And lastly his tail and his antler head rack
then over he'll turn and sprawl out on his back.
I thought he would lie there and just rest and soak

but soon he was doing a rhythmned back stroke.
A one and a two and a three and a four
he moved through the water, what next was in store?

Then from his muzzle, the stream went straight up
like geyser "Old Faithful" the water erupt.

He stroked and he sputtered and sang out his tune
'til his skin shriveled up and he looked like a prune.

It's time to get out and get on with his day
his breakfast is waiting - a field full of hay.

He'll scoop up Bill Webber, his scrubby-dub brush
his Mr. Moose Bubbles, this bath's been too much.
He'll head for dry land and pick out a spot
he'll locate his towelsies of which he had brought.

And then as he's dripping, he'll plant down all fours
he'll throw back his head and let out a roar.
He'll start at his ears and give them a shake
it's a ripple effect, that one shake it did make.

Down his nose and his back to the tip of his tail,
I thought for a moment, he's starting a gale.
    For the water you see, it went up with such power,
it sure did resemble an early spring shower.

When every last drop of mere wetness is gone,
he'll pick up his Moose robe of which he will don.

He'll scoop up his towelsies and give them a toss
over antlers just perfectly they'll go across.

He'll look to the East
and look to the West
    he'll pick out a sunspot
that suits him the best.
    There he will lounge
and slurp on his leaf juice
    he'll look to the sky
and be glad he's a clean moose.

Have you ever seen a Moose taking a bath?
You will giggle and snicker and out-'n-out laugh.
It's an absolute stitch; it's a sight to behold.
So be sure and see it before you get old!

'14 May A78

**Friday** — original arrival ...

... hell. Pam, Tom & me ...
... hell. Pam ... arrived ...
... Mothers Day. finished ... for a ...
... good place run. ... 2:5 ... ...
... on nice rabbit. Kept weekend of Pam ...
... mother. ... A very good run over next three
miles ... ... best & best OK.

---

11 JUNE 78 — TRY — BELL ½ mile (14.2 mi). Temp 80° ...
**Saturday** — Marine 7/5 ... finished 30 in
... Timmy finished 9 overall. Made Room very 46%
all. Sheah run 4 mi race 116 over all. dear & Pam
... a good time. Andy & allison were w/ me ...
... place glue to extreme heat & run ... best &
publicity before 80 min race a course 1.1 mi ...
... ... ... ... 1.1 mi
... ... & no atmos
... nice ... & no atmos
... speak of. ... NICE Day ...
NYC 19 78 — 22.09   2:46:23   318 ... ...
... 30° too hot  pun amount 11800 ... Temp ...
**Sunday** ... & finished ...

... Manhattan (...) & andy ...
... Pam & andy Room ... present. Ron good
... pace had to pick up ... for Mase ...
... comet & drive ... Marriage ...
... turk ... Sean. shot Chinese food
... sheer ... Cruisalarm name ...
... cheer cheer. Working 4P to 12

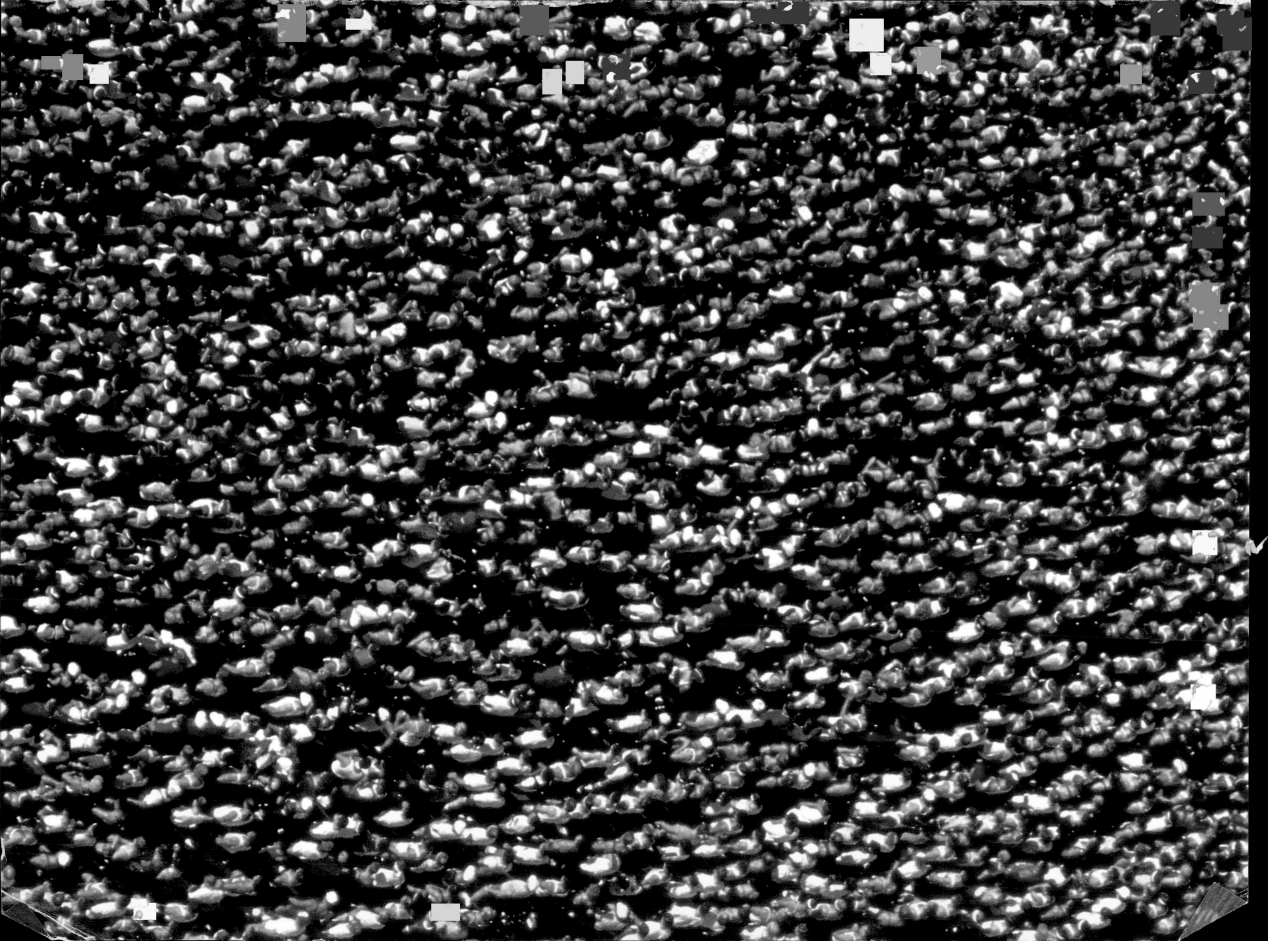

# The New York City Marathon

## TWENTY-FIVE YEARS

Text by Peter Gambaccini

Foreword by Fred Lebow   Preface by Grete Waitz

Edited by Charles Miers

Designed by Leslie Pirtle   Photography edited by Nancy Coplon

Published in association with the New York Road Runners Club, Inc.

RIZZOLI
NEW YORK

**ACKNOWLEDGMENTS**

This book celebrates the vision of those who have daringly dreamed that a marathon in New York was a reachable goal for themselves and for others. In creating this publication, it has been our great pleasure that both the pioneers and the most accomplished participants were able to share with us their passion for the event. Almost without exception, from the winners to the survivors, the New York City Marathon is the most memorable athletic achievement for anyone who participates. The emotions (as well as the words and pictures) that accompany such an experience are enthusiastically shared.

We must first thank Fred Lebow and Allan Steinfeld of the New York Road Runners Club for their rare commitment to realizing a historical record of their activities. Without the extraordinary editorial guidance of Raleigh Mayer and the professional acumen of Brian Crawford, the desire to capture the New York City Marathon's wondrous journey could not have been fulfilled.

The club's professional staff responded to the exceptional demands of such a comprehensive publication with great dedication and skill. We were most fortunate in working with photography researcher and editor Nancy Coplon, a running devotee and photographer; our thanks go to Nancy Rowe, Rob Hustick, Cara Taback, Sue Ellen Silber, and Don Mogelefsky; and to Barbara A. Withers and Gloria Averbuch for reading the manuscript and providing valuable suggestions. Marilyn Shaw, Dr. Andres Rodriguez and his family, and the entire race production, promotion, and administrative staff create the race year after year.

At Rizzoli, Judith Joseph and Antonio Polito supported our vision of a book worthy of such a spectacle as the marathon; Elizabeth White, Steve Sears, Sieg Widmer, Mary Albi, Robert Lemstrom-Sheedy, and Patrick Jennings helped to make it possible, along with Jane Dekrone. Jen Bilik, the unsung hero of this project, kept the steadiest pace when the distances to be covered sometimes seemed immeasurable.

Our particular thanks, also, to George Hirsch, Steve Jones, Eamonn Coghlan, Tom Fleming, and Markus Ryffel for their generous assistance; to Christoph Herle, Jim Grogan, Martin Ryan, Martin Hemsley, and Pete Schuder for their unerring advice on matters of road and track; to Alan Turner, Fritz Mueller, and Rick Shaver of the Central Park Track Club for supplying vital details and refreshing our memories; to Derek Pell, Jessie Adair, Jeff Kisseloff, and Merrell Noden for serving as sounding boards; and to Hope Carr and Lawrence Stanley. Photographers in New York and throughout the world generously cooperated in our search for the finest images.

Above all, designer Leslie Pirtle and consultant Woody Pirtle envisioned both the intensity of the athletic competition involved and the exuberant and festive venue that is New York City, providing us with a special look at both sides of this magnificent event.

Charles Miers
Peter Gambaccini

**DEDICATION**

The New York Road Runners Club, organizer of the New York City Marathon, dedicates this book to the hundreds of thousands of runners who have crossed the finish line, to those who have yet to begin, to the people of the city of New York, and to all the volunteers, spectators, and sponsors who make the five-borough event an unforgettable journey.

# Contents

# FOREWORD

I never take the New York City Marathon for granted. It opens my eyes anew each year and still boosts my spirits. New Yorkers and visiting runners have created an epic marathon that is an astonishing testimony to the power of human cooperation. It is a day of urban magic.

Pope John Paul II called the New York City Marathon "a fantastic event" when I met him in 1982. The fantasy would not be real without the brilliant technical director, Allan Steinfeld, the club's tireless staff, the event's thirteen thousand dedicated volunteers, and various city departments. The "teamwork" required by literally millions of complete strangers is a miracle that has sustained twenty-four editions of our marathon. As race director, I feel I fell into the right place—New York—at the right time, when the popularity of running was peaking.

The New York City Marathon showcases world-class athletes, but the race embraces runners of every age, ambition, and ability level. We have welcomed at least one representative from every state and participants from over one hundred countries—a true affirmation of the global camaraderie of the sport.

So many people want to enter that we could easily fill two marathons each year.

When I ran the race myself in 1992, it was exactly as everybody had told me—the five-borough New York City Marathon really *is* the experience of a lifetime. **—FRED LEBOW**

marathons, the first sub-2:30, and four world records. When the International Olympic Committee saw what people such as Grete Waitz, Allison Roe, and Patti Lyons Catalano could do in New York, they *had* to add a women's marathon to the Olympic schedule—especially after intense lobbying from pioneers like Nina Kuscsik who had put the New York City Marathon on the map.

Many people deserve credit for the growth of the peerless event, but we must point first to the industrious and ingenious race director, Fred Lebow. He shies away from the epithet "visionary," insisting, "I'm just a person who plans ahead. Not everything that we planned works." The New York City Marathon works quite well, thank you very much, far more splendidly than Lebow could have predicted back in 1970 or 1976.

New York City tends to hold itself in high regard, but today it actually *is* the world's running capital. Twenty-five years ago, before its marathon, New York would not have ranked in the top two hundred. The New York Road Runners Club, organizer of the event, has grown to over twenty-nine thousand members and sponsors more than one hundred races and clinics annually. The club's headquarters are one city block from the 1.6-mile circuit around the Central Park Reservoir—during its peak time, the loop is circled by five hundred runners per hour.

It took several decades for the Olympics to have the athletic and social impact the New York City Marathon made with its first five-borough incarnation. In the post–World War II period, the only new sporting event to have affected the American landscape as drastically as the New York City Marathon is the Super Bowl. But that football game does not have imitators on every continent, and participation is limited to about ninety large men.

The New York City Marathon is a show, with a chorus of twenty-seven thousand marathoners and standing-room-only audiences along miles and miles of sidewalk. The longest-running musical in New York is *The Fantasticks,* but these marathoners are the real "fantastics," and their long run, New York City's strongest advertisement for itself, is not likely ever to post a closing notice. —PETER GAMBACCINI

# MARATHON HISTORY

In the minds of most people, long-distance runners in the late fifties and early sixties were the lunatic fringe, small bands of puffing guys exercising in their underwear in public. The running scene, such as it existed in New York, was primarily concentrated on the city's northern edge in the borough of the Bronx, around Macombs Dam Park and nearby Yankee Stadium. By 1959, a cadre of stalwarts was staging an annual marathon in that area, called the Cherry Tree Marathon because it was held on Washington's Birthday and because a prominent tree on the course served as a turn-around. Race officials *assumed* it was a cherry tree, but no one could be absolutely certain. The champion of the inaugural Cherry Tree Marathon, in 2:38, was 1952 Olympian Ted Corbitt, who was also the first president of the Road Runners Club of America, New York Association, later to be called the New York Road Runners Club.

The race was held in February to serve as a tune-up for April's Boston Marathon, and according to Joe Kleinerman, a busy road-race director and coach of the fabled Millrose Athletic Association, "What we had at the Cherry Tree Marathon was a fear of freezing." Kleinerman recalled being chastised by the mother of a sixteen-year-old who suffered frostbite while running in the marathon.

By the late sixties, the Cherry Tree's future was imperiled by increased traffic created by a new highway ramp in the Bronx and by a proliferation of high-rise apartment buildings along the course. From the apartments' balconies, kids threw rocks at runners.

In 1969, reigning New York Road Runners Club president Vince Chiappetta began a campaign to stage a new marathon in Central Park. The park and its 6-mile perimeter loop roadway would come to be internationally recognized as a perfect running venue, but this was not the case twenty-five years ago, and the city's Department of Parks and Recreation did not warm to Chiappetta's dream.

By the following year, matters had changed. There was a new parks regime, and Mayor John Lindsay declared a ban on automobile traffic in Central Park on Sundays. And Chiappetta had met a fellow enthusiast, an aggressive entrepreneur from New York City's garment district, Fred Lebow. In the late sixties, Lebow had forsaken tennis for running. After circling Central Park's 1.6-mile reservoir loop for the first time, he was a convert and later noted, "I've never lost a tennis match since." His debut road race was a 5-miler in which the runners repeatedly circled Yankee Stadium. Lebow, who was in his thirties, came in next to last, beating only one competitor, a fellow in his mid-sixties. That man merits our eternal thanks. "I've always felt since then that if I hadn't beaten that old guy, there wouldn't have ever been a New York City Marathon," Lebow wrote in his 1984 autobiography, *Inside the World of Big-Time Marathoning*. "If I had been dead last in my first race, I would have been so discouraged that I would have given up running."

Chiappetta and Lebow served as codirectors of that first, very modest New York City Marathon, held entirely in Central Park on September 13, 1970. By 1985, 95 percent of the marathon's starters would complete the 26.2-mile jaunt through the five boroughs. This was not so in the early Central Park days—in 1970, only 55 of the 127 starters completed the marathon. The early fall date of the race was too close to the summer for runners to have established a sufficient mileage base over the warm months. Except for the 1972 race, held on October 1, the park marathons from 1970 to 1975 took place in September. It was often hot, and water stops, especially in the first year, were few and much too far between.

The course, four full loops of Central Park plus a smaller, 2-mile loop, forced the runners to negotiate the roller-coaster northern hills four times. These climbs are exponentially more demanding than any hill in the later five-borough course, which enters the park just below the hills and has the good sense to keep heading south. Most entrants either lived near the park or could leave their cars on its perimeter. It was easy to convince oneself, during the third attack on those hills, that one had suffered enough and it was time to go home.

Gary Muhrcke (left), the first New York champion, celebrated with runner-up Tom Fleming after the inaugural 1970 race.

Joe Kleinerman, here directing New York's predecessor, the Cherry Tree Marathon, was a New York Road Runners Club pioneer.

# 1970-1975

**1970** The budget for the 1970 New York City Marathon was one thousand dollars, and the entry fee was one dollar. Out of his own pocket, race codirector Fred Lebow purchased a few inexpensive wristwatches for the winners, who also received recycled trophies.

Gary Muhrcke, twice the winner of the Yonkers Marathon in the late sixties, when its status in the East was second only to that of the Boston Marathon, was a New York City firefighter. The night before the 1970 race, he has recalled, "We had a lot of fires and a couple of close calls, and I was up all night. It was a major decision just to go to the marathon the next morning. I wanted to go to bed, but we had three small kids and my wife wanted to get out of the house." A family outing in Central Park was in order.

As temperatures hovered in the eighties, Muhrcke wended his way up from tenth place after 14 miles to fourth place with one remaining 6-mile lap. He was first at the finish in 2:31:38, with nineteen-year-old Tom Fleming of New Jersey's William Paterson College second in 2:35:44. Fifty-four-year-old Ted Corbitt placed fifth in 2:44:15. Muhrcke was crowned with a laurel wreath fashioned by his wife, Jane, who would continue making such wreaths into the nineties.

"Nobody knew the marathon would explode," Muhrcke has reflected. "When I won, it was unimportant. But fifty years from now, someone will ask, 'Who won the first?' I'm lucky to have won it. I'm lucky I even *went* to it."

Muhrcke took disability leave from the fire department in 1973 after suffering a herniated disk on the job. His win in the 1977 Empire State Building Run-Up became a cause célèbre; many people did not distinguish between running stairs recreationally and carrying heavy loads in life-and-death situations. Having started a business selling shoes out of the back of his van, Muhrcke eventually became principal owner of the Super Runners Shops, with six stores in New York and one in Bermuda.

The Amateur Athletic Union (AAU), the sport's national governing body, had not yet sanctioned female marathoners, but the New York City Marathon progressively defended women's right to race from the very beginning. As Vince Chiappetta pointed out, "We decided we were a nongender sport. Anybody could run."

Lebow made sure that Nina Kuscsik, a well-established fixture on the fledgling New York road-race scene, made it to the inaugural starting line. Though Kuscsik had trained assiduously, she suffered from a virus and fever shortly before the September 13

22

**Connecticut's Gray Ghost, Norm Higgins, still ranks as the race's oldest male winner.**

**In 1971, Nina Kuscsik (403) and Beth Bonner (402) became the first women officially to run the marathon in less than 3 hours.**

race date. "It was devastating for the lone woman in a marathon not to finish," commented Kuscsik, who dropped out after 14 miles.

A mere one hundred spectators gathered at the ground-breaking marathon's finish line. There were cans of soda waiting for the runners but, in the era before pop-tops, no can openers.

**1971** There had been reports that an Australian woman, Adrienne Beames, had run a marathon in 2:46:30 in practice, but as of September 1971 no woman had officially broken the 3-hour mark. One prime candidate to smash the formidable barrier was Beth Bonner, a lean, bespectacled nineteen-year-old student at Delaware's Brandywine College. Bonner had placed 11th in the 1971 World Cross Country Championships and had run the Philadelphia Marathon in 3:01:42 in May. She triumphed in Central Park in 2:55:22, which was recognized as a new United States record. Nina Kuscsik was close behind in 2:56:04, joining Bonner to make history as the first two women in the world to officially run the marathon in less than 3 hours.

Norm Higgins, thirty-four years old in 1971, still ranks as the race's oldest male champion. He had the grayest hair, which is half of the reason he was known as the Gray Ghost; he was also a figure of some mystery in the close-knit New York running community.

Higgins, from eastern Connecticut, made the latest decision to enter New York of any winner in the marathon's annals. He was headed to a 5000-meter cross-country race in the Bronx's Van Cortlandt Park when he heard of the new 26.2-miler and opted for it instead. Higgins was easily the class of the field. His creditable 2:22:54, winning by 10:27 over Chuck Ceronsky of the Twin Cities Track Club, was the largest men's margin of victory in the history of the race.

In 1966 Higgins had run 2:18:36 in Boston; it was the fastest time to date on that course by an American, but he finished in fifth place behind four Japanese runners. His greatest renown, however, came as the coach of Jan Merrill, an archrival of Francie Larrieu and Mary Decker, who scored many middle-distance victories on the indoor boards at New York City's Madison Square Garden.

**1972** The unenlightened AAU finally agreed to sanction women as marathoners, but the national organization mandated a segregated start for the New York City Marathon; women were to begin the race 10 minutes before the men. Finding this unacceptable, the women who came to run in Central Park on October 1 staged a well-publicized sit-in at the starting line and would not commence running until the men did. "It became the only event where women voluntarily added 10 minutes to their times," noted Nina

Kuscsik, who spearheaded the strike. The AAU was subsequently sued for discrimination in a public place. In 1973, there was no separate start.

In April, Kuscsik, a registered nurse, former competitive roller skater, and mother of three, had been the first official women's champion of the Boston Marathon. On October 1 she became the first woman to win the Boston and New York City marathons in the same year; her New York time, 3:08:41, bested runner-up Pat Barrett by 10:52.

The men's winner, former New Jersey schoolboy runner and lifelong iconoclast Sheldon Karlin, was a senior at the University of Maryland who had recently fallen out with the school's cross-country coach. On the first weekend in October, he was available to run 26.2 miles in Manhattan. "My impression was that it was a good local marathon to get into," he commented.

Karlin will forever remember his four circuits around the park's northern hills. "The first time it went very easy. The second time it was a little more difficult. On the fourth time, I was pushing with all my might to get up [the hills]. I was aware that it was all downhill from there." Karlin's 2:27:52 placed him ahead of Glenn Apell of the New York Athletic Club, who took second place in 2:32:51.

The growing marathon's notoriety had by now extended beyond the New York metropolitan area and the press began covering the event. Karlin was pleased and amazed to discover unanticipated acclaim: "I was a celebrity for a day. It made the *Washington Post* and the *Washington Star.* People knew about it when I got back to my dorm."

**1973** Nina Kuscsik, now thirty-four, won her second consecutive New York City Marathon by a hefty margin over Kathrine Switzer, 2:57:07 to 3:16:02. For Kuscsik, 26.2 miles was a trifle; she later set an American record for the 50-mile road race in 6:35:53.

A longtime member of the New York Road Runners Club's board of directors, Kuscsik chaired the women's subcommittee of the Long Distance Running Committee of The Athletics Congress (TAC) in 1981 (TAC had replaced the AAU as the governing body of track, field, and road running in the United States). She was forthright, bold, and politically active in athletics, and sought to institute a women's marathon in the 1984 Los Angeles Olympics. The curmudgeonly president of the International Amateur Athletic Federation (IAAF), Adriaan Paulen, disagreed with her stance. When the opportunity arose, Kuscsik publicly presented Paulen with a lapel button that read, "I Support Fast Women." In 1981 the International Olympic Committee's executive board voted 7–1 to add the women's marathon in 1984. Through

**Above: When the AAU ruled that female marathoners had to start 10 minutes before the men, it was an insult the women would not take lying down—so they sat in.**

**Opposite: Nina Kuscsik breasted the tape to win in 1972.**

the 1980 Olympics, the longest women's running event was 1500 meters—less than a mile.

Tom Fleming, second in the inaugural 1970 Central Park marathon as a teenage college student, now competed for the New York Athletic Club. This time he won his battle and set a course record of 2:21:54. Runner-up Norb Sander finished in 2:23:38. Fleming's windfall was exceptionally lavish by 1973 road-race standards: he won a round-the-world ticket worth twelve hundred dollars from Olympic Airways, one of the marathon's sponsors.

**1974** Twenty-six-year-old Wesleyan University graduate Bill Rodgers was the early leader in 1974, but he wilted in the heat and 93-percent humidity. Dehydrated, he faded to fifth place in 2:35:59.

Norb Sander had been a member of Fordham University's championship four-mile relay team in the 1963 Penn Relays. In 1973 he won the Yonkers Marathon despite chronic appendicitis. In Central Park, Sander added a New York City title to his list of wins. His 2:26:30 prevailed over Boston Athletic Association member Art McAndrew's 2:28:16. Today, Sander is one of New York's most renowned internists and sports medicine specialists.

Kathrine Switzer, a former collegiate lacrosse player who now represented the Central Park Track Club, was the women's winner in 3:07:29. Her record margin over runner-up Liz Francheschini was 27:14, the biggest margin of victory in the history of the race by a male or female.

Switzer had achieved national fame in 1967 for entering the Boston Marathon when women were still prohibited from the race. To cloak her gender, she had registered as "K. Switzer" and wore a bulky sweat suit and cap at the Hopkinton start, but race official Jock Semple uncovered Switzer's ruse and attempted physically to remove her from the race. Famous photos of their clash were emblazoned across the nation's newspapers, the most indelible images of women's struggle to gain sanctioned legitimacy as distance runners. Switzer completed the race; in the coming years, hundreds of thousands would follow in her path. Seven years later in Manhattan, women were welcome if not plentiful.

Switzer would become one of the sport's most important administrative figures. In 1980 she testified before the IAAF in Paris, pressing the federation to favor the inclusion of a women's marathon in the 1984 Olympics. Switzer was also a part of ABC's broadcast team for many New York City Marathons and anchored New York 1's coverage of the race in 1993.

**1975** Tom Fleming, now twenty-four, had a tendency to set blistering paces. In the 1979 Boston Marathon, he would soar through the Natick 10.5-mile checkpoint in 50:08, inspiring Bill Rodgers to an American record of 2:09:27. Rodgers always generously credited the New Jersey runner for his pacesetting in that race.

By 1975, Fleming was one of the leading road runners in the world. He had significantly enhanced his road-racing stature with a 2:12:05 finish for third place that year in Boston. But eight days before the New York City Marathon, Fleming had gotten married, and except for his prerace warm-up, he had not run since the wedding. He nevertheless won his second New York City Marathon title by a comfortable margin, nearly 6 minutes ahead of his New York Athletic Club teammate, William Bragg. Fleming's 2:19:27 broke his own Central Park course record and made him the first—and, as it turned out, the last—man to run the park marathon course in less than 2 hours and 20 minutes.

The AAU, formerly opposed to allowing women to compete in the marathon, designated the 1975 New York race as the women's AAU championship, prompting twenty-year-old runner Kim Merritt to travel to Manhattan from Parkside, Wisconsin. In Merritt's 26.2-mile debut, she beat Beth Bonner's four-year-old New York record by more than 9 minutes, in 2:46:14. Miki Gorman placed second in 2:53:02 and Gayle Barron of Atlanta took third place in 2:57:22. All three women were Boston Marathon champions in the seventies.

The field for the 1975 New York City Marathon totalled 534, the second straight year it had surpassed 500; in Boston that year, the field had been 2,090. Keeping track of laps for so many runners on a four-loop course was becoming a knotty problem, necessitating a single loop or point-to-point layout.

The stature of the race had grown to the point that Manhattan Borough president Percy Sutton agreed to stand on the awards dais in 1975. He placed the victor's laurels on Kim Merritt's head, but the wreath quickly fell off. The incident made the cover of the *New York Daily News*, something Sutton, who had mayoral aspirations, had never been able to do with his political achievements. Sutton instantly saw the public-relations potential of the New York City Marathon.

By 1975, Ted Corbitt had decided it was time to give this marathon a fresh boost. He envisioned a competition of some sort between runners who each would represent one of New York's five boroughs—the Bronx, Manhattan, Brooklyn, Queens, and Staten Island—and mentioned his notion to his friend and fellow runner George Spitz. Legend now has it that Spitz mistakenly thought Corbitt was talking about a race that would actually be run *through* the five boroughs, though something more ambitious than four laps in Central Park may already have been festering in Spitz's mind. After experiencing the Boston Marathon that April, he wondered why New York could not have an extravaganza at least equal to Beantown's long journey on city streets from Hopkinton to Prudential Square.

Spitz mentioned his brainstorm to Lebow, whose initial enthusiasm was lukewarm. Logistically, the race in its current state was challenging enough for Lebow. Spitz's proposal would at the very least require closing off over three hundred intersections.

Spitz was not dissuaded by Lebow's doubts. As luck would have it, Spitz knew Sutton, that recent convert to marathon enthusiasm. Well-connected Sutton saw the five-borough marathon as a chance to literally tie together the city's polyglot ethnic neighborhoods.

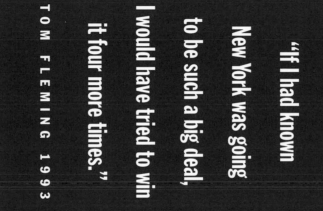

> "If I had known
> New York was going
> to be such a big deal,
> I would have tried to win
> it four more times."
>
> TOM FLEMING 1993

In ensuing discussions, Sutton parried Lebow's reservations, one after the other. Police protection and other support services along the route could be secured. Mayor Abe Beame was persuaded that a marathon through all five boroughs would be an ingeniously favorable way to showcase the city. Sutton even got the financing Lebow said he needed—twenty-five thousand dollars—from real-estate moguls Jack and Lewis Rudin, who sponsored the race as a tribute to their recently deceased father, Samuel, a long-distance runner. The initial twenty-five-thousand-dollar estimate proved insufficient: the Rudins contributed further and additional sponsorship came from Manufacturers Hanover Trust (now Chemical Bank) and *New Times* magazine, whose founder, George Hirsch, was a marathon runner, an active Democrat, and later the publisher of *The Runner* and *Runner's World*. The Rudin family, Chemical Bank, and *Runner's World* are all current sponsors.

Lebow had run out of excuses. Spanning the boroughs would be complex, but once the apparent obstacles had been removed, how could he *not* proceed with the most audacious and ambitious urban road-running venture ever attempted? The race across five major bridges and through city streets would be a test of trust, faith, and cooperation unlike anything America's original melting pot had ever seen. The jump from the intimate 1975 Central Park junket to the citywide 1976 marathon was a quantum leap, a daring, giant step for race director Lebow and his staff and volunteers. It took more than a bit of bravado to transform the whole city and reshape the entire health and fitness landscape in the United States.

Above: In the days before spandex, Kathrine Switzer wore her tennis dress to best the 1974 women's ranks by 27:14.

# 1970-1975

Below: Tom Fleming (10) copped the first of his two New York City Marathon titles in the 1973 race. Norb Sander (6) would win his New York laurels in 1974.

**Left:** Kurt Steiner's booming voice welcomed thousands of runners across the finish line over the years—he was one of the race's earliest volunteers and certainly its most loyal. **Bottom right:** Fred Lebow (clapping) fell in love with running from the instant he tried it. Codesigner of the five-borough route, Olympian Ted Corbitt (running) placed fifth in the 1970 New York City Marathon at the age of fifty.

**Below:** When politician Percy Sutton fumbled the laurel wreath onto 1975 champion Kim Merritt's head, the publicity prompted him to think of the marathon on a grander scale. **Middle right:** George Spitz's misunderstanding was the genesis of the five-borough marathon.

# 1976

On October 24, Fred Lebow almost became the first marathon director to be arrested at his own race. Near the Pulaski Bridge, he got into a wrestling, pushing, and profaning altercation with a police officer who had incorrectly arranged police sawhorse barricades. Lebow turned apoplectic at the prospect of two thousand confused and impeded runners attempting to maneuver from Brooklyn to Queens. He rearranged the barricades, and his staff hustled him into the lead vehicle just as the officer was preparing to drag him to jail. That catastrophe was averted, as was Lebow's worst nightmare—that the runners would make the brief turn into the Bronx and keep going, deep into the heart of the northernmost borough.

Indeed, the venture that some called impossible went off without a major hitch. In America's bicentennial year, the marathon finished near the Sheep Meadow in Central Park. Manhattan's First Avenue, that monument to Sunday brunch, was at that time off-limits to the runners, who instead plodded along the East River Park paths. This meant the marathoners struggled not only with the 26.2-mile distance, but also with car exhaust from the thick traffic on the FDR Drive congealing with pollution from industrial smokestacks.

Jack Maguire, who became chairman of Vermont Pure Natural Spring Water, a future sponsor of the race, recalled that the East River route even included flights of stairs: "Bill [Rodgers] wondered, 'What kind of marathon is it that makes you run up stairs?'"

Rodgers, squeezing in 140-plus-mile training weeks while teaching emotionally disturbed children in Everett, Massachusetts, had achieved a momentous

breakthrough with his third-place finish in the 1975 World Cross Country Championships in Morocco. After the race, he quipped about retiring, assuming he could never surpass that performance. But Rodgers kept running, and later that spring he won his first of four Boston Marathon titles, in 2:09:55. At the end of the year, he won the Fukuoka (Japan) Marathon. The United States now had another internationally competitive marathoner to rival Olympic gold medalist Frank Shorter.

Rodgers made the 1976 Olympic team, but his Montreal experience was a severe disappointment—he took 40th place. A New York City Marathon title would be redemptive, but Rodgers, in the first phase of an often-stormy history of negotiations with Fred Lebow, asked for two thousand dollars to appear. Lebow paid Rodgers out of his own pocket. Most of the country still imagined that even the most elite runners, officially categorized as amateurs, were indeed just that, despite the time commitments training required.

Frank Shorter, who had just added an Olympic silver to his 1972 marathon gold, agreed to run the inaugural five-borough extravaganza because, he said, "I just wanted to show up and see how the police would clear the streets. That alone would be an accomplishment." To add a necessary international dimension to the spectacle, Lebow invited Englishman Chris

**Above: Olympian Frank Shorter actually ran with a fractured ankle in the new-and-improved bicentennial marathon and placed second. Opposite: Bill Rodgers made up for his Olympic disappointment with a 2:10:10 sojourn over a 1976 course that included flights of stairs.**

Stewart to race. Initially reluctant to make the trip, Stewart was enticed when Lebow agreed to arrange a series of dates with models Lebow knew from his halcyon days in the garment district.

In the race, Pekka Paivarinta of Finland became the first in a long line of overeager front-runners. Navigating a maze of potholes that proved deeper and more problematic than anticipated, Paivarinta had an early margin of 500 yards, but that diminished to 125 yards after 10 miles. Rodgers, wearing his Greater Boston Track Club singlet, trademark white gloves, and—having forgotten his shorts—a pair of borrowed soccer pants, soon took over. At the 18-mile mark he was 2 minutes ahead of Shorter and Stewart, who would take second and third places, respectively. Rodgers's victorious 2:10:10 was the world's fastest marathon time in 1976. Stewart ended the race with painfully bloodied feet from the grating on the Queensboro Bridge. Since 1977, a carpet has been rolled over the grating to provide a smoother surface.

Five-time world cross-country champion Doris Brown Heritage made her first marathon sojourn, but she was broken at the halfway point by diminutive Miki Gorman of Los Angeles. Almost 14 minutes ahead of Heritage, forty-one-year-old Gorman crossed the finish line in 2:39:11, history's second-fastest women's marathon.

At some moment during Bill Rodgers's historic run, his illegally parked car was being towed. The New York Road Runners Club forked out ninety dollars to retrieve it. "That would never happen in Boston," marveled Rodgers. Later that day, *Boston Globe* scribe Joe Concannon encountered physician and marathon maven George Sheehan in the Barbizon Plaza Hotel. Sheehan, whose writings treated running as more than mere sport and conveyed how fulfilling and exhilarating the running life could be, told Concannon that New York would soon outdistance Boston as the top United States marathon.

Right: When she was forty-two, Miki Gorman won her second straight New York victory and set an American masters record.

# 1977

In its second incarnation, the five-borough marathon was already the world's largest, with 4,823 starters. The crowds were growing, too. The route now took runners from the Queensboro Bridge onto First Avenue, where the Sunday brunchers were the most vociferous segment of a throng along the course that would come to exceed two million.

Since her 1975 triumph in New York, Kim Merritt had won the 1976 Boston Marathon and established a new American marathon record of 2:37:57 in the 1977 Nike-Oregon Track Club Marathon in Eugene. But ninety-pound Miki Gorman, born in China to Japanese parents and twenty years older than Merritt, handily thwarted Merritt's challenge, 2:43:10 to 2:46:03. Gorman, who had a five-year-old daughter, was the first mother to capture the five-borough marathon title, but many more would follow.

Four of the top six men from the 1976 Olympic marathon in Montreal were entered in New York, including American Don Kardong and Canadian Jerome Drayton, who had won in Fukuoka and Boston. With much of the Brooklyn segment run against 10-mile-per-hour headwinds, Victor Mora of Colombia, Englishman Chris Stewart, and Neil Cusack of Ireland were the leaders at the halfway point. They were soon absorbed by a larger pack, and upon arrival in Manhattan the battle was down to Bill Rodgers and Garry Bjorklund. After a tenacious 3-mile struggle, Rodgers dropped Bjorklund and proceeded unchallenged to the Central Park finish line in 2:11:28.

Stewart took third place, as he had the previous year. Bjorklund hung on for fifth. The runner-up was fast-closer Drayton, who discovered that New York City Marathon spectators were ecumenical in cheering their support: "The crowd really helped me, especially in Central Park. It was their encouragement which inspired me to make my mad rush from seventh to second in the last 3 miles."

# 1978

Once again the year's designated AAU women's championship, New York City surpassed Honolulu as host to the largest women's marathon field in the world. Joe Kleinerman, a New York Road Runners Club pioneer and an ardent advocate of women's running, promised, "New York's marathon will show the world that we have high-caliber women marathoners. If marathoning for women is ever put into the Olympics, our runners will be prepared."

An early consensus favorite was young Marty Cooksey, a vegetarian who had played basketball and volleyball at California State University, and who had been a runner for less than two years. Cooksey had been unknown before 1978, when she won the Avon Women's International Marathon in Atlanta in 2:46:15 and captured the California International Marathon in Sacramento. In New York, Cooksey wanted to beat Christa Vahlensieck's 2:34:48 world record, set in West Berlin in 1977; Cooksey's coach was even boasting about a possible sub-2:30. Cooksey herself surmised, "Nobody knows how fast women can run marathons. I know we are capable of doing more than we think we can." Vahlensieck, earlier world-record-holder Jacqueline Hansen, and new American-record-holder Julie Brown would also be at the Staten Island start.

Norwegian schoolteacher Grete Waitz was a late entrant, and Fred Lebow displayed limited enthusiasm for her presence before deciding that she might make a good "rabbit." Though Waitz had ranked first in the world at 1500 meters in 1975 and was top-ranked at

3000 meters in 1977, she had failed to make the 1976 Montreal Olympic final in the 1500 meters, the longest Olympic event for women until 1984. The disapproval she endured after disappointing the Norwegian public had nearly driven her into retirement.

Waitz was rejuvenated in March 1978 in Glasgow as she took the first of what would be five World Cross Country Championships. Two weeks prior to the New York City Marathon, she had traversed 10 miles in 51:50, hitting the 10-kilometer mark in 32:00

**Above: Despite the heat, Bill Rodgers captured his third consecutive New York title in 1978.**

**Opposite: Grete Waitz was surprised by her fame, but handled the attention with a shy grace.**

at a time when the world best for 10 kilometers was 31:45. But that was as far as she had ever raced, and Waitz claimed, "I had never thought about running [the New York City Marathon] until this unexpected invitation came. My husband and I thought this would be the only chance to see this famous city."

Local hero Doreen Ennis of New Jersey held the women's lead in Brooklyn, but Cooksey took command after 9 miles and covered the first 13.1 miles in 1:17:45, with Vahlensieck and Waitz trailing by only 30 seconds. The Norwegian was in uncharted territory, but she found it friendly. Cooksey commented, "I didn't think there were any women near me and suddenly there she was. She had a huge lead before I knew it." Waitz passed Cooksey near the 18-mile mark on First Avenue, never to look back. She negotiated the second half of the race in 1:14:15; her 2:32:30 at the finish line was a new world record by 2:18.

Cooksey collapsed a half mile from the finish, got up, and fell once more. Finally, she crawled the last few yards. Despite her difficulty, she was the runner-up and

34

In 1978, after her **first** NYC Marathon title. There would be **eight** more.

had cut her best time by nearly 5 minutes, to 2:41:49. New York in 1978 was an epochal turning point in women's marathoning. Only twenty-three women had entered with times under 3 hours. But by early afternoon, forty-two females shattered that standard in Central Park.

Waitz's historic performance verified for all certainty that the New York City Marathon was a world-class competition. For Waitz, 1978 was the beginning of a new road-racing career that would transform her into the most recognizable female runner and an international figure of unprecedented stature in the sport. Yet the slender Scandinavian had not found the experience aesthetically or athletically pleasing. She took off her shoes and thrust them toward her husband, Jack, with some exclamation along the lines of "never again." She responded to a later query by gasping, "Another marathon? I don't think I feel like running another one, ever!"

She had been completely unaware that she was setting a world-record pace and was not initially impressed by what she had accomplished. "Once some of the European women track runners take up marathoning, the record is bound to go even lower," Waitz theorized, not knowing that she herself would be the track runner to bring the record down.

**Despite collapsing during and after the 1978 race, Marty Cooksey captured second place.**

In its coverage of the 1978 marathon, *New York Running News*'s headline inquired, "Who Is Grete Waitz?" In the following years, Waitz would answer that question quite emphatically, over and over again—and her response would not be free. "I was probably the last world-record holder who didn't get paid," Waitz reflected in 1993. In 1978, however, an all-expenses-paid trip to New York and a plunge into the race that would change her life were enough.

**Forty-six-year-old New Zealander Jack Foster set a New York masters record in 1978 with his sixth-place finish in 2:17:28; the mark went unbroken for ten years.**

Bill Rodgers came back in search of his third New York title, but many pundits favored Olympic 10-kilometer finalist Garry Bjorklund, who had battled Rodgers for so many miles in 1977. Fred Lebow commented, "I'm picking Bjorklund because he's hungry."

Ian Thompson, the 1974 European and Commonwealth champion, led early. But after 8 miles, Bjorklund was briskly in command, reaching the halfway point in 1:05. "I was furious with Garry," Rodgers remarked later. "He was crucifying both of us." But the defending titleholder had already observed that Bjorklund was struggling.

It was Rodgers who survived and persevered, assuming the lead before reaching the Queensboro Bridge and going solo from there. Rodgers became the New York City Marathon's first three-time winner with his 2:12:12, precisely 2 minutes ahead of Thompson. In the last 5 miles, Bjorklund plummeted from second to 76th place in 2:29:59. Like many lesser athletes, he found the marathon's proverbial "wall" to be a punishing and insurmountable barrier.

She had not yet become accustomed to the frenzy and publicity that now surrounded New York City Marathon champions. "What is the *Today* show?" Waitz wondered aloud. "They're going to pick me up in the morning, but it's so early. What kind of show is that?"

36

# 1979

In its fourth year as a five-borough affair, the New York City Marathon awarded prize money based on performance rather than paying hefty appearance fees. The financial arrangements went unpublished and remained generally unknown to the public; most still perceived running as an amateur sport. In 1982 Bill Rodgers would comment, "Amateurism is dead and should be buried as deeply as possible." This attitude, already prevalent among athletes, was accepted, grudgingly or otherwise, by officials and sponsors of premier United States road races.

*Running Times* noted that New York had become "a near necessity for the world's top runners, due to the attention it receives from the world's media." Coverage included a syndicated television broadcast anchored by Bill Mazer, Marty Liquori, and Gayle Barron—a telecast so beset by transmission mishaps that only meager portions of the marathon actually went out over the airwaves.

Rodgers was none too pleased that despite 1978 victories in Boston and New York he was ranked second in the world to European Championship winner Leonid Moiseyev of the Soviet Union. In April 1979, Rodgers had clocked the fastest marathon of his life, triumphing in Boston in 2:09:27. He was the new world-record holder at 25,000 meters, a seldom-run track event. But his 1979 calendar was also riddled with losses and dropouts, perhaps an indication that Rodgers, who customarily took on a heavy load, was overracing.

One of his stronger adversaries was likely to be twenty-three-year-old University of Colorado graduate

Kirk Pfeffer, who had won the Enschede Marathon in the Netherlands in 2:11:50 two months earlier. Pfeffer's New York entry was an eleventh-hour decision, one of the latest ever by an elite athlete. "I was lying in bed Saturday morning and I said I thought it would be nice to run in New York," he explained. "My wife, Kim, laughed, but I called up Fred Lebow."

A *New York Post* reporter who would eventually finish in more than 4 hours had fantasized about a story titled, "I Led the New York City Marathon." In his eagerness, the journalist prematurely broke away from the Verrazano-Narrows start halfway through the 10-second countdown, and a major portion of the men's field followed suit. Rodgers spent most of the first mile winding his way through the overzealous masses.

The lesser pretenders drifted away and Pfeffer was in front after 7 miles, passing through the 10-mile mark in 48:48 and the halfway point in 1:03:50. It was a pace meant to shatter the five-borough course record, but temperatures were reaching into the seventies. Pfeffer characterized his own mistakes: "When you get into a 4:50 [per mile] pace and go with it, you're caught in a trap." He fell prey to his own mental commitment to maintain a rigid and unrealistic speed. Rodgers was adhering to his plan to start slowly and pick people off in the heat. "Psychologically, that's a good way to run," he noted. "As you catch people, you get stronger."

After 17 miles, Rodgers was contending for second place with Benji Durden of Atlanta, who later made the 1980 Olympic squad that boycotted Moscow and would become a leading marathon coach in the nineties. Pfeffer still held a 74-second margin af-

**"I was one of the first in this sport to call myself a professional runner, and I'm proud of that."**

BILL RODGERS

**Above: Achilles Track Club president Dick Traum (175) watched Kirk Pfeffer (96) lose his huge lead over Bill Rodgers (2).**

**Right: George Sheehan—running columnist, raconteur, and guru—staggered through the 80-degree heat of 1979.**

ter 20 miles, and his pursuer "was seeing the headline 'Pfeffer Upsets Rodgers.'" Two miles later, Pfeffer's arms and legs were coming undone and *he* knew he was a goner. "Those hills annihilated me," the valiant Coloradan said of the Central Park inclines. Rodgers caught him beyond the 23-mile mark and sensed that the twenty-three-year-old was spent, too exhausted even to turn his head and acknowledge his rival's presence. Rodgers proceeded to an unprecedented fourth New York City victory in 2:11:42, with Pfeffer hanging on for the next spot in 2:13:09. Olympic gold medalist and 1976 runner-up Frank Shorter had returned to New York and he placed seventh in 2:16:15. As the seventies came to a close, Rodgers stood as the only man to better 2:13 in New York, a task he had accomplished four consecutive times.

Although the public identified her as a marathoner, Grete Waitz claimed she was "still a track runner." Great Britain's Gillian Adams would be the 1979 runner-up, but she commented, "The only time I saw Grete was when we were talking together at the starting line." After Waitz's 1978 New York victory, she had been awarded an endorsement contract. Her deal with Adidas now enabled her to support herself by running.

As in 1978, Waitz negative split the 26.2 miles, accelerating after 13.1 miles in 1:14:51 to reach the finish line in 2:27:33. She had set another world record, easily breaking the women's 2:30 barrier. Among the forty-two hundred runners in the America's Marathon in Chicago that same October 21, Waitz's time would have taken second place *overall*.

"It'll make a lot of men sit up and think," Gillian Adams said of the Norwegian's accomplishment. "She is a bit of an inspiration, but it would be nice to have someone closer to her." Adams was a full 11 minutes behind Waitz in 2:38:33, with future Boston Marathon winner Jacqueline Gareau of Montreal in third place and Patti Lyons in fourth.

Right: Behind her
cool reserve, Grete
Waitz's calm
concentration hinted
that she might
win her second New
York title.

Above: Jacqueline
Gareau, the 1980
Boston champion,
finished a distant
third behind
Grete Waitz.

# 1980

Alberto Salazar was a National Collegiate Athletic Association (NCAA) cross-country champion and had secured one of three 10,000-meter spots on the forsaken 1980 United States Olympic squad. But before running from the Verrazano-Narrows Bridge to Central Park, he was probably best known for his strenuous effort in the 1979 Falmouth (Massachusetts) Road Race: the oppressive heat left Salazar in a state of severe hyperthermia; he had to be packed in ice and he received the last rites. Salazar was tenacious, and he understood more than most mortals about pushing the limits. Bill Dellinger, Salazar's coach at the University of Oregon, had made three Olympic teams and ultimately won the bronze medal in the 5000 meters in Tokyo in 1964.

In the autumn of 1980, Alberto Salazar's NCAA cross-country eligibility had expired, so the New York City Marathon fit nicely into his schedule. Neither Salazar nor Dellinger was concerned that Salazar had never run an event longer than 8 miles. "The longer the race, the more time you have to think about it, and that's where Alberto's toughness comes in. You have to want to stay with a killing pace, and Alberto does," insisted Dellinger, who theorized and hoped that the marathon would be up for grabs in the last 6 miles, "a distance Alberto was familiar with. At that point, it would be little more than a 10,000-meter race."

Those who pay attention to such things were rankled by Salazar's pronouncement that he was looking to break 2:10 in his first marathon venture. He explained his confidence: "Some people tell me that you have to run a lot of times to be able to run a good marathon. I'm not at all sure that's true. It's just a race." Craig Virgin, another member of the boycotting 1980 United States Olympic squad, was doubtful: "I'll eat a lot of crow on Monday morning if Alberto can run 2:10," he stated. With a forthrightness that made the bold seem timid, Salazar said, "When someone asks me what I think I can do, I'll tell him. I'm not going to be like some guys and have false modesty. If I think I can do it, I'll say so."

**Former world-record holder in the mile Filbert Bayi of Tanzania (57) and college 10-kilometer ace Alberto Salazar (K661) pushed forward. Bayi wilted; Salazar won.**

The runners enjoyed 45-degree weather and tailwinds for the first 20 miles, but blustery headwinds dogged the final 6 miles. A sizable pack went through the 10-mile mark in 49:05. Steve Floto, a good marathoner and an even better fashion model, made a bid for glory and maintained a 25-meter edge after 15 miles.

Meanwhile, Bill Rodgers's tumble from the marathon throne was quite literal. At the 14-mile mark, his heel was clipped, apparently by Dick Beardsley. "I hit somebody, tripped, and went flying through the air," Rodgers reported. "It took me a mile to get moving again. It popped into my mind that the same thing happened to Lasse Viren [in the 10,000 meters] in the 1972 Olympics. I tried to emulate Viren, but I guess I'm not gold-medal material."

**Opposite: The ever-exuberant Patti Lyons Catalano demonstrated what an ecstatic occasion a new American record could be. Her 2:29:33 made her runner-up to Grete Waitz, who earned her third world mark in New York.**

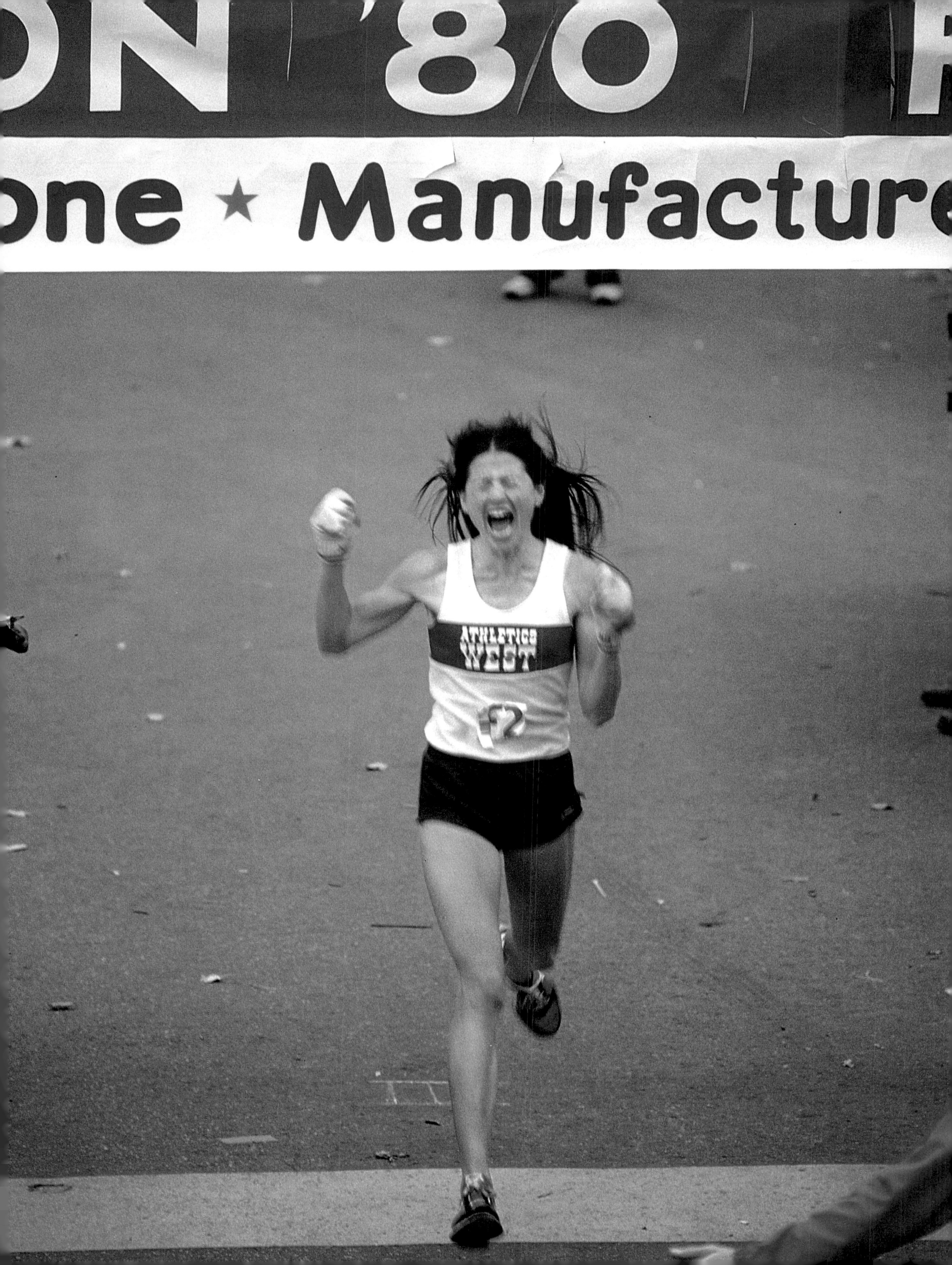
ON '80
one ★ Manufacture
ATHLETICS WEST

In 1981, six months after her stunning breakthrough in Boston, Allison Roe (F2) of New Zealand wrested the world record and New York championship from Grete Waitz (F1),

Rodgers was, however, a four-time New York City Marathon champion, whereas Viren would drop out of the race for the third time in a row.

Other challengers were succumbing to the rigors of the race. Filbert Bayi of Tanzania, former world-record holder in the mile, overreached his range and faded. Bayi and many other champions at shorter distances were finding mastery of the marathon to be frustratingly elusive; the 26.2-mile road test demanded its own particular set of skills, physicality, conditioning, and character.

Gerard Nijboer, the Dutch silver medalist in the marathon at the Moscow Olympics, had quipped that there was only one hill in the Netherlands and that he ran up it every day. Such training did not help him in New York; he suffered leg cramps and ceased and desisted after the 18th mile. At the exit from the Queensboro Bridge onto First Avenue, the battle was coming down to Salazar, Rodolfo Gomez of Mexico, and John Graham of Great Britain. Salazar, in his yellow and green University of Oregon shirt, turned on the juice between the 19th and 22nd miles; on an upgrade and into the wind, his 21st mile in 4:57 was the clincher. He proceeded to the tape in 2:09:41, a course record, the fastest marathon debut in history, and the second-best American time after Rodgers's 2:09:27 in 1979.

Gomez and Graham took the next two spots in 2:10:13 and 2:11:46, with Jeff Wells of Dallas in fourth place in 2:11:59. Rodgers finished an unfamiliar fifth with his trademark white gloves, a green ski cap (with his own "BR" logo), and blood caked on his knees.

Salazar, meanwhile, was "surprised how easy it was. I thought I'd have to kill myself, but it wasn't any more difficult than some 10,000s I've run. I didn't feel real pain until the final 300 yards. The first 10 miles were easier than some training runs I've done."

Grete Waitz arrived for her third New York City Marathon looking more formidable than ever. In the spring, she had demolished the field at the Mini Marathon (a 10-kilometer race for women that finished at the same Central Park spot as the New York City Marathon) in a performance *Track & Field News* termed "Waitzian." She had become an adjective.

Seven weeks earlier in Montreal, Patti Lyons Catalano had established a new American marathon standard of 2:30:57. Yet in New York, after speeding through 5 miles in 27:00, Catalano had to let the defending titlist go. Waitz ran near-even splits, with a halfway time of 1:12:37 on the way to her third straight world record in New York in 2:25:42.

With an ebullient burst at the finish, Catalano took second place in 2:29:34, setting a record as the second woman, and the first American woman, to better 2:30. It was difficult to distinguish joy from agony and fatigue in Catalano's gritty facial expressions. She put a very human face on women's marathoning in the early eighties.

There was by now an undeniable phenomenon hovering around Grete Waitz, observed and best-explained by Olympian Don Kardong: "There was always a group of men who wanted to run with her. They sort of closed in around her, but when she started to run the second half of the race, she left them all. There wasn't anyone who could stay up with her. But the greatest moment still was when she passed Lasse Viren at 10 miles."

One fellow who missed seeing Salazar, Waitz, and just about everything else was Harlem resident Ernest Conner. He ran backwards for the entire 26.2 miles. The effort Conner termed "my crucifixion and resurrection" lasted 5:18. He was pounding New York's pavement considerably longer than Hendrik Doornekamp of the Netherlands, who finished 26.2 miles in 4:27 wearing wooden shoes. More and more foreigners, both serious and wacky, were taking the five-borough tour of New York. The New York City Marathon was that rare event that accommodated both the relentless striver and the shameless exhibitionist.

# 1981

ABC was broadcasting the New York City Marathon nationally for the first time, having paid $290,000 for the privilege of a four-year deal. The network, as it would turn out, could not have asked for a better show.

Mayor Ed Koch, up for reelection (he would win), pronounced Grete Waitz to be "the only one who can beat me in November." In truth, her prospects of a record-setting fourth New York crown were clouded by excruciating shin pain.

In the months since Waitz's third triumph, the sport had discovered a dazzling new star, the stately Allison Roe of New Zealand. A former high jumper and tennis player, and later a secretary at an architecture and engineering firm, Roe was New Zealand's cross-country champion when she was eighteen years old. She had progressed steadily in her 26.2-mile endeavors, but it was a major shock when she won the 1981 Boston Marathon, defeating (and flabbergasting) Patti Lyons Catalano with a sizzling 2:26:46. Roe, twenty-five years old in 1981, was admittedly "a bit overwhelmed by the magnitude of all this"—her newfound status as a major contender in New York and all the expectations and attention that go with the role.

Julie Brown had made the 1980 United States Olympic team at 800 and 1500 meters; her leg speed was unquestioned. Brown scorched the first 6 miles of the New York City Marathon in 33:06. After 8 miles, she held a 200-yard lead, but 4 miles later Waitz, Roe, and Norway's Ingrid Kristiansen were

catching up. The agonized Waitz realized she could not stay in the hunt. At the Pulaski Bridge, she told Roe, "You go ahead. Don't let [Brown] get too far ahead. I'm dropping out."

By the time she arrived on First Avenue, Roe had overtaken Brown. Spurred on by two million screaming spectators, Roe gave New York its fourth women's world record in four years, bringing the mark down to 2:25:29. Ingrid Kristiansen, from whom a great deal more would be heard in the years ahead, took second place in 2:30:08, a personal best by 4 minutes. Julie Brown drifted back to ninth in 2:40:08.

On the eve of his first New York City Marathon, Alberto Salazar had "suspected it would be just like any other race, just longer and with about fifteen thousand more runners. I believed I would win." What he might not have anticipated was the impact of his 2:09:41 triumph. "In one race, I achieved what many others called instant fame," he explained. "I had won national championships before, but all those races combined did not give me the exposure or media attention I received from the New York City Marathon."

Salazar had not been idle in 1981. In January he set a road-race world best of 22:03 at 5 miles, followed by an American indoor 5000-meter mark of 13:22.6 at Madison Square Garden. In June Salazar won the TAC 10,000-meter title. Later that summer, he set a course record of 31:55.6 at the 7.1-mile Falmouth Road Race—the event in which he had nearly died two years earlier. He was, after all, Alberto Salazar, named in part for his great-great-great-

All alone and feeling anything but blue, Alberto Salazar finished in 2:08:13 and sheared 21 seconds from a 12-year-old world record that some had deemed invincible. How wrong they were.

grandfather Peter Bauduy, of whom George Washington said, "He is not afraid of hard work." Neither, obviously, was his namesake.

The world marathon record, 2:08:34, had stood for twelve years since Australian Derek Clayton established the mark in Antwerp in 1969. Clayton's was a controversial distinction; questions about the measurement of the Belgian course persisted. Methods of measuring marathon courses were not globally standardized, and some officials recognized Clayton's achievement only as a "world best" rather than as a "world record."

Salazar wanted to render such uncertainties moot. Two days before the 1981 race, he again promised, "I've said I'll run 2:08, I'll stick by it." His former coach, Bill Squires, warned, "There are three things that you don't bet against. They are taxes, death—and Alberto."

Clayton himself said, "The only one I know of who could [break my record] is Alberto Salazar. He's reckless. He's the gutsiest runner I have ever seen. I admire him tremendously, the way he runs." But John Graham, third in New York in 1980, had more recently conquered Rotterdam in 2:09:28 despite a side stitch and said, "I can feel it in my legs that [Clayton's] record could be mine."

A third intriguing prospect was Jukka Toivola of Finland, a hospital technician who performed blood tests in a lab. Toivola was one of his own customers. "I check mostly for testosterone, cortisone, and hemoglobin levels," he noted. "If any of them are low, I cut back on training."

Salazar, Graham, and Mexico's José Gomez reached the halfway point in 1:04:10. But the 6-foot, 145-pound Salazar's surges in Manhattan were unlike anything New York had ever seen. He blazed the 17th mile in 4:33. No one was able to maintain contact. "Instead of worrying about them," Salazar later said of his foes, "I ran away from them." He reached the 20-mile mark in 1:37:29, clearly within range of Clayton's record.

Salazar's final solo stretch was dramatic enough, but he could have strolled in at the end as his 2:08:13 took the global mark down by 21 seconds. It was the first men's world marathon mark to be set on American soil since 1947. Blood-monitoring Toivola was a distant second in 2:10:52. Tony Sandoval, the 1980 United States Olympic trials winner, placed sixth in 2:12:12.

"It's like Roger Bannister's first 4-minute mile," a jubilant Allan Steinfeld, the marathon's longtime technical director, said of Salazar's landmark achievement. The marathon trailblazer would have company soon enough. Two months later, Rob de Castella of Australia clocked 2:08:18 at Fukuoka. A new marathon era had begun.

Roe's and Salazar's records were, as one headline blared, a "Double Fantasy." In reality, Fred Lebow, ABC, and the New York City Marathon's sponsors had probably not dared to dream that big.

**Above: Runner-up Ingrid Kristiansen joined her compatriot Grete Waitz in making her mark on the New York City Marathon. Opposite: Before 1981, Allison Roe was unknown in road-running circles. By that October, she was the fastest female marathoner in history.**

**Tony Sandoval, the 1980 United States Olympic trials winner, had his best New York showing in 1981, finishing in 2:12:12 for sixth place.**

**Above: Poland's Ryszard Marczak, fourth in 2:12:44 at the age of thirty-six, later became a standout masters marathoner.**

**Above: Julie Brown was the 1982 New York runner-up only two years after making the United States Olympic squad at 800 and 1500 meters.**

**Opposite: New York had never witnessed a 26.2-mile duel like the one between Alberto Salazar (left) and Rodolfo Gomez (right). Salazar literally emerged from a cloud of dust to break the finish tape in Central Park for the third consecutive year.**

# 1982

In an interview with the *Eugene Register Guard*, Alberto Salazar spoke admiringly about his bullterrier puppies. "I'm intrigued that such a small dog can be so friendly and then such a terror among other dogs," he said. "In a fight, they will never give up."

Salazar could have been speaking about himself. He was the reigning terror among marathoners, a man for whom the fiercest struggle ended only when he had somehow emerged on top. In Boston in April, he had been in his first 26.2-mile dogfight, forced to summon everything within him to overcome Minnesotan Dick Beardsley by just 2 seconds, 2:08:51 to 2:08:53. The two rivals would again go head-to-head in New York City. "People are trying to make it out as a Muhammad Ali–Joe Frazier situation," Beardsley complained. "It's just not that way."

The temperature was 47 degrees at the Verrazano-Narrows start as runners departed into headwinds that would reach 20 miles per hour. Beardsley briefly moved to the front after 15 kilometers, but his legs were ailing and he would not last. The winds kept the two leaders' halfway time down to 1:04:55; there would be no new record. A pack of nine was intact as the runners reached Manhattan, where Salazar tossed in a pair of 4:44 miles intended to break the pack. Rodolfo Gomez, Carlos Lopes, Jon Sinclair, and David Murphy remained in close proximity, but not for long.

Salazar's sole companion as he entered the Bronx was Gomez. Lopes, Portugal's 1976 Olympic silver medalist at 10,000 meters, had never run more than 18 miles, and he would not complete this marathon. Yet as he explained years later, it was in New York in 1982 that "I learned I could be a marathoner for the future." The future arrived in 1984, when, at thirty-seven years old, he won the Los Angeles Olympics marathon.

As he tussled with Gomez, Salazar had a bit of a side stitch. "I wish I had known," Gomez later commented. "I would have increased the pace." The

Mexican, sixth in the 1980 Olympic marathon, shared a considerable history with Salazar. They had finished in first and second place in New York in 1980, with Salazar enjoying a comfortable 32-second edge. They had competed together twice in the NCAA Cross Country Championships; in 1978, Salazar won the individual title for the University of Oregon while Gomez, from the University of Texas at El Paso, placed a fairly dismal 40th.

However, Gomez had won his three most recent marathons. Salazar suspected that Gomez, who had previously been a 5- and 10-kilometer runner in the 1972 Munich Olympics, might possess superior speed. "I was really scared to death," Salazar said later, "because I know Rodolfo is faster than I am. I had to make sure he was very tired. The plan was to wear him down."

Salazar would almost run out of territory before he could execute that plan. He threw in a series of 150-yard surges in Central Park, "designed to soften [Gomez] up. And I didn't slow down to a normal speed again after each one. The tempo was constantly picking up." The final segments were staggering—30:13 for the closing 10 kilometers, 4:35 for the 26th mile. Yet barely an eyelash separated the two men as they passed the Plaza Hotel on Central Park South with one mile left.

The pair reached Columbus Circle, reentering Central Park for the closing burst. The runners had to travel over a brief stretch of lawn before returning to the park's roadway. A motorcycle escort passed over the dry grass, raising a cloud of dust that obscured visibility. When the dust cleared, spectators could see that Alberto Salazar had managed to pull ahead of Rodolfo Gomez; Salazar eked out a 4-second victory in 2:09:29.

Salazar had now won all three of his New York City Marathons and stood undefeated in four marathons overall. His courageous performances earned him his second consecutive number-one world ranking. Gomez, valiant but vanquished, had improved his personal best by 40 seconds.

Salazar and Gomez gave the two million spectators and the television audience the most exhilarating duel in the annals of American road racing. "The last six years we've had winners, but never a race," noted an ecstatic Fred Lebow. "No one has ever entered Central Park with company. It was my dream that we have not so much world records, but a race. And we did." The marathon had never been thought of as a down-to-the-wire event. Salazar injected unprecedented drama into a race that usually played itself out over two hours, a verdict that was decided by minutes rather than seconds.

Running steadily and picking off stragglers to take third was Dan Schlesinger of Raleigh, North Carolina, in 2:11:54. His academic résumé may have been the most impressive of anyone ever to place in New York's top three. Schlesinger was a Yale graduate, a Marshall scholar at Oxford, and a Harvard law student. He also spoke fluent Japanese, Korean, and French.

For Grete Waitz, New York City in 1982 represented a bit of a comeback. She had dropped out of her previous two marathons, New York in 1981 and Boston in 1982. The woman who had assumed her New York crown and record a year earlier, Allison Roe, had an Achilles tendon injury and was serving as an ABC commentator.

Headwinds impeded Waitz early on; she barely bettered 18:00 for the first 3 miles. She was in command soon enough, however, grabbing her fourth New York City Marathon win in 2:27:14. Julie Brown of San Diego, no longer a middle-distance star but a bona fide marathoner, was next in 2:28:33, her best time by 5:07.

At the awards ceremony that evening, Rodolfo Gomez spoke in Spanish, at length and with passion. The only available translator was Alberto Salazar's Cuban-born father, José. The elder Salazar simply informed the audience, "Rodolfo says he loves New York, and he loves Alberto."

# 1983

Grete Waitz's supremacy extended far beyond the five boroughs in 1983. In April she had tied Allison Roe's world best of 2:25:29, winning the London Marathon. The record was hers for the briefest of interludes; Joan Benoit conquered Boston in 2:22:43 the very next day. But Norway's favorite daughter retorted in August by capturing the first World Championships marathon in Helsinki in 2:28:09, prevailing with an ease and dominance that were truly Waitzian. Marathon pundits and top runners began to speak of the 2:20 barrier for women as something epochal but no longer unattainable.

The New York field had doubled in each of the first three five-borough years, reaching 9,875 entrants in 1978. It had grown steadily to surpass 15,000, but there was still only one unsurpassable Grete Waitz. A full 4:49 ahead of Italy's Laura Fogli, who moved up to second place after two previous fourth-place finishes in New York, Waitz's 1983 victory in 2:27:00 was a relative cinch. At the finish, the five-time, five-borough champion triumphantly tossed her white gloves into the crowd. A few minutes later, Great Britain's Priscilla Welch, thirty-eight years old and getting swifter with age, placed third in 2:32:31.

As a child, Rod Dixon had run on the beach and to school barefoot. In 1972 he was a twenty-two-year-old Olympic bronze medalist at 1500 meters for New Zealand. Four years later, he was left out of the medals in a four-man blanket finish in the 5000 meters. New Zealand boycotted the 1980 Moscow Olympics, accelerating Dixon's metamorphosis into a road runner. He established an American base in the tranquil Amish countryside of Pennsylvania. He won the 1980 13.1-mile Philadelphia Distance Run, and in 1982 set a course mark of 35:07.6 in the San Francisco Bay-to-Breakers, a 12-kilometer race. In one stretch in the early eighties, Dixon took first in sixteen of twenty road races.

He was joyful about this fresh phase of his athletic life. "In track, people like you are in the stands," he observed in *Running Times*. "In road racing, you're on the course with me at the same time, running the same hills, taking the same water. You can relate to me. And I can relate to you."

Dixon had run 2:11:20 in a New Zealand marathon in May 1982. Through calculations known only to himself, he quoted 2:07:38 as his projected time in New York, supplying a dramatic boost to a race that would not have Alberto Salazar. The event was also facing a formidable challenge from the America's Marathon in Chicago, which had heavy funding from one generous sponsor, Beatrice Foods, and a pancake-flat course that proved highly conducive to record-setting times.

The rain was steady and puddles pockmarked New York's marathon route in 1983, but the conditions seemed merely to goad the elite athletes into trying to arrive in Central Park sooner. Tanzanian Gidamis Shahanga was the most anxious, clocking his second mile, albeit on a somewhat downhill stretch, at 4:28. He breezed through the 10-mile mark in 48:06, arriving at the halfway point in 1:03:12. Only Geoff Smith, an Englishman who had attended Providence College, stayed close. On the carpet of the Queensboro Bridge, Smith swept past a tired Shahanga.

> "That win ten years ago was the topping off of my whole career. New York is the one you have to win."
>
> ROD DIXON 1993

Dixon, meanwhile, slipped while coming off the bridge and aggravated a right hamstring injury; later, he began periodically grabbing his leg. "I thought for sure I'd let them get too far ahead," he said. "I really didn't think I was going to catch them."

Smith was pouring it on; one of his First Avenue miles was clocked at 4:39. He had a 35-second bulge at the 20-mile mark, but he started to get cramps and hamstring spasms. Dixon's agony, on the other hand, was gone. At 23 miles the gap was down to 22 seconds.

"My track background gave me the confidence that if it came down to a kick, I was ready for it," Dixon said later. In fact, both men were stellar milers, Dixon at 3:53 and Smith at 3:55. The last stages of the marathon could be scorching—if the runners had anything left.

"Just before we got into the park, I noticed that he was a little more upright going up the hill," Dixon observed of Smith. "I felt he really wasn't leaning into it, attacking it." Dixon was also doing a superior job of running the route's tangents, saving precious yards of endeavor, whereas Smith thought he might fall at several points in the final mile. His face and form were contorted in delirium, pain, or both.

Dixon was gaining. When he passed Smith at the 26-mile mark, Dixon was on the right side, closer to the crowd and gaining nourishment from its enthusiasm. Smith was in the middle of the roadway, barely on his feet. "When Dixon passed me, the air went out," he sighed after the race. "My legs were just gone. I was just running on memory."

Dixon finished in 2:08:59, stretched his arms upward, and jubilantly, with the broadest of gleaming smiles, gazed to the skies. Then he fell to his knees and kissed the pavement. He was the champion, perfectly self-possessed, in glaring juxtaposition to Smith, who had barely arrived at the finish line before crumpling into a heap. After his valiant effort Smith bravely admitted that he was "more disappointed than hurt."

In a deep field, eleven men had finished in under 2:12. Smith's 2:09:08 qualified him as the fastest-ever debut marathoner, but that was small consolation. For Dixon, "It was fantastic. In the space of 30 seconds, I went from being the hunter to the winner." He had resisted the urge to narrow the gap between himself and Smith too quickly.

"The thing I learned today is that you need patience and concentration to be successful in the marathon."

Among all New York City Marathon champions, Rod Dixon could race at elite levels in the widest range of distances. In the nineties he would be reincarnated as a miler on a burgeoning masters circuit. Still, he realized that he would be remembered most for his torturous human struggle with Geoff Smith. "That win ten years ago was the topping off of my whole career," he reflected. "New York is the one you have to win."

By 1983 the running boom was an established fact, a healthy and competitive outlet embraced by millions of athletes of all sizes, ages, and levels of aspiration. Still prevalent was the impression that those drawn to the sport were unusually intelligent overall. Magazines printed articles with headlines asking, "Are Runners Smarter?" According to a 1983 *New York Times* study, 83 percent of runners polled had attended college and 45 percent had gone to graduate school.

**Above: In 2:09:08, Geoff Smith, the front-runner on a wet course, clocked New York's fastest nonwinning time and, at the 26-mile mark, held the latest lead of anyone who did not emerge victorious.**

**Opposite: New York's most transcendent moment may have been Rod Dixon's exultation after vanquishing Smith, who lay sprawled at the finish.**

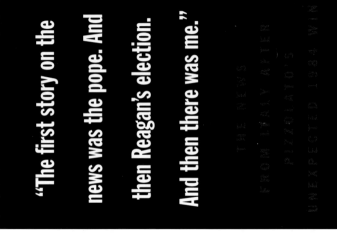

# 1984

Ed Koch has called the New York City Marathon "the city's greatest sporting, cultural, and entertainment event, because it's all of them mixed together." To the mayor, there was no argument: "New York is *the* international marathon in the world."

The race had a challenger, however, in the Windy City. The America's Marathon in Chicago, held the week before New York's 26.2-miler, had a cast of competitors in 1984 that included Steve Jones, Rob de Castella, Geoff Smith, Rosa Mota, Lisa Martin, and Ingrid Kristiansen—and Fred Lebow, who explored the Chicago course in 3:55. Rosa Mota had topped the women in 2:26:01; ahead of her, Steve Jones established a new world record of 2:08:05.

Lebow remained adamant in praise of his own race. "Any runner with a business sense knows [they would] be penny-wise and pound-foolish to pass up New York," he insisted. "Winning New York is like winning the Olympics." One runner who concurred was defending champ Rod Dixon. "There's magic to New York," he said. "You can't buy that feeling."

Lebow had an additional new headache. His autobiography, *Inside the World of Big-Time Marathoning* (with Richard Woodley), confirmed what many had suspected or privately known: that Lebow and the marathon's sponsors had paid out hundreds of thousands of dollars in prize money and appearance fees to top runners since 1976. Mayor Koch may have spoken hosannas about the race, but he was peeved that Lebow had gone public with the money "secret." The mayor sent Lebow a $300,000 bill, primarily for city services. With nothing to hide,

the New York City Marathon boasted a published prize structure that totaled $273,800.

In the week after the Chicago race, the weather had turned unseasonably (one might say unconscionably) torrid. The high temperature on October 28 was 79 degrees and the humidity climbed to over 90 percent. Fog and steam rose from the Verrazano-Narrows Bridge at the starting line.

The heat slowed the early pace only slightly. Pat Petersen of Long Island was among those who covered the first 10 miles in 49:31. An Italian named Orlando Pizzolato surged through the 14th mile in 4:52 and found himself ahead of the pack. Pizzolato had yet to register a set of fast times, but he had run well in the heat at road races in Italy. Virtually unnoticed, Pizzolato had run in New York before, clocking 2:15:28 for 15th place in 1983.

Pizzolato kept extending his lead, but his mile splits were inflating as he ran through Harlem. In the 22nd mile, he came

"The first story on the news was the pope. And then Reagan's election. And then there was me."

THE NEWS
FROM ITALY AFTER
PIZZOLATO'S
UNEXPECTED 1984 WIN

to a full stop and grabbed his side. Rod Dixon had dropped out with stomach cramps after 21 miles, leaving Englishman David Murphy as Pizzolato's closest pursuer, trailing by 250 yards. Pizzolato came to a halt six more times; he ran his 23rd mile in 6:01. Murphy ran more smoothly and Central Park spectators yelled to him that Pizzolato was vulnerable, but Murphy himself was also wilting. "I gave out," he conceded, telling reporters that Pizzolato "was brave, and it paid off." A police officer on a motorcycle may have been Pizzolato's savior; each time the Italian runner paused, the policeman yelled, "Cinquantamila dollari!" (fifty thousand dollars). It was the encouragement Pizzolato needed to get going again.

Above: Aggravated by the heat, stomach cramps forced defending champion Rod Dixon out of the chase after 21 miles. Below: Englishman David Murphy had the best shot at beating a faltering Pizzolato in Central Park, but Murphy had given away too much ground and finished second.

Pizzolato won in 2:14:53, the slowest victory in any five-borough marathon, with Murphy 43 seconds behind him. Germany's Herbert Steffny was third in 2:16:22. "I ran the race in USA shorts to get the cheers of the spectators," the German racer noted. "It was a trick." An actual American, Pat Petersen, was fourth in 2:16:35.

Pizzolato, a twenty-six-year-old physical therapy student in Ferrara, had his name mispronounced more often than all previous New York City Marathon champions combined. Asked about his biggest previous triumph, he conceded, "There wasn't any." American winners get congratulatory calls from the president. Pizzolato received one from Primo Nebiolo, president of the IAAF. In Italy, as the unexpected New York victor was delighted to learn, the news of his win ranked only behind stories on the pope and on Ronald Reagan's election.

After so many years of lobbying, the inaugural women's Olympic marathon had finally taken place in Los Angeles. Grete Waitz earned a silver medal, finishing behind champion Joan Benoit but ahead of Rosa Mota, October's Chicago winner.

Chasing her sixth New York title, Waitz confessed, "Sometimes I feel more like a New Yorker than a Norwegian." It never gets as swelteringly hot in Norway as it was on the day of the marathon; though the conditions slowed her down to 2:29:30, the weather was her only competitive threat as she came in 4:28 ahead of Great Britain's Veronique Marot. Waitz's time was far from her finest, but on a day when so many men faded in the heat, she placed 57th overall. The top American woman was Judi St. Hilaire, fifth in 2:37:49.

By the end of the afternoon, twelve hundred runners required medical attention, mostly for afflictions connected to the oppressive heat. The 1984 experience was the main impetus for permanently pushing the marathon to November after 1985.

56

# 1985

The New York City Marathon had a tough act to follow in the America's Marathon in Chicago, which was again blessed with an extraordinary pair of victors: Steve Jones and Joan Benoit Samuelson clocked 2:07:13 and 2:21:21 respectively, barely missing Carlos Lopes's 2:07:12 and Ingrid Kristiansen's 2:21:06, world records set that spring in Rotterdam and London. Benoit's time, however, set a long-standing American record.

Grete Waitz, seeking her seventh New York victory, was unstinting in her allegiance to the race that had made her world famous. "I would not trade my New York victories for fast times in Chicago," she affirmed. "The victory is mine forever; a record is meant to be broken."

As an obvious corollary of the New York–Chicago competition, bidding for marathon stars was becoming costly. Reports indicated that Carlos Lopes, now both the reigning Olympic champion and the world-record holder, could have made $150,000 in performance bonuses by running in the 1985 New York City Marathon, but he stayed home.

Lopes and Kristiansen had made a huge impact on the marathon in April, also the month of perhaps the most glorious moment in the history of Djibouti, the tiny former French colony sandwiched between Ethiopia and Somalia on the Horn of Africa. Djibouti's three-man squad had captured the team title in the World Cup Marathon in Hiroshima. The individual cup winner was the swiftest Djiboutian, Ahmed Saleh, who clocked 2:08:09.

Saleh admitted that the tall buildings and many cars of Manhattan made him nervous, but he predicted he would set a world record, talking openly about running a 2:05. He was a bit disappointed, however, that Djibouti had dispatched him to New York rather than Chicago, sending Djama Robleh to the America's Marathon instead, ostensibly because Saleh would do better on New York's hillier course. Placing second to Jones in Chicago, Robleh had finished in 2:08:08, supplanting Saleh as the fastest Djiboutian by one second.

The main players in the 1983 New York City Marathon drama, Geoff Smith and Rod Dixon, would each have crucial roles in the 1985 race, but it is doubtful they were as proud of their 1985 performances. Smith shot through the first 10 kilometers in 29:20, clocking a manic 47:37 in the first 10 miles. Was this the behavior of a man expecting to run 26.2 miles, or the showmanship of one paid to secure 45 minutes of coveted airtime for Tofutti, whose huge logo was emblazoned across Smith's shirt? Tofutti had, apparently, introduced a new flavor—Marathon Orange.

Dixon, meanwhile, was working for ABC. The network had equipped the former champion with a helmet mounted with a minicamera. Dixon's assignment was to jump into the race at assorted intervals to provide a fresh, expert view of the elite competitors; instead, he supplied jittery glimpses of their rear ends. It was not a proud innovation—to Phil Stewart of *Running Times*, it was part of ABC's "relentless invasion of the sanctity of the sport." By the end of the race, the Dixon experiment had yielded little journalistic value.

As Geoff Smith drifted out of the lead, Saleh and Bill Reifsnyder reached the halfway point in a still-brisk 1:03:01, after which Reifsnyder faded. Orlando Pizzolato, the surprise 1984 New York winner, had been sixth in the World Cup that Saleh won, but Pizzolato's 2:10:23 had been a significant personal improvement. Now Pizzolato was 2 minutes behind Saleh and in 20th place, but he was precisely on schedule for his plan to combine two 1:05 halves for a 2:10 marathon.

Bill Rodgers would comment that Saleh "made the classic mistake of the beginner" in ignoring the fact that this marathon's first miles were relatively

easy while the later ones were more difficult. After 19 miles, Saleh was slowing down. Pizzolato had shifted into fourth position but could not see Saleh; oblivious to the leader's fatigue, Pizzolato was nearly prepared to settle for second place. But as the Italian recounted, "People were telling me, 'Saleh doesn't look good.' They said he was in bad condition. I got closer, step by step."

Saleh ran his 23rd mile in 5:43—his force was spent. Pizzolato pulled even with him at the 24th mile. The World Cup victor hung in for another half mile, but Pizzolato applied pressure on an upgrade near 72nd Street in Central Park and the contest was over. Overlooked as a contender in prerace speculation, Pizzolato scored his second New York victory in a creditable 2:11:34. Saleh kept second place in 2:12:29, with Pat Petersen, now of Brooklyn, in third place in 2:12:59.

A gregarious gentleman who speaks nearly fluent English, Pizzolato expressed gratitude for the crowd support he had received. "Nobody knew me last year," Pizzolato said. "People thought I won by mistake. Now everyone's a friend of mine. They help me very well."

A tailwind and "Lisa Martin breathing on my ear for 10 miles" sent Grete Waitz out faster than usual, but by the 11th mile she seemed to have broken Martin, the Australian challenger. From that point, Waitz's fiercest foe was an unsettled stomach. A lucky Waitz won her seventh New York City Marathon crown in 2:28:34. She was followed by Martin in 2:29:48, Laura Fogli in 2:31:36, and Lorraine Moller of New Zealand in 2:34:55. Forty-year-old Priscilla Welch placed fifth in 2:35:30.

Above left: Rod Dixon's helmet camera failed to provide useful vantage points. Right: With Lisa Martin close behind, Grete Waitz won her seventh New York title.

Above: Ahmed Saleh of
Djibouti (2) was big news
after his World Cup
victory in Japan, but
Orlando Pizzolato (1)
proved that his 1984 New
York upset was no fluke.

Above: By 1985, the
marathon throng had
swollen to 16,705
and massive lead
packs stormed
across the Verrazano-
Narrows Bridge.

Gianni Poli was New York's least-anticipated champion, and its most exhausted. Poli prevailed over his Italian countryman, two-time winner Orlando Pizzolato, and also beat the heavily favored Rob de Castella.

# 1986

In an interview with Don Kardong in *The Runner*, Lisa Martin discussed her 1985 New York experience with the invincible Grete Waitz: "Last year I ran with her for 11 miles, and I looked across at this woman they made a statue of in Oslo, and I was thinking, 'Wow!' And she took off and I was thinking, 'Wow!' I thought about it afterwards, and you have to knock people off pedestals before you can beat them."

By 1986 Waitz was feeling the competition: "The pressure is mounting. Everyone just takes it for granted that I'll win. There are people who always want to beat you. And they seem to be getting closer and closer."

A former collegiate 400-meter hurdler, Martin was now the 1986 Commonwealth Games marathon champion, having run 2:26:07 in Edinburgh in August, but Waitz showed no sign of slowing down. Her new personal record was 2:24:54, which she ran to win the London Marathon in April. With a strong performance in New York, Waitz could earn another number-one world ranking to follow the five she had secured in 1978, 1979, 1980, 1982, and 1983.

The New York City Marathon women's crown would remain on Waitz's head. After leaving Laura Fogli behind at the 15-mile mark, the woman whose statue stands in Oslo proceeded without impediment to her eighth New York City triumph in 2:28:06. Martin returned for second place in 2:29:12, with Fogli third in 2:31:44. The finishing order of the top three duplicated 1985.

Marathoning's 1986 imbroglio had already been dubbed "Car Wars." Mercedes-Benz supported the sport by putting its money into major events and by awarding automobiles to winners. Mazda subsidized headline-caliber individual athletes with its Mazda Track Club. In April, Rob de Castella had set a

**Above: De Castella (2),** back on top after his 2:07:51 Boston win, was shocked at his inability to break free of Poli (10), who took the lead in the Bronx.

**Left: Laura Fogli** accepted her roses after placing third behind Grete Waitz and Lisa Martin, duplicating the 1985 win-place-show. **Below: A men's pack led** as the press truck caught every stride.

personal record of 2:07:51, taking the Boston Marathon, while Ingrid Kristiansen was the women's victor in 2:24:55. "Deke" and Kristiansen had worn singlets with "Mazda" written in conspicuously large letters across their chests. The two had posed after the race with their Mercedes prizes, in outfits again labeled "Mazda."

At long last, Fred Lebow wanted de Castella in New York. The Australian had dethroned Alberto Salazar in Rotterdam in 1983; later that summer, de Castella had triumphed quite handily in the marathon at the first World Championships of track and field in Helsinki. After his 2:07:51 in Boston, "Deke" was once again the hottest property in the marathon. But Lebow worried about alienating Mercedes-Benz. De Castella had allegedly been paid forty thousand dollars to wear the Mazda logo in New York. After negotiations between all parties, the logo was reduced to a size virtually unreadable on television screens. Many media outlets avoided mentioning or displaying the logo at all. More significant to the 26.2-mile race itself was the fact that de Castella, also a Commonwealth Games victor in August, would be attempting his third marathon in seven months, potentially overextending himself.

Orlando Pizzolato was back in a bid for a third win in New York. This time he warmly played to the crowd, blowing kisses as he journeyed through Brooklyn. But the most formidable Italian in the 1986 race was Gianni Poli, fourth in Chicago in 1985 and holder of the Italian national record, 2:09:57.

Djama Robleh had hopes of placing one spot higher than fellow Djiboutian Ahmed Saleh had finished the year before, but for Robleh the quest proved futile after 12 miles. The highly celebrated de Castella had his hands full with the unheralded Poli; a surge on the Queensboro Bridge, intended to drop Poli, did not have the desired effect. After 18 miles, de Castella was laboring. On the bridges in and out of the Bronx, Poli sealed his triumph.

Poli persevered to win in 2:11:06. In a furious finish virtually unnoticed until it was a fait accompli, Antoni Niemczak passed de Castella for second place. "Another quarter-mile and I would have had first place," insisted Niemczak. "I just waited too long." A Niemczak victory would have been a monumental embarrassment; he tested positive for anabolic steroids and was disqualified despite his claim of innocence. In the adjusted standings, de Castella was second in 2:11:43, with Pizzolato third in 2:12:13 and Ibrahim Hussein of Kenya fourth in 2:12:51.

An unhappy Pat Petersen was a distant also-ran, placing 101st in 2:30:55. Great things had been expected of Petersen on the basis of his 1984 and 1985 showings, but he had found himself at the heart of the marathon's publicity whirl for the first time and the distractions were painfully uncomfortable. And, as his father Henry explained, "He just can't say no to anyone. He put up a few friends in the hotel suite last night because they needed a place to stay."

"Running 20 minutes longer in a marathon is a lot tougher," Petersen deadpanned. "And you get a lot colder." He tried to reassure supporters disappointed by his performance. "Don't look so depressed," he told his brother Edward. "I'll get over it . . . in a couple of years."

The field of 20,502 runners, an increase of nearly 4,000 from 1985, showcased athletes from eighty countries. The big story was the success of the Italians; four Italian men and three Italian women placed in their respective top tens. Rumors of "blood doping"—a method of increasing oxygen levels in the blood—had plagued Italian runners since Alberto Cova's gold medal in the 10,000 meters at the 1984 Olympics (Cova had been suspected of the practice), and ABC gave ample currency to the rumors. Petersen, however, had trained with top Italians on their home soil and swore he never saw any evidence of the practice; no proof was ever supplied to the public.

# 1987

Into her thirties, Priscilla Welch had been a pack-a-day smoker who enjoyed drinking with her colleagues in the British Royal Navy. When she took up running, the communications officer was thirty-four years old and weighed 150 pounds. Five years later, at thirty-nine, Welch placed sixth in the marathon at the 1984 Los Angeles Olympics in 2:28:54.

While stationed with the navy in the Shetland Islands, Welch ran wearing a miner's helmet so she could train in the dead of winter. In 1987 she did much of her running on the mountain paths of Boulder, Colorado, where her only companions were birds of prey.

With the running boom more than a decade old, the demographics of the sport showed a significant number of masters (over forty) runners. There was a healthy curiosity as to just how fast these athletes could run.

Now it appeared that a forty-two-year-old competitor had a definite shot at winning the New York City Marathon.

Welch was not sure that the age distinction held any importance. "I don't know how *you* feel at 40," she commented, "but I don't think I've grown up properly yet." As if to prove it, Welch was anything but cautious in the race. Before the women merged with the men at the 8-mile mark in Brooklyn, she already held a sizable lead. She led Belgium's Ria Van Landeghem by 65 seconds after 10 kilometers. Welch's blistering pace forced Allison Roe, the 1981 champion and course-record holder on a comeback venture, to cease and desist after 10 miles. Welch's halfway time was 1:12:17.

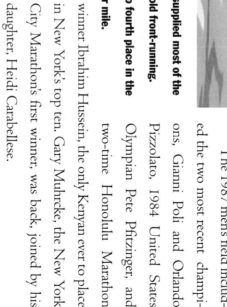

**Local hero Pat Petersen supplied most of the 1987 drama with his bold front-running. He slipped from second to fourth place in the final quarter mile.**

Even Welch could not maintain that breakneck schedule; she slowed down in the race's latter stages, but the huge edge she had built up could not be eradicated, despite the efforts of Frenchwomen Françoise Bonnet and Jocelyne Villeton (the bronze medalist in the marathon at the World Championships in Rome that year) who gained ground through Manhattan. At the finish, Welch won her New York laurels in 2:30:17, setting a New York masters record that still stands. Bonnet placed second in 2:31:22, Villeton third in 2:32:03, and Van Landeghem fourth in 2:32:38.

"I think old age is a social disease that people think they cannot overcome," the victorious master theorized. "For those who really want to go for it, I hope this will be an inspiration." In 1992 Priscilla Welch was diagnosed with breast cancer. By 1993, she had sufficiently recovered to enter her first Race for the Cure, a national series of races that promotes breast cancer research and education.

The 1987 men's field included the two most recent champions, Gianni Poli and Orlando Pizzolato, 1984 United States Olympian Pete Pfitzinger, and two-time Honolulu Marathon winner Ibrahim Hussein, the only Kenyan ever to place in New York's top ten. Gary Muhrcke, the New York City Marathon's first winner, was back, joined by his daughter, Heidi Carabellese.

"Mentally fried" by the publicity demands of the 1986 race, Pat Petersen returned in 1987 determined to maintain a low premarathon profile. "Everybody dreams of the Olympics. I'd rather win the New York City Marathon," affirmed Petersen, a financial

analyst based in Long Island and owner of all 340 known Elvis Presley albums. "There are few days that go by when I'm not thinking about being in first place coming into Central Park, with the crowds going crazy."

The multitude at the Staten Island start had grown to 22,523. Nerves and adrenaline seized control of Petersen, who sped to such a dominating lead by the 4-mile mark that he turned and asked pace-car passenger Fred Lebow where everyone else was. Petersen had planned on a 1:04 opening half but "I screwed up and went faster"—he ran 29:37 for the opening 10 kilometers and clocked 1:03:16 at the halfway point. ABC's coverage was dominated by Petersen's characteristic swaying gait, rocking like a ship from port to starboard. In reality, the extraneous motion was all above the waist; Petersen was a very efficient runner.

Only Ibrahim Hussein stayed close. "I could not leave a serious runner like him alone," the Kenyan had decided. "He had a way to go, but he was moving." Petersen, meanwhile, was discovering that "running by yourself is the loneliest feeling in the world." He was actually relieved when Hussein joined him after 14 miles. Hussein led for the next 12 miles, never seeming to be exerting himself too much. "I wasn't running fast because I wanted to be fresh," he said. "I was expecting those guys to be coming up to me." They never did; Hussein ran the rest of the race virtually unchallenged.

Petersen seemed ready to take second place, but Gianni DeMadonna, Pete Pfitzinger, and Tommy Ekblom gave chase in Manhattan. They ran as if they were attached at the hip, appearing to gain strength from one another symbiotically.

Hussein was the champion in 2:11:01. ABC, occupied with another part of the race, actually neglected to telecast his breasting of the tape. Since Hussein was the New York City Marathon's first black winner, the oversight prompted allegations of racism. The following April in Boston, Hussein would outsprint Juma Ikangaa to the tape, 2:08:43 to 2:08:44, in a duel of once-and-future New York kings.

Very close to the 26-mile mark, DeMadonna and Pfitzinger passed an unsuspecting Petersen. DeMadonna took second place in 2:11:53, Pfitzinger third in 2:11:54, Petersen fourth in 2:12:03, Ekblom fifth in 2:12:31, and Pizzolato sixth in 2:12:50. Poli did not finish the race. Along with so many who had admired his bravado, Petersen was crushed to see second place slip away so late in the game. "I set the tone, I set the pace for the race," he reassured himself. Lebow thanked him for giving "a great show." Petersen had demonstrated his mettle. "They've got respect for me now. They know I've got balls," he said.

There was consolation for New Yorkers as one local hero, research chemist Fritz Mueller, won the over-fifty age-group category by 5 minutes in 2:38:18. In his forties, Mueller had run under 2:30 in seven consecutive New York City Marathons, with a best of 2:25:25.

By 1987 Fred Lebow suspected that some elite athletes were accepting appearance fees while hiding the fact that they were in no condition to contend for victory. Chicago had lost its primary funding and was no longer a major rival, so Lebow elected to pay appearance fees only to previous winners and Olympic gold medalists. "New York doesn't just buy stars," asserted Lebow. "New York creates them."

64

Opposite top: Runner-up Gianni DeMadonna continued the string of Italian accomplishments in New York.

Opposite bottom: American Olympian Pete Pfitzinger was edged into third place in the final strides.

Below: Forty-two-year-old Priscilla Welch's top New York honors highlighted her remarkable career—she had been an overweight chainsmoker in her thirties.

Above: Ibrahim Hussein, the first of the great Kenyans to excel at the marathon, led for the last 12 miles in the most one-sided New York men's race since 1981.

American-record holder Joan Benoit Samuelson (F3) never scored a New York title to go with her Olympic, Boston, and Chicago wins, but she finished a valiant third in 1988.

In recent seasons, Fred Lebow had been steadfastly parsimonious in his dealings with elite athletes who hoped for glory *and* riches in New York, but now he was faced with a new reality. There were big-budget fall and winter marathons in China and Japan, and greater largesse was required to keep pace in bidding for the world-class runners. To the rescue came John Hancock Financial Services and the company's senior executive vice president, David D'Alessandro, whose sponsorship of the marathon included negotiations with and payments to a "Hancock team" of top marathoners.

Steve Jones was thirty-three years old and had recently retired from his long stint as an airplane mechanic in the British Royal Air Force. More than any other athlete, he had given credibility to the America's Marathon in Chicago with his Windy City triumphs in 2:08:05 and 2:07:13 in 1984 and 1985.

In the 1988 Boston Marathon, however, all Jones could manage was 2:14:21 and ninth place. On the basis of that disappointment he was left off Great Britain's Olympic squad for Seoul. There was a late reversal of that verdict, but Jones demurred. He had

marathoner to journey to the high altitudes of Boulder for several weeks of preparation. In New York he would face Wodajo Bulti. Bulti had run his first marathon in Rotterdam in 2:08:44, taking second place behind fellow-Ethiopian Belayneh Densimo, who set a world record of 2:06:50.

Mark Nenow had set the American 10-kilometer marks in road and track, but he had not made the Olympic team and was in New York for his debut marathon, aspiring to be America's first great 26.2-mile hope in five years.

Ireland's John Treacy, silver medalist in the 1984 Olympics, would also compete. In road, track, and cross-country events, Treacy and his friend Jones, both in their thirties, had raced against each other too many times to count.

Spain's Juan Romera controlled the lead for the first 12 miles, after which Jones took over and settled the outcome of the 1988 New York City Marathon. Jones ran the 14th mile in 4:47. "Steve was flying," Treacy realized. But Jones was merely beginning; with no one at his heels, he left nothing in reserve. He scorched the second (and more difficult) half of the course and was all done in 2:08:20.

Jones's time was seven ticks slower than Alberto Salazar's New York record, but the route had been re-measured since 1981. In the minds of many—including Jones himself—the 1988 victor was the new course-record holder. John Treacy estimated that his friend's effort was "probably equivalent to a 2:06 in Rotterdam," a much flatter course. Jones, the only man to win the Chicago, London, and New York City marathons, believed this latest victory to be "my best run ever."

Jones's winning margin, 3:21, was the largest among the men in the history of the five-borough marathon. The runner-up, Italian Salvatore Bettiol, had hushed the horrified Central Park onlookers when cramps forced him to lie in the road at the 24-mile mark for 45 seconds before valiantly resuming

**1988**

**Below: Salvatore Bettiol faltered and even lay down in the road in the race's closing miles, but he managed to hold on for second place.**

**Opposite: An exuberant Steve Jones resolutely conquered the men's field in the second half of the race. His 2:08:20 was New York City's fastest time in seven years, and his 3:21 winning edge was the biggest in five-borough history.**

his mission. Treacy placed third in 2:13:18. In his first marathon, Nenow finished in 2:14:21 for eighth place.

For Grete Waitz, New York in 1988 represented another comeback. Injuries had kept her out of New York and prevented her from defending her title in the World Championship in 1987, and recent arthroscopic knee surgery had left her out of shape, causing her to drop out of the Olympic marathon in Seoul.

After dispensing with 13.1 miles in 1:22:39, Waitz, Laura Fogli, and Joan Benoit Samuelson were the trio of front-runners. Samuelson, winner in Boston and Chicago and the 1984 Olympic gold medalist, was making her New York debut, attempting her first marathon in three years. Stomach problems soon forced Samuelson to drift behind, and Waitz drew a full 2 minutes ahead of Fogli after the 20-mile mark.

As Samuelson gamely struggled to get back into contention, an overzealous child volunteer stepped into the roadway at the 20-mile water stop, toppling the Maine native (children are no longer accepted for volunteer assignments). Samuelson rose and continued, but was unable to move out of third place. Waitz won an astonishing ninth New York City Marathon crown, possibly her sweetest, in 2:28:07. Fogli was the

runner-up in 2:31:26 and Samuelson finished for third place in 2:32:40.

Both the upper and lower spans of the Verrazano-Narrows Bridge were used to accommodate runners at the beginning of the 1988 race, allowing for the field's expansion: 23,463 men and women ran, of whom 22,405 crossed the finish line.

# 1989

Many good things had happened to Ingrid Kristiansen since her previous visits to the New York City Marathon, where she had taken third place in 1980, second place in 1981, and fifth place in 1982. She had run three of the five fastest women's marathons in history, including the world record, 2:21:06, set in London in 1985. Kristiansen had also established world records in track at 5000 and 10,000 meters, and had won both the 1987 World Championship in the 10 kilometers and the 1988 World Cross Country crown.

She was now ready to take on New York in the race that had been so kind to her absent compatriot, Grete Waitz. "I've seen a Norwegian girl winning so many times," quipped Kristiansen. "It looked great."

No one had been predicted to mount a serious challenge to Kristiansen, but Kim Jones of Spokane, Washington, decided to try. New York took place only four weeks after the Twin Cities Marathon, which Jones had won, but she defied the conventional wisdom that recommended a far longer interval between marathons. "I'm going to explore the unknown," she explained.

Kristiansen was never challenged; no one could approximate her 1:09:59 in the opening half. She slowed a bit at the end, costing herself the ten-thousand-dollar bonus paid to course-record setters. Her 2:25:30 missed Allison Roe's New York City mark by just one second, but Kristiansen did not seem to mind.

Kim Jones, gathering momentum as she ran mile after mile, displayed no weariness as she finished in second place in 2:27:54, a time fast enough to have

"Losing to Grete is an honor. She owns New York."

JOAN BENOIT SAMUELSON

won earlier New York City Marathons overall. Laura Fogli of Italy placed high once again, coming in third in 2:28:43, her best New York time.

A star-studded men's field conspired with the mildest marathon weather since 1983 to guarantee an assault on Alberto Salazar's long-lasting New York record, 2:08:13. Steve Jones returned for a shot at back-to-back victory, but when it was suggested that his familiarity with the course might be an advantage, Jones retorted, "I can't remember a single bit of it."

Belayneh Densimo of Ethiopia had set a world record of 2:06:50 in Rotterdam in 1988 and had then seen his nation boycott the Seoul Olympics. He came to New York brashly confident of victory and a course record. The Italian hopes rested with 1988 Olympic champion Gelindo Bordin, 1986 New York winner Gianni Poli, and Salvatore Bettiol, the runner-up to Jones in 1988. Mark Plaatjes, a swift South African residing in the United States, was also in the fold, as was diminutive Tanzanian Juma Ikangaa, arguably the world's best-traveled marathoner. Ikangaa had scored victories in Cairo, Beijing, Melbourne, and Tokyo, but he had also finished a heartbreaking second in Boston three times in a row and invariably seemed vulnerable in a sprint finish. Ikangaa, one of six children in a cattle-farming family, was an army major and the first African to run a sub-2:10 marathon. A high-altitude trainer who practiced in Alamosa, Colorado, Ikangaa was known to run 200 miles in a week, tapering to 100 miles before races.

Ken Martin, a former University of Oregon steeplechaser who lived in New Mexico, had made the conversion to marathoning. He and his ex-wife, Lisa Martin, had been the first married couple to top the men's and women's divisions of a major United States marathon in Pittsburgh in 1985. Ken's recent performances had not impressed the New York organizers; he was offered a very small appearance fee. "I thought I'd come anyway and do well," Martin decided.

Ikangaa had insisted that someone have the courage to lead, and placed himself within a pack that ran the first 13.1 miles in 1:03:44. Steve Jones tossed in a surge at that point, but Ikangaa covered it and kept forging ahead. "He'll come back to us," Martin, searching for assurances, told Jones. "No, he won't," was Jones's dark realization. Jones later marveled at Ikangaa's performance: "He ran incredibly. His knee lift was good and his back kick was coming up high. He looked so good, it was demoralizing."

Ikangaa was not going to let the race come down to a kick at the tape. The Tanzanian triumphantly shattered Salazar's mark with a personal best of 2:08:01, saying, "I could have run another 5 miles." As if to prove it, Ikangaa jumped into the air, his heels almost touching his shorts, some six times. He was thrilled to shed the yoke of the runner-up. "My mother had complained that I never win the car," noted the owner of a new Mercedes-Benz.

Ken Martin had become one of the first serious marathoners to do the bulk of his long-haul training on a treadmill, efficiently calibrating his pace. It worked wonders for him. After Ikangaa zoomed off, Martin ran alone in second place for much of the closing half, but kept his wits about him and held his position to finish in 2:09:38.

His performance was a much-needed shot in the arm for United States marathoning, the first sub-2:10 by an American since 1983. Martin earned over thirty thousand dollars and was reportedly awarded an adjustment in his appearance fee.

Characteristically, Gelindo Bordin closed quickly, but he had too much ground to make up and just missed catching up to Martin. After his 2:09:40, the gold medalist from Venice was haggard and wan and required medical attention. Bettiol came in fourth in 2:10:08. Defender Steve Jones placed eighth in 2:12:58, one notch ahead of Densimo, who finished in 2:13:42.

Opposite: Too often outkicked at the end, Juma Ikangaa finally jetted to a New York City record in 2:08:01. Ingrid Kristiansen missed Allison Roe's course mark by a single tick in 2:25:30, but her New York laurels made her smile. Above: Densimo (2) and Ikangaa (3) set the pace for (back row, left to right) Poli, Nenow, Garcia, Plaatjes, Jones, and Martin. Below: Gelindo Bordin tried to catch Martin but settled for third place. Right: Kim Jones ran just four weeks after winning the Twin Cities Marathon and was pleased with her 2:27:54 second-place finish.

# 1990

The running community had watched with a mixture of deep concern and admiration as Fred Lebow battled brain cancer. Under the slogan "Fred, This Run's For You," the 1990 New York City Marathon was a fundraiser for Stop Cancer, an organization created by industrialist Armand Hammer.

The unique nature of the 1990 race largely accounted for the return of Grete Waitz, who was no longer training with her former intensity. Her transformation from anonymous track runner and schoolteacher to the world's most recognizable road racer was primarily based on the astonishing nine New York City Marathon titles she had won. Through the years, she and Lebow had forged a special bond. The customarily neutral Lebow announced, "I'm rooting for Grete, and I don't feel guilty about it."

Waitz would have to contend with the 1989 runner-up, Kim Jones, and with Katrin Dorre, the first athlete from the former East Germany to compete in the five-borough race. The overall favorite, however, was Wanda Panfil, a thirty-one-year-old Polish woman. Earlier in 1990, Panfil had won the Nagoya and London marathons and the 10,000 meters at the Goodwill Games.

Although the race took place on November 4, the city's temperature soared to 73 degrees. Early on the heat did not seem to bother Panfil. She separated herself from the other competitors after 9 miles, but in the final 5 kilometers she was visibly struggling. Kim Jones suffered from a form of asthma that flared up when her pace dipped below 5:30 per mile, which may have been the reason she conceded such a wide margin to Panfil in the first half of the race.

Jones trailed by one full minute at the 20-mile mark, but after reentry into Manhattan from the Bronx the American challenger heard that she was narrowing the gap. "They really wanted me to catch the leader," the popular Jones later said of the spectators lining the race route. "Some of their faces were red with excitement. And they kept telling me how many seconds I was in back of Wanda."

Panfil's impassive countenance betrayed nothing, but by the time she arrived in Central Park she was in no condition to resist a late challenge, if it should materialize. Tension—an element not traditionally conspicuous in New York women's competition—was palpable until the final seconds of the race when Jones simply ran out of space and time to close the gap. Panfil prevailed by 5 seconds, 2:30:45 to 2:30:50. Jones steadfastly refused to feel miserable. "I think I ran as fast as I could today," she concluded. "Five seconds is a long time." Waitz traversed the familiar 26.2 miles in 2:34:34 for fourth place, 1:13 behind Dorre.

Juma Ikangaa returned to New York the year after his record-breaking triumph, but he warned, "What somebody did last year is not what he is going to do tomorrow." An arduous trainer, Ikangaa noted, "The will to win means nothing if you have not had the will to prepare." Ikangaa was adored by the press for his sweet bluntness and wisdom.

The race's soaring star was Douglas Wakiihuri of Kenya, who had journeyed to Japan when he was nineteen years old to train with Kiyoshi Nakamura, the mentor of Toshihiko Seko. Wakiihuri won gold medals in the 1987 World Championships and 1990 Commonwealth Games marathons and won the silver medal in the 1988 Olympic marathon. In April he had triumphed in London in 2:09:03.

**John Campbell of New Zealand placed fifth in 2:14:34, a New York City masters record. He won the 1990 masters triple crown—Los Angeles, Boston, and New York.**

74

Above: Garcia (9) looked but found no weakness in Wakiihuri or Ikangaa (1). Below: Panfil (F5) kept pace with (left to right) Jones, Groos, Waitz, Dorre, Sirma, and Isphording.

Ikangaa and Wakiihuri displayed entirely different personalities. An insider who knew both men observed, "Ikangaa is a diplomat. When he's not running, he's watching CNN for hours. He understands *you* much better. Douglas understands *himself*."

Wakiihuri conveyed an aura of invulnerability and impermeability. One reporter stated that interviewing the Zen Kenyan was "like root canal." He was given to making such statements as: "There is the truth about the marathon and very few of you have written the truth," and "Even if I explain it to you, you'll never understand it, you're outside of it."

Wakiihuri, who had trained in rural New Zealand, declined an advance glimpse of the route. "I think I'll know the course better when I run on it, after I've finished the race," he asserted. He betrayed no sentimentality about New York's legendarily enthusiastic crowds. "It's not important," he said. "You either win a race or you lose; you can't care about how crowded it is. It's a matter of how ready I am that day." Of two things he was certain: "Running is my satisfaction. To me, it's everything. The most important thing is to win each and every race I run."

Through much of Manhattan, Wakiihuri and Ikangaa were in a tight group of four that also included Steve Brace, an Englishman who had won the Paris Marathon, and Salvador García, whom New York–area runners remembered from his victory in the 1989 New Jersey Waterfront Marathon. García trained in Mexico City with his Doberman, La Mafia, and was rather intimidating. Ken Martin, who had missed a month of training due to illness and would eventually be forced to abandon the race, said, "When I saw [García] at the

start with a shaved head and an earring, I figured he was kind of motivated today."

Wakiihuri was the most upright and effortless of the top four. His decisive break came after 20 miles, but even the invincible Wakiihuri felt the heat in the final miles. He took the race easily, but his 2:12.39 was the slowest winning time since the infamous swelter of 1984. Wakiihuri was 40 seconds in front of García, who proudly displayed his gruesomely bloody and blistered feet at a postrace press conference. The upstart Brace was third in 2:13:32, one minute ahead of

**In 1990, only the Mercedes pace car and Fred Lebow, bullhorn in hand, could keep up with Douglas Wakiihuri.**

Ikangaa, who had struggled with severe cramps.

In fifth place was forty-one-year-old John Campbell of New Zealand, whose 2:14:34 established a New York City masters record. As the masters winner in the Los Angeles, Boston, and New York City marathons, Campbell reaped a seventy-five-thousand-dollar bonus from John Hancock. "I just can't believe what I achieved today," beamed an ecstatic Campbell. "Today is probably going to change my life." His life had previously consisted of seven-day workweeks spent

operating a convenience store, sneaking out to run "when it's convenient."

Interest in Campbell's triple win was an indicator of how long it had been since running's initial boom. The early "boomers," graying and reaching the far side of forty, were taking masters competition quite seriously. Many were surely people like Campbell, who had been a promising if not world-class athlete in his youth. For years, he had been a seriously overweight smoker and drinker. A friend flatly told him he would soon be dead, so Campbell decided to start running again.

For the first—but certainly not the last—time, American men had been shut out of the New York City Marathon's top ten. The first United States runner, Gerry O'Hara, placed 29th in 2:26:15.

# 1991

Liz McColgan of Dundee, Scotland, had been an NCAA champion in the mile for the University of Alabama as Liz Lynch. She topped off an eminently successful road-racing season by winning the 10,000 meters at the 1991 World Championships by a full 21 seconds. In spite of her many athletic achievements, McColgan felt that her greatest accomplishment of the year had been "having Eilish," her baby daughter. In New York, McColgan was attempting her first marathon; her closest competitors were expected to be mother-of-two Joan Benoit Samuelson and Lisa Ondieki, who had a new daughter of her own, Emma.

Ondieki, the New York runner-up in 1985 and 1986 as Lisa Martin, had married Yobes Ondieki of Kenya, the 1991 world champion at 5000 meters. Motherhood had given Lisa Ondieki her first respite from athletics since she was eleven. "I feel more relaxed," she declared. "Perhaps it's the distraction of taking care of a child. I don't sit around and stew over my training all day." Bert Rosenthal of the Associated Press dubbed the 1991 women's competition "the race of the mothers."

McColgan, defying what had been conventional wisdom, had trained hard until the very late stages of her pregnancy. Where exercise during pregancy had once been almost completely discouraged, it was later recommended that women not train in the third trimester. It has since been shown, however, that active athletes tend to have shorter labors, easier deliveries, and very healthy babies.

Though she was attempting her first marathon, McColgan was undaunted by the approaching race, but she was not as brazenly confident as some reports indicated. Arriving in New York a few days before McColgan, Lisa Ondieki claimed that her competitor had announced a goal of 2:16 for herself. McColgan was baffled. "If I thought I could run 2:16 here, I might as well think I could fly without wings," she stated. Her preparation in Gainesville, Florida, however, was staggeringly impressive: she was clicking off ten 5-minute miles, alternated with recoveries of only 30 seconds. "If your training's gone well, you've got every reason to be confident," she maintained. "I'm here to win."

Samuelson had won an Olympic gold medal and the Chicago and Boston marathons, and held the American marathon record by more than 5 minutes. Only one title was missing from her résumé. "It would mean more for me to win in New York than come back and do another Olympic marathon," she said.

An overzealous official's premature signal caused the women's field to start 9 seconds early. Samuelson, suffering from significant asthma-related fluid loss, ran well in the first half of the race but barely made it to the finish, taking sixth in 2:33:40.

With her ponytail sticking straight up like Stone Age cartoon character Pebbles Flintstone, McColgan characteristically ran in front while Ondieki kept her on a short leash. The leaders had company from two

> "Everything else is just a stepping stone.
> The marathon is what I'm going to be best at."
>
> LIZ McCOLGAN BEFORE THE 1991 MARATHON

Left: Liz McColgan, a Scot who had won an NCAA title in the mile for the University of Alabama, came to New York as the new reigning world champion at 10,000 meters. The focus of heady speculation about her marathon prowess, she did not disappoint and triumphed with a debut world record of 2:27:32. Below: Lisa Ondieki stayed close for 23 miles before finishing in third place.

Soviets, Ramilia Burangulova and twenty-three-year-old Olga Markova. Markova's venture into the lead group after the 23rd mile prompted McColgan to find a faster gear. "She kind of got me going at that point, and I started to stride out," the Scot would explain. McColgan won in 2:27:32, the world's fastest debut marathon by 3 minutes. She was the latest star to feel the encouraging power of the roaring New York City crowd. Markova took second place in 2:28:27 and had lowered her personal best by 5 minutes. Ondieki finished third in 2:29:02.

Graziella Striuli of Modena, Italy, had topped the masters category in Boston in 2:39:32 and finished in 2:40:13 in New York, placing her ninth in the overall women's ranks. The oldest finisher, eighty-year-old Lois Schieffelin, was subsequently a *Late Night* guest of talk-show host David Letterman, who quipped, "It took her 6 hours and a bit to run the marathon. You could fly to California in that time."

By 1991, Mexicans rivaled Kenyans as the dominant force in United States road racing. Mexican army sergeant Salvador García had run with a shaved head in 1990, but now sported a full head of hair. The men's race was sorted out at the 17-mile mark on First Avenue when García bolted from a pack that included his countryman Andres Espinosa, Ecuador's Rolando Vera, and Kenyans Andrew Masai and Ibrahim Hussein. "I thought he was responding to the crowds and would not last," Hussein later said, but García lasted, winning in 2:09:28, 32 seconds in front of Espinosa. Hussein placed third in 2:11:07, followed by Canadian Peter Maher in fourth in 2:11:55.

**Salvador García had grown his hair since 1990. The change in style propelled him one spot higher and into the winner's circle.**

The French contingent in the marathon now numbered more than two thousand, and there were almost as many Italians and Germans. When Jean Baptiste Protais took eighth in 2:14:54, however, he was the first Frenchman in New York's top ten since 1977. Eamonn Coghlan, an Irishman who had thrilled New York and New Jersey audiences with his world records in the indoor mile, ran the 26.2 miles in a very creditable 2:25:13.

Foreign hopefuls often carry to New York enormous pressures from their home countries. Rolando Vera, a Pan American Games silver medalist, found that the largest overseas press corps at the 1991 New York City Marathon was from his native Ecuador, where he was the third most popular man behind the nation's president and French Open tennis champion Andres Gomez. It may have been too heavy a burden for the five-foot-one-inch Vera to bear. He made his bid for the lead but faded to 14th place in 2:17:21.

The Memorial Sloan-Kettering Cancer Center sponsored a "Put Cancer on the Run" campaign in conjunction with the marathon and raised $650,000. The runners also made a lot of money: advantageously cool weather and a system of rewards based on finishing times brought prize totals to a record $327,500.

Anticipating a reduction in foreign entries due to the Persian Gulf War, marathon officials had permitted 1,500 wait-listed Americans to start in Staten Island, but the international athletes arrived in full force. The field thus reached a record 26,900, of whom 25,797 completed the race. At a midafternoon peak, over 300 runners per minute entered the finish chutes.

# 1992

For some couples, the New York City Marathon is more than just an occasion to run. The day before Sunday's marathon, entrants Anthony Borough and Sylvia Matthews were married at the finish line on the Central Park roadway by a vicar from Aberdeen, Scotland. According to a friend, Borough had been "next to last this year in the Paris Marathon." On the morning of the race, Mike Paolillo proposed to Linda Harris on the local telecast in front of fellow marathon volunteers near the finish line. Harris accepted.

Lisa Ondieki had journeyed to Barcelona as the 1992 Olympic favorite in the marathon, but she felt mysteriously flat and listless in the heat and dropped out. Almost immediately she thought about returning to New York City for a shot at the crown she had never won. "I was in the best shape of my life for Barcelona, but it didn't do me any good," Ondieki said. "I came here for redemption."

She had trained at a 7,000-foot altitude in Flagstaff, Arizona, following a demanding regimen prepared by her husband, Yobes. "I almost cracked several times," she confessed in *Runner's World*, calling her husband "unforgiving when it comes to training. He can be merciless.... Still, I don't want him to change. I learned so much from him."

Ondieki was not the unanimous New York favorite. Olga Markova of St. Petersburg, Russia, had been an unknown when she finished ahead of Ondieki in New York in 1991 but had since captured the Boston Marathon in 2:23:43. Her Boston time alerted the marathoning world to her prowess and lifted her from obscurity to the forefront of race speculation. Markova was a former army sergeant whose assignment was "only running." The Soviets,

**Above: Willie Mtolo (1) dogged the steps of Andres Espinosa (2) before the two switched places. Opposite: Cleared to compete outside South Africa, Mtolo soared to a 2:09:29 win.**

**Left: A jubilant Lisa Ondieki finally got her New York triumph.**

now competing as the Unified Team, had selected their Olympic women's marathon squad on the basis of results from the Los Angeles Marathon in March. They ignored Markova's Boston feat and left her off their Barcelona squad.

Kim Jones also returned to New York, giving the marathon three leading contenders who were all former runners-up. Surely one of them would stand a place higher on the awards podium. It would not be Jones. Still recovering from bronchitis, she abandoned her effort after 17 miles.

Ondieki never allowed Markova or anyone else into the race. "I didn't come here to waste my time running a 2:30 marathon," she affirmed later. "If someone beat me today, that was fine, because I was going to run as fast as I could." After an overcrowded 6:04 first mile, Ondieki raised her tempo and reached the 10-kilometer mark in 33:46, one minute before Markova and Poland's Kamila Gradus. At the halfway point, Ondieki was 2 minutes ahead of Markova in 1:11:45.

Ondieki never faltered, never appeared fatigued, and never seemed to be making anything close to a maximum effort. After all the grueling work in Flagstaff, the marathon itself "felt like jogging." It was abundantly clear long before Ondieki arrived at the finish line that Allison Roe's 1981 course record of 2:25:29 would be eradicated. No one could have guessed that a woman would make 2:24:40 in New York look so easy. Markova, the runner-up for the second year in a row, had to be astonished that she sped through the five boroughs in an exceptional 2:26:38 yet was never in contention. For Ondieki, the silver medalist in the 1988

Olympic marathon, this triumph was an indubitable career highlight. "New York is the jewel in the crown," she affirmed. "It's the one I've always wanted to win."

Willie Mtolo, a banker from Durban, South Africa, and a son of a Zulu cattle farmer, had set his personal marathon best, 2:08:15, in 1986 on a Port Elizabeth, South Africa, course. The legitimacy of the course's length had always been questioned, so the marathoning world was not sure how good Mtolo was. They had been unable to find out because IAAF sanctions against South Africa for its system of racial apartheid prohibited Mtolo from competing virtually anywhere outside his own country. In 1992 he was the first South African to run in New York since the ban had been lifted. A spectator in the marathon press truck in 1991, Mtolo returned to South Africa, where "all of my training was on hills because I know at the end of the New York City Marathon there are some hills." The night before the race, Mtolo set off a smoke alarm in his hotel room while preparing Zulu corn porridge. The field also included young Kenyans such as twenty-one-year-old Lameck Aguta; the Kenyans had displayed raw talent at various distances but were untested as marathoners. Ibrahim Hussein had warned Mtolo, "Don't pay attention to what the Kenyans do" on First Avenue in Manhattan, where surges are made.

The field had swelled to 28,656 starters, including runners from the newly sovereign nations of Croatia, Slovenia, and Kyrghizstan. The numbers were becoming too large to handle. Marathoners in the 2:20 to 2:35 range were permitted to line up just behind the

**Race director Fred Lebow's post-cancer marathon effort left him and running-companion Grete Waitz emotionally charged.**

elite entrants. In the squeeze, the men were too eager and began before the starting gun. Miraculously the women, who could observe the premature departure, waited 55 seconds for the proper start.

Paul Pilkington, a designated "rabbit," led the men through 13.1 miles into strong winds in 1:04:10. Lameck Aguta and Andres Espinosa, the 1991 runner-up, stayed with Pilkington and hammered away at each other along First Avenue as Mtolo and South Korea's Wan-Ki Kim followed about 80 yards behind. Espinosa shed Aguta at the 19-mile mark, but the effort proved costly. Mtolo pulled alongside Espinosa after 21 miles and assumed the lead a mile and a half later. Mtolo, whose full first name, Bhekisizwe, means "gift to the nation," won in 2:09:29. With time-based bonuses, Mtolo earned fifty thousand dollars and a thirty-five-thousand-dollar Mercedes-Benz, his first big payday in sports. Espinosa finished next in 2:10:53, one second ahead of Kim. Antoni Niemczak, disqualified and suspended in 1986 after placing second and testing positive for anabolic steroids, returned and took fifth place in 2:13:00 at the age of thirty-six.

Runners with social, political, medical, or environmental causes had begun to use the New York City Marathon as a pulpit. The heir to the Dutch throne, Prince Willem Alexander Claus George Ferdinand, ran with an entourage of thirty-five and finished in 4:33:04. The prince, who was raising funds for cancer-stricken children in the Netherlands, also made a generous donation to Memorial Sloan-Kettering. As they slogged through the streets, the prince and twenty-eight thousand other runners were entertained by an

eclectic array of musical acts, including Who Killed Bambi, Squirrels from Hell, and They Call Me Chaos, recruited by organizers to play along the course.

Fred Lebow, celebrating his sixtieth birthday, had decided to do something he had not attempted since 1970: he would run his own New York City Marathon. It would be his first five-borough race. "Running the marathon is not only the most dramatic way I know to fight my illness," pronounced Lebow, "It is also my message to the many other sufferers of this disease who have sought from me a bit of advice or inspiration." After cancer surgery, Lebow began doing laps in the hospital's corridors as soon as possible. "The question is not why I'm doing it," he informed people who inquired about his exercise zeal. "The question is, 'Why aren't you doing it, too?'"

He was raising money for Sloan-Kettering, his siblings from Brooklyn and Tel Aviv were present as well-wishers, and, through five boroughs, Grete Waitz would provide support and guidance. Lebow followed the progress of the elite

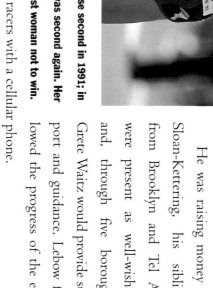

**Olga Markova was a surprise second in 1991; in 1992, as the favorite, she was second again. Her 2:26:38 made her the fastest woman not to win.**

racers with a cellular phone.

In the 23rd mile, octogenarian Joe Kleinerman, a fixture on the New York running scene for over half of a century, rushed out of the New York Road Runners Club headquarters and planted a kiss on Lebow's cheek, moving Lebow to tears. Lebow and his entourage finished in 5:32:34. "I never knew a marathon could be so long," gasped Lebow. More emotionally than physically spent, he and Waitz both wept. The next day Waitz reflected, "The first [race] was the most important, but yesterday—that was the best."

# 1993

It was predicted that the 1993 women's battle would come down to Uta Pippig, Anne Marie Letko, and Kim Jones, three buoyant and genial women who said only the nicest things about one another. At a prerace press conference, Pippig even gave debutmarathoner Letko some friendly advice.

Pippig, a Berlin medical student who had won her hometown marathon twice, had placed ninth in the 10 kilometers at the World Championships in Stuttgart in August. "It was a big disappointment to run so poorly in my own country," she confessed. She had bounced back with ten hard weeks of training in Boulder. Pippig was experienced and had never "bombed out." She could run in the heat, a significant factor though the race was slated for November 14, the latest race date in New York City Marathon history.

Twenty-four-year-old Letko was a road-racing phenomenon who had placed eighth in the Stuttgart 10 kilometers, one spot ahead of Pippig. The New Jerseyan insisted upon moving up to the marathon. Even her coach, 1973 and 1975 New York winner Tom Fleming, was unsure whether it was the right moment to do so, but Letko felt strong and invoked the example of Ingrid Kristiansen, who had handled the move from the 10 kilometers to the marathon with record-setting aplomb. Letko would be one of seven thousand first-time marathoners in the race.

Jones patiently deflected questions about her many second-place finishes, most recently in Boston in April when she ran in 2:30 behind Olga Markova's

2:25:27. Jones felt she performed up to her capabilities, but one woman always seemed to run faster. Overlooked in the prognostications was Mexico's Olga Appell. Though Appell's personal best was only 2:30:22, she had won three marathons in 1992 and had recently clocked a scintillating 1:10:38 in the Sapporo (Japan) Half-Marathon.

Before the 8-mile merge with the men, Nadia Prasad of France found herself ahead of Pippig and, astonished at her rift of protocol, quickly tucked in behind the German. Letko, who had been warned against a rapid early pace, stayed close. "I just got sucked into it," Letko acknowledged later. "I guess it was just habit and adrenaline and feeling like I was invincible."

Pippig was as hot as the weather. She covered 13.1 miles in 1:11:21 and the race was hers. Jones, plagued by asthma, stopped after 17 miles and went to the hospital. Pippig proceeded unchallenged at less-than-full throttle in the end, managing a 2:26:24. Thoroughly unfazed, she gave the thumbs-up sign and blew kisses to fans assembled at the finish line. "I couldn't believe I could win so easily," she marveled.

Pippig was never aware of the progress of Appell, who had begun conservatively and spent the second half of the race picking off stragglers, including a dehydrated Letko, who stopped after 23 miles. Appell placed second in 2:28:56. Prasad, coached by 1993 world-champion marathoner Mark Plaatjes, improved

**After two second-place finishes, Andres Espinosa held together in the final miles to capture his cherished New York title.**

**Opposite: Uta Pippig, a Berlin medical student, was drained but joyous after adding New York honors to her pair of hometown wins.**

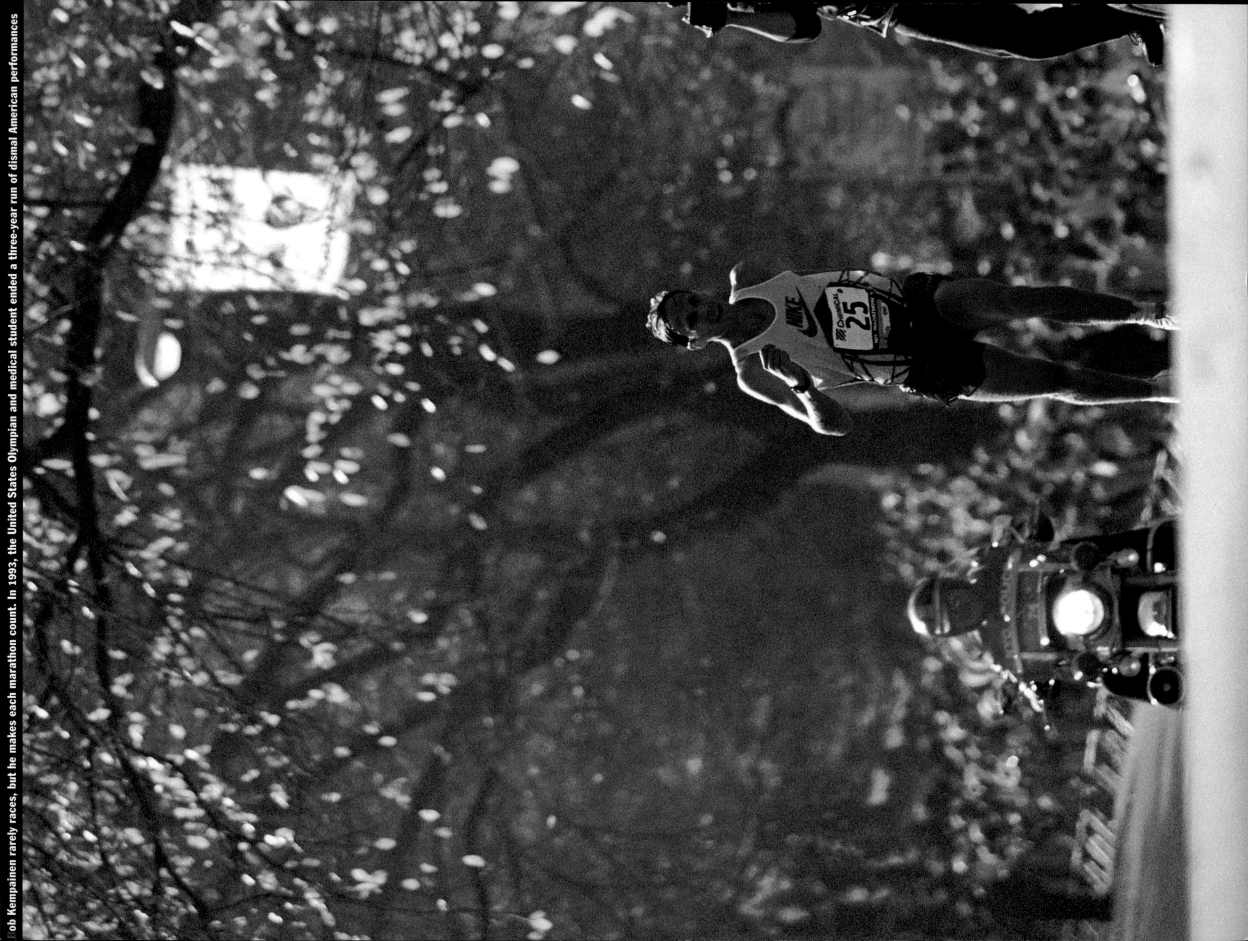

Previous Page: © Mike Powell, Allsport USA. This Page: © 1993 Andy Lyons, Agence Shot. Opposite: © duomo 1993, William R. Sallaz.

her personal record by 7 minutes with a third-place finish in 2:30:16. With Jones and Letko out of the race, the top American was forty-two-year-old Ellen Gibson of Utah, who placed 16th in 2:50:17. Rae Baymiller, a New Yorker who had been a runner for only eighteen months, shattered New York's all-time over-fifty record in 2:53:53, taking 22nd place among the women's field. Baymiller had been the *overall* women's winner of the 25-kilometer New York City Marathon Tune-Up in October. Californian Mavis Lindgren, eighty-six years old, became the oldest woman to finish the New York City Marathon. Lindgren, who also worked out on a trampoline, toured the city in 7:20:47.

Marathoning in the United States had been moribund at the elite level for quite a few years, particularly in New York, which had not crowned an American men's champion since 1982. An American woman had not won since 1977. No American man had placed in New York's top ten in three years. The dearth of domestic heroes was a cause for conjecture and concern; ABC informed marathon officals that a homegrown champion would boost ratings.

The problem, to a large extent, was money. Americans had been opting for other fall races—the Twin Cities Marathon in Minneapolis–St. Paul and the Columbus Marathon in Ohio—where generous cash prizes were easier to come by. In 1993 the New York City Marathon announced that any American to finish in the top five would earn twice the listed prize amounts; a winning American would receive a one-hundred-thousand-dollar bonus.

Steve Plascensia, Don Janicki, Keith Brantly, and Bob Kempainen were the most promising Americans in the men's ranks. A Dartmouth graduate, Kempainen was a University of Minnesota medical student who had taken a break to train with his college coach, Vin Lananna, now at Stanford. "Just running without the burden of school is a joy," Kempainen declared. On a previous visit to New York in 1990, Kempainen had been the surprise victor at the National Cross Country Championships in Van Cortlandt Park.

Brantly hailed from Florida and had been quartered in Concord, Massachusetts, with several Kenyan runners, whose single-minded work ethic had him in respectful awe. "They don't suffer lifestyle burnout like we do," he found. "They don't worry about anything except running. Their focus is their talent."

The favorites were Arturo Barrios of Mexico, a preeminent road runner and former 10,000-meter world-record holder in track, and Moses Tanui of Kenya, who had the world record in the half-marathon. On the eve of his debut, Tanui said, "I need to compete with the distance before I compete with other runners."

**Virtually unnoticed, Mexican-born Olga Appell came from well behind to finish in second place after champion Uta Pippig.**

Little was said about Andres Espinosa, the runner-up in 1991 and 1992. Like many Mexican runners, he had been inspired by seeing compatriot Rodolfo Gomez battle Alberto Salazar in New York. Gomez was now Espinosa's coach. In Mexico, Espinosa had ripped the Volkswagen symbol from his Jetta, replacing it with a Mercedes-Benz ornament to represent the spoils of a New York victory. "I didn't want to settle for second place anymore," Espinosa later explained. "Winning New York was all I cared about."

Espinosa had done his training in a forest near Mexico City at a 9,000-foot altitude. The 1991 winner, Salvador García, had supposedly gone to Bolivia to train at 13,000 feet, thought to be humanly impossible, or at least inadvisable.

The thermometer reached 72 degrees at noon on the warmest November 14 ever recorded in New York City. García led at the halfway point in 1:04:35. Kempainen followed 100 yards behind in a group with three other Americans. Sammy Lelei of Kenya tried to assume command on First Avenue but soon faded. Espinosa caught him after 20 miles, where Tanui was losing his battle with the distance. The ABC camera failed to catch the next important surge. Kempainen in his bid to win. Don Janicki reported, "All of a sudden, he zoomed! He took off like a locomotive and kept on moving until he caught the pack."

**Anne Marie Letko (F22) and Nadia Prasad of France (F21) stuck with the more experienced Uta Pippig (F3) on Brooklyn roads.**

After 22 miles, Kempainen pulled alongside Espinosa, for whom this was déjà vu. "At that point I thought I had a crack at winning," said Kempainen. "But I was working harder than [Espinosa] was," Espinosa surged at precisely the spot where Willie Mtolo had abandoned him in 1992. "Espinosa had another gear left," Kempainen said. "I clearly didn't." Espinosa earned his cherished victory in 2:10:04.

"When someone takes something very seriously and works very hard, this is the result," concluded Espinosa, who received a congratulatory post-race phone call from Mexico's president Carlos Salinas. Kempainen preserved second place in 2:11:03. With American and time bonuses, Kempainen's earnings totaled forty-five thousand dollars. Blisters had caused Barrios to fall behind on First Avenue; he placed third in 2:12:21. Cofavored Moses Tanui finished in 2:15:36 for tenth place.

Keith Brantly closed strongly for fifth, ahead of his Kenyan training mates. The New York City Marathon did not have its American champion, but second- and fifth-place finishes were better than anybody expected, possibly providing a respite from headlines like the *Village Voice's* "Why U.S. Marathoners Suck." Kempainen, however, had little time to ponder the situation. He flew back to Minnesota, where he had neurology rounds at eight o'clock the next morning.

# BILL RODGERS

With virtual simultaneity, the New York City Marathon and Bill Rodgers bombarded the American consciousness in the mid-seventies. One was a mammoth, urban, athletic street carnival, unprecedented and unparalleled in flavor and scope. The other was a meek-looking, unassuming blond man who reminded everybody of their best friend—but a tad wittier, a bit bolder, and a whole lot less beatable in the long, long run.

It is difficult to establish which of the two phenomena was more responsible for the revolutionary prominence of the other. We can only be grateful for the fortuitous and synchronous match enjoyed by American running from 1976 to 1979, when Bill Rodgers conquered four New York City Marathons in a row, man and event boosting one another's stock in the process.

More than a decade after his last major marathon victory, Rodgers remains the best-known and most popular distance runner in the United States. "He's like an appealing kid," observes Fred Lebow. "He has a great smile and ambience. He's always the man in demand. He's the most recognizable name in running."

As the media and the international running community were being introduced to the five-borough marathon, Rodgers was a perfect and much-needed figurehead for the new race. The champions of running, Rodgers demonstrated by example, did not have to be huge, hulking, scary, standoffish, monosyllabic, glower-

ing brutes. Rodgers was cheery and chatty and had an unintimidatingly scrawny regular-guy physique. "He was nice-looking, personable, an all-American boy," explains Jack Brennan, a New Yorker who ran in the 1980 Olympic marathon trials. No contemporary athlete has replaced Rodgers in the affections of the average runner. Notes Brennan, "There's no one else people can latch on to as their fair-haired boy."

A product of Wesleyan University, Rodgers was forthright and articulate without being self-absorbed. Rather than celebrating himself or other stars, Rodgers preferred to salute the efforts of the runners who struggled in the middle. "It's hard for everyone, the way I look at it," Rodgers concludes of the mid-pack racers. "Everybody pays the price and feels the fatigue. And when you're out there longer, you feel it longer." Rodgers always asserted that running merited as much respect as the more celebrated sports; he once told a reporter that throwing a football, by comparison, was "a questionable skill."

As a senior in high school, Rodgers topped his division in Connecticut's venerable Manchester Road Race and in college he ran the two-mile in a fine 8:58. But Rodgers understood that "I needed to go to a longer distance than that" to truly distinguish himself. When his Wesleyan roommate Amby Burfoot won the 1968 Boston Marathon, Rodgers knew exactly what that distance would be.

The Vietnam War and the student strikes of 1970, however, threw Rodgers into turmoil, and his marathon mission would be sidetracked for nearly two years. He

Above: Bill Rodgers, sans socks, posed with his suave Wesleyan University teammates in the late sixties. Opposite: Rodgers earned the prestigious Abebe Bikila Award (donated by Tiffany & Co.) in 1989 for contributions to distance running.

Opposite: Bill Rodgers spent many moments alone in the lead with the press truck in the seventies; in 1978, a dog tried to join him en route to his third New York triumph.

Top: At age thirty-seven, Rodgers (6) placed seventh in 1985, four spots behind Pat Petersen (21). Left: In 1980 Rodgers ran ahead of Englishman Chris Stewart (36) and (lower left) with heir-apparent Alberto Salazar on his shoulder. Lower right: Rodgers vied with Garry Bjorklund (17) in 1978 before surging ahead in Queens.

smoked cigarettes, wore his hair in a long ponytail, rode a motorcycle, and earned conscientious-objector status.

When Rodgers began watching the Boston Marathon each spring, he saw some of the same runners he had dusted in college doing exceptionally well. His motorcycle was stolen, "which was good for me," Rodgers says—because he hated the public trolley, he found himself jogging to work.

Rodgers came to New York in 1974 for four 6-mile laps in Central Park. "It was a killer course," he recalls, twenty years after the ordeal. "I had a large lead. I was trying to run away with it." He ran himself into severe dehydration and faded to fifth.

In March 1975, he scored a stunning, breakthrough third-place finish in the World Cross Country Championships in Morocco; running in the Boston Marathon one month later, he set an American record in 2:09:55, *9 minutes* and 39 seconds below his previous personal best. The victories seemed like miracles from out of the mist. In truth, he had labored arduously and without reward for nearly two years before his startling payoff. Says Rodgers, "My body took that long to be able to train hard and recover to do that kind of effort."

He returned to New York in 1976 for the first five-borough race. On the original course, complete with its stairs and potholes, he finished in 2:10:10, only 15 seconds over his American mark. Despite the magnificent showing, Rodgers was "on cruise control" for the final 3 miles and could have smashed 2:10.

Rodgers was the one male marathoner who delivered world-class results in New York City in the seventies, proving that it was humanly possible to break

2:13 there. "I didn't *like* to race in the heat," Rodgers claims, "but I could *win* in the heat," which he did in the swelters of 1978 and 1979. He remembers "dueling with Garry Bjorklund. It was like a boxing fight, surging back and forth." And he prevailed in the 1979 race after he had been given up for lost behind the leader, Kirk Pfeffer. "I never saw him until 22 miles," reports Rodgers. "It took a long time to work my way up. It was nerve-racking. I was probably about 100th." His catch-up was made easier by fans along the route: "They yelled, 'You're 60 seconds back! You're 45 seconds back!'"

Of the elite American athletes, Rodgers most clearly straddled the amateur and professional eras of running. He was determined to kill amateurism, with all its hypocrisy and unfairness, and bury it for eternity. He unabashedly argued that the serious and talented runner had a right to make a living; his crusade to professionalize the sport riled those who misinterpreted his mission and feared its economic impact.

"For me, it was never a thing of wanting money," Rodgers insists. "What upset me was an underestimation of what marathoners were worth, what the value of their effort was. Our country is totally out of the loop when it comes to understanding what endurance sports are about. People have no idea what it takes to excel at them." Some folks must have understood. Lucrative endorsements came Rodgers's way, and by 1978 he had his own signature line of running apparel. His 1978 and 1979 New York City triumphs made the covers of *Sports Illustrated.*

When he started winning in Boston and New York, Rodgers was teaching emotionally disturbed

> ## "The tension builds—can you knock someone off? I took defending my title very seriously."
>
> BILL RODGERS

children in a Massachusetts school; he would change in the boiler room before going out to train. "They put pressure on me not to run on my lunch hour," he recalls. The moment had arrived for Rodgers to become one of America's first full-time distance runners.

"Boston Billy" captured his hometown race in 1975, 1978, 1979, and 1980, and in 1977 placed first in Fukuoka, the world's premier marathon before being surpassed by New York. Rodgers conquered the great marathons of the world, winning in Stockholm, Kyoto, and Melbourne, twenty marathon triumphs in all.

With his brother, Charlie, Rodgers now runs his own Bill Rodgers Running Center in Boston's historic Faneuil Hall area and he markets his line of running gear to teams. All manner of companies continue to solicit Rodgers to promote their wares.

Married to a former New Yorker, the Central Park Track Club's own Gail Swain, and the father of two young daughters, Rodgers maintains an en-

during and fruitful running career. His overall total— twenty-eight official sub- 2:15 marathons—has yet to be surpassed. In 1993 he set new American road-race standards at 5 kilometers, 8 kilometers, 10 kilometers, the half-marathon, and 30 kilometers in the 45–49 age group.

Rodgers still gets a "great kick" out of the New York City road show that made him famous (or was it the other way around?). "It's such a meticulously organized mass marathon," he says. "The magnificence of the city comes through pretty powerfully, and it may be the most spectacular marathon course there is."

It is exceedingly apt that the champion of the first four incarnations of the race is such a decent, regular fellow, not so far removed from the tens of thousands who, in some modest measure, yearn to emulate his success.

**Being a marathon king is not all sweat and toil.**

**In 1985, Bill Rodgers fulfilled a softer duty as a recipe judge.**

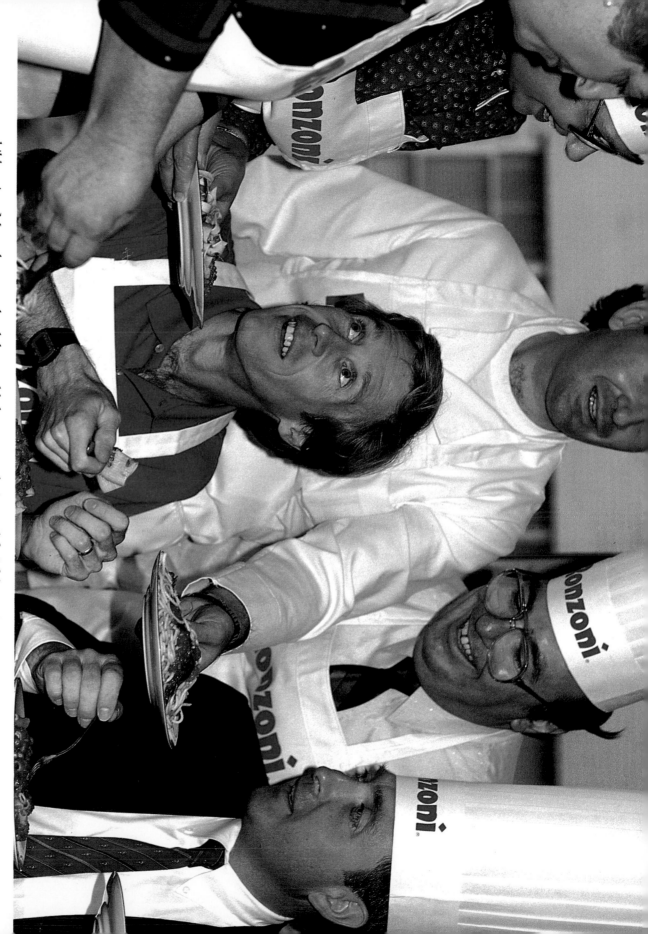

"You have to
almost take for **granted**
that there isn't
**anyone**
in the race
who wants to **win**
**more** than Alberto."

BILL DELLINGER

SALAZAR'S COACH

# ALBERTO SALAZAR

Alberto Salazar does not squander many moments pondering his lasting contributions to the marathon—until you ask him. "I think of Bill Rodgers as being the first cult hero among the masses, the soft-spoken, very likable nice guy," he then submits. "I was the first guy to come in when television really covered it. My brash statements captured the imagination of people, beyond just runners themselves. They were curious to see what this loud-mouthed kid was going to do in his next marathon. Fortunately, I was able to put together a string for a while. They could see the same runner win; I was able to produce."

For three years in New York City, Salazar produced everything marathon officials and spectators could have begged for, and then some. The young man known to his University of Oregon teammates as "the Rookie" had his marathon initiation in 1980, a premiere performance that resulted in a 2:09:41 triumph, the first sub-2:10 in New York, and the fastest 26.2-mile debut anywhere on the planet. A year later Salazar blithely predicted a world record on the challenging five-borough course and, in 2:08:13, he delivered it. One year after that, he prevailed in the longest, closest mano-a-mano test of fortitude ever witnessed at the New York City Marathon. For all of 26 miles its outcome was uncertain, until Salazar finally (and literally) dusted Rodolfo Gomez, the Mexican who would not flinch. It was old hat for Alberto; in Boston that April he had gutted out a win over Dick Beardsley in a similar down-to-the-wire duel.

No one before had won battles of that pitch in the United States's two preeminent marathons in the same year, and no one has done it since. Alberto Salazar was unquestionably the ultimate warrior of marathoning. As long as he was standing and conscious, surrender was inconceivable to him. "I believed that I could take as much as anyone else," he maintains. "I was willing to pay more than anyone else. Someone would have to break, and I thought it would be the other guy."

**Young prodigy Salazar won the Eastern States High School two-mile in 1976 in 9:09. Outdoors, his scholastic best was 8:53. At sixteen, he set a world 5-kilometer mark of 14:14 in his age group.**

Alberto Salazar burst into the marathoning realm as something entirely new. Marathoners had been a quiet, clubby bunch who lived and breathed as if the 26.2-mile event were their little secret, a combination of mysticism and ardor meant for the proud few, the athletic elite—the marathon specialists. They most certainly were not the sorts to make brazen proclamations about ambitious trailblazing expectations, comments that would haunt them if those goals exceeded their grasps.

Salazar had developed from one of the nation's leading high-school runners in Wayland, Massachusetts, into an Oregon NCAA and TAC cross-country champion before arriving in New York, where he had the temerity to make the sacrilegious declaration that the marathon was just a long race. In the tradition of Muhammad Ali, Joe Namath, and Moses Malone, Salazar stated precisely what he felt his heart and legs could do. He was not bragging—with honest certainty, he answered what he was asked. Interviewing Salazar in the early days could be a

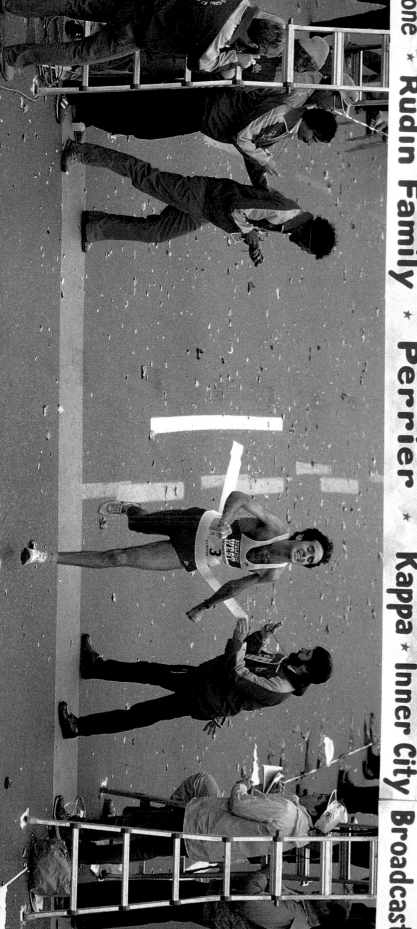

K CITY FINISH MARA THO

one · Rudin Family · Perrier · Kappa · Inner City Broadcast

CITIZEN WATCH
2:08:13
CITIZEN WATCH

bove: A contender kept his eye on Alberto Salazar (1) early in the 1982 marathon. Below: In 1981, Salazar hurled himself into marathon history when he shattered the 1969 world recor chilling experience. Reporters had never encountered someone with such an aura of invincibility, someone impervious to frailty and devoid of doubt.

His sole mission was to excel, and his steely resolve was crucial to its accomplishment. "You can't have any excuses," Salazar says. "You can't say, 'Maybe I'll run 2:09 today, maybe 2:14.'" The cliché "giving 100 percent" is physically impossible, but Salazar came closer to doing it than any elite runner. "I did whatever I had to do to try to be the best. It really was an obsession," he admits.

Amid the circus atmosphere of the New York City Marathon, he maintained his tunnel vision. Even coming off the Queensboro Bridge onto First Avenue, where the roar of the fans is the loudest, little registered with Salazar apart from the competitive quest. "I'd see it for a second and say, 'Wow, that's nice, the crowd's big,' and then it was back to business. I would concentrate so hard."

Yet Salazar did have the luxury of enjoying his world record even before he set it in 1981; he knew "for certain" after 20 miles that he would finish faster than Derek Clayton had when he clocked his 2:08:34 in Antwerp in 1969. Salazar's halfway split was slower than he wanted and "I got a little scared. I didn't like the idea of being behind." But he scorched his legendary 17th mile in 4:33, putting the record well within reach.

The epic struggle with Gomez in 1982 remains vivid for Salazar. "I decided I had to break him mentally" with sets of 200-meter surges, he reveals. With only 1000 meters left, one such spurt did the trick, and Salazar told himself, "On the next one, if I just keep going, he won't be able to beat me." The cloud that cloaked the two men as they reentered Central Park created a memorable but deceptive image: "On television, it looked like I made a move right then. [The move] was actually *before* I went into the dust. I already had 20 meters on him. I'd broken him, and he knew it."

The Cuban-born Salazar (his father, José, soured

on Castro and moved the family to Connecticut when Alberto was two years old; the family later settled in Massachusetts) held his reign as the dominant marathoner even while remaining engaged in other world-class pursuits. In 1982, along with the classic Boston and New York victories, he was runner-up to Ethiopia's Mohammed Kedir at the World Cross Country Championships in Rome and set United States track records at 5000 meters in 13:11.93 and at 10,000 meters in 27:25.61.

Salazar had appeared immortal but it could not last. "Expectations were high," he says. "My first four marathons went so well. You either maintain that or you go down." The first drop was a loss to Rob de Castella and Carlos Lopes at their ballyhooed "match race" in Rotterdam in 1983.

**Salazar's family crest reads "Never Without Hope." After his 1982 triumph, glad tidings from Salazar's son, Antonio, provided an inspiration of a different sort.**

102

**Leading the field after the Verrazano start, Salazar bided his time in his 1981 bid for the world record before he broke the race open with a 4:33 17th mile.**

Salazar had suffered from some common runners' injuries, but what ultimately undid him was a severe endocrine imbalance, Salazar concludes, "probably as a result of my never taking breaks. I didn't work too hard, but I'd always go from one season to another." His body needed respites. If he had it to do over again, Salazar says he would spend one month each year without running.

Salazar's career has apparently become an object lesson for aspiring distance runners, but he questions whether they are attentive students. "Guys think, 'I don't want to end up like Salazar and be burned out.' Gee, you're thirty-four, what are you waiting for? Better to have achieved it once than to not have achieved it at all. Runners have to try for it all. They have to shoot for the stars."

He never wavered on the gigantic stage that stretches through the five boroughs. "The New York City Marathon has the most reach with the general public of any event, more than the Olympics," Salazar says. "I went from being a relatively obscure collegiate runner to all of that fame." But he neither lapped up nor fell prey to the notoriety: "Being so tunnel-visioned, focusing on doing well, it didn't really bother me."

Back in Oregon today, Alberto Salazar is, as Fred Lebow observes, "a good father, a good husband," and a devout Christian. He works in Nike's marketing department and coaches a handful of the company's most promising contract runners. He strives to imbue his charges with the same unshakable sense of purpose that he possessed in his racing days. "Every day was very, very important. I want them to have the same drive. But," an experienced Salazar now understands, "I have to be there to make sure they don't overdo it."

"When I came to New York in **1978**, I was a full-time **schoolteacher** and track **runner**, and determined to **retire** from competitive running. But **winning** the New York City Marathon kept me running for another **decade**."

GRETE WAITZ

# GRETE WAITZ

Her number, 1173, was not even listed among the prerace entries of the 1978 New York City Marathon, and when Fred Lebow inquired who had won the women's division while he had been scurrying around the course, all the respondent could tell him was "some blond girl."

The "blond girl" was Grete Waitz of Norway, and all she had done was set a world record. It was the first of three she would establish in consecutive 26.2-mile sojourns through New York. She had emerged in the world's media capital as marathoning's first world-class woman competitor.

The Waitz era was still intact in 1988 when she tasted five-borough victory for the ninth time, a tenured witness to all the growth and upheaval in her sport. Grete Waitz is a history maker, one of the truly epochal athletes in women's sports. She has been the constant thread through the elite ranks of the New York City Marathon. Former mayor Ed Koch anointed Waitz "a New Yorker by adoption," and the millions who shouted "Grete!" from the sidelines embraced her on a first-name basis.

Her slender frame and quiet, retiring manner lent Waitz an air of fragility, but her ferocity in battles of the road confirmed her strength. Her decisive early breaks and her control in the races' second halves required a rare balance of courage and savvy, supreme ability and conditioning.

Persuaded to run in New York by her husband, Jack, Waitz saw that first marathon merely as a one-time chance to visit the United States and almost stayed home when Lebow was reluctant to pay for Jack's transit. She had no idea what she was getting into in 1978; she imagined "3 hours of hard work before you can rest." More familiar with kilometers than miles, Waitz came off the Queensboro Bridge and "didn't realize I still had 10 miles to go; I thought I was close to the finish. In 3 or 4 miles, I wanted this to end. Each time I saw trees, I thought it was Central Park."

The Norwegian schoolteacher and track runner who had never covered more than 12 miles at a stretch

**Teenagers Grete Andersen and Ingrid Christiansen competed in Oslo's Bislett Games in 1971.**

**Waitz's career began when the longest women's Olympic race was less than one mile.**

tried to drink water en route and spilled it in her face and up into her nose. Her quadriceps and calves cramped from dehydration and insufficient training. These things did not happen on the track. When the marathon was over, she was extremely miffed at Jack. "I wanted him to know how much I suffered," Waitz says.

Almost single-handedly, she set the standard for women's distance running as the sport began to proliferate on American roads. In 1980 Waitz set world records at 5 miles, 10 kilometers, 15 kilometers, 10 miles, and 20 kilometers. Three of her five world cross-country titles came by margins so enormous that the sport will never see the likes of them again. At the Mini Marathon, the foremost 10-kilometer women's road race, New Yorkers saw her flash to victory an astonishing five times, setting three world records.

The public came to view her triumphs as givens even before the races were run. "Everyone just takes it for granted that I'll win," she said somewhat ruefully. But, after all, it was Waitz who gave them reason to believe.

If anything, her peerless accomplishments deserve even more credit than they have received. In her nine New York City triumphs, the vanquished included Ingrid Kristiansen, Lisa Martin Ondieki, Patti Lyons Catalano, Julie Brown, Jacqueline Gareau, Priscilla Welch, Laura Fogli, Lorraine Moller, Charlotte Teske, and Joan Benoit Samuelson.

Waitz was sure of herself, even when others thought her supremacy was faltering. Lisa Martin's 1986 New York challenge seemed like a serious threat, but the Australian competitor stayed with Waitz for slightly more than half of the marathon before drifting back into second place. As Waitz explains, "I knew what I had done in preparation. I knew I was in good shape. I always think of myself as the strongest in the field. In the marathon, nothing is over until the finish. That's why I didn't worry that [Martin] ran with me for so long."

The New York City spotlight was more luminous than Waitz might have preferred. "To suddenly be a hero on a world basis was hard for me to understand," she reflects. "God gave me a gift. I got the chance to use it. I felt uncomfortable with the credit. I'm doing what I love doing. I didn't think I deserved what people were saying. My talent is just more visible than theirs." In 1979 she told Marc Bloom of *The Runner* that the mantle of fame and its pressure could be too much to bear: "Sometimes I wish I could throw the whole thing away… and be a common girl." To deflect attention when her fame was fresh and at its height, she chose not to have a telephone at her home in Norway; she would call her mother from a public phone a half mile away.

If people could not identify the lanky Norwegian

**Upper left: After running a marathon in the 2:20s became a sure thing for Grete Waitz, bands of men with that goal kept her company through Manhattan. Lower left: Waitz, Lisa Martin (F2), and Laura Fogli (F3), placed first, second, and third both in 1985 and in 1986.**

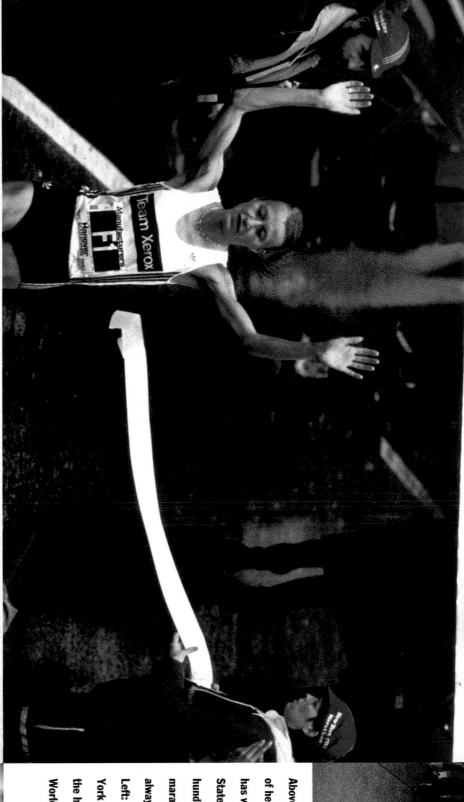

Above: Waitz's husband, Jack, persuaded Grete to accept an invitation to come to New York in 1978. Left: Waitz was equally masterful at cross-country, earning five world titles, often in a runaway.

Above: Over the course of her nine wins, Waitz has waited at the Staten Island start with hundreds of thousands of marathoners—but she always stands apart. Left: Waitz's fifth New York City crown came on the heels of her 1983 World Championship.

with the blond pigtails when she showed up in New York in 1978, it was only because they had not been paying attention. A high-school teacher of Norwegian literature, grammar, history, and geography who trained twice a day, Waitz had ranked first in the world at 1500 and 3000 meters in 1975, and had previously set two 3000-meter world marks, winning the World Cup at that distance in 1977. In effect, she was the West's best hedge against Eastern Europe's middle-distance monopoly. Waitz had already earned her first world cross-country crown in 1978 and clocked the year's fastest mile in 4:26.9. Even after five victories in New York City, she still called herself "a track runner who occasionally runs marathons."

Born Grete Andersen, Waitz grew up in the suburbs of Oslo with two older brothers. A young girl who preferred running to piano lessons, she became Norway's junior champion at 400 and 800 meters when she was sixteen years old. By 1971 she was Norway's national 800- and 1500-meter champion. But by 1978, as Waitz recalls, "I felt I had reached my potential on the track. The longest distance would be 1500 meters at the 1980 Olympics. In those days it was normal that you retire in [your] mid-twenties and raise a family and follow the pattern."

Yet at the point when she might voluntarily have put herself out to pasture, the United States running boom took hold and all it lacked was a world-class female standard-bearer. For Waitz, the New York City Marathon was an unanticipated bonus, "a new era of running that I didn't know existed. It was more friendly and social than eight people in a 1500."

By 1980 in New York, male marathoners had begun buzzing around queen-bee Grete. They may have hoped that she would guide them to a marathon in the mid-2:20s, or perhaps it was their way of saying, "Hi, mom, I'm on TV." Or maybe they just liked being with her. She was not one to complain: "It didn't really bother me as long as they didn't get too close, talk to me, bother my concentration, or get in my way. They wanted to run with me because I run such an even pace. Some guys dropped out when I passed them."

She set her fourth world record in London, won the marathon at the inaugural World Championships in Helsinki in 1983, and earned the silver medal in the first women's Olympic marathon in 1984. The very existence of the latter two races owes so much to Waitz, who had demonstrated that women could excel and prosper at the classic road distance.

She had metamorphosed from a shy, reluctant visitor into a gregarious and generous spirit. In 1992 she accompanied Fred Lebow on his post-cancer marathon trek. "I was worrying about being out there for five hours," Waitz observed. "It went by so quickly. All of the time I paid attention to Fred. I got tears in my eyes. I didn't know I was that emotional."

In 1993 she waited for Zoe Koplowitz, a runner with multiple sclerosis, to finish the race, 24 hours after Koplowitz had begun. "I told her, 'I'm going to be there for you.' I got [to the finish line] at 6:30 A.M. and the weather had slowed her down. No one had a medal for her. I rushed back to my hotel to get her Jack's medal. I don't have multiple sclerosis and I don't do half of what she does. It puts my whole life in perspective." Anyone who thinks of Waitz as emotionally restrained should have glimpsed her with Fred and Zoe.

Waitz now lives in Florida for several months of each year, leading running clinics and making appearances. She comes to New York each spring for the Trevira Twosome, where in 1993 she coasted through the 2 miles with Lynn Swann, the former Pittsburgh Steeler, who visibly toiled next to Waitz. She has been part of the New York City Marathon for long enough to see it soar "from a regular road race to *the* road race." Now, on Marathon Sunday, Waitz shouts loudly, trying to coax husband Jack to a superior effort...or she might just be trying to get back at him for dragging her to New York in 1978.

"There are people who are visionaries and people who are bookkeepers. Fred brought running up centerstage.

He's done radical things and he's made mistakes but you need people with imagination and Fred has it."

NORMAN GOLUSKIN

CENTRAL PARK TRACK CLUB PRESIDENT, 1984

# FRED LEBOW

The leader stands in an open touring car, gunning through the streets of his city. He is well known, but his uniform identifies him beyond mistake. His rigid stance is authoritatively upright. His gaze is sweeping, but it can zero in as he vigilantly surveys his domain for glitches in the established order. He barks his instructions into a bullhorn, snapping at anyone who might disrupt the flow of the day's proceedings. He presides over a vast army of staff members and thousands of volunteers. He is field marshal Fred Lebow, in running togs on New York City Marathon Sunday, riding at the crest of a wave of world-class athletes. In their wake will follow a polyglot horde of exceptional people from every state and from over one hundred nations on the globe, a remarkable feat of international diplomacy and solidarity.

This is perhaps our most indelible image of race director Fred Lebow. If not, maybe we recall his annual presence at the finish line, a veritable whirling dervish with arms wildly gesticulating as if his frantic exhortations might help a winner squeeze a smidgen more time-shaving effort from the final 100 meters. It could be Lebow's agitation that works the magic; many records and speedy marathons have been run on this five-borough course that is far from easy.

We have also grown accustomed to seeing Lebow on his endless circuit of promotional appearances, stoking interest in his unsurpassed New York City Marathon. Does he ever get tired? By midnight after

the marathon, Lebow is in—for him—rare form. He is speechless, hoarse, and fatigued after 48 sleepless hours. Yet he somehow manages to crank it up for one last television appearance. Fred is the one they want. Journalists who know virtually nothing about distance running know Lebow and trust in what he says. The most indifferent and least enterprising among them are infected with his enthusiasm for the race that he nurtured into one of the glorious miracles of American athletics.

In more recent memory, the most enduring image

**Lebow transformed a community footrace into the most popular marathon in the world, changing the fitness landscape of America.**

of Fred Lebow may be a singular and moving one. In 1992, less than two years after being diagnosed with brain cancer, Lebow vowed to complete the five-borough journey he had so often studied from that open car. "I've never seen it from the pack," he stated. "I've heard how great it is, but I'd like to see for myself." His far-flung relatives wanted to see him try; in an expression of pride and love, they united in support at the Manhattan finish line, coming from Tel Aviv, Chicago, and Brooklyn.

Lebow's crusade became a heroic human story that left few eyes dry. His own eyes, and those of Grete Waitz, who accompanied him for the 5:32:34 trip to Central Park, were no exception. Neither had cried in public before, but both now wept. It was Lebow's moment, but he gazed at nine-time New York City champion Waitz and asked, genuinely concerned, "Are you hurting?" At the finish, he kissed the ground. The marathon route was, after all, his Holy Land.

He was born Fischel Lebowitz in 1932 in Arad, a city in Romania's Transylvania near the borders of

112

Hungary and Yugoslavia, the sixth of seven children of an Orthodox Jewish produce merchant and his wife. As a young teenager, Fred was forced to flee from the Nazis, and later from the Soviets. He made his way across Europe by smuggling sugar and diamonds, "learning about living by your wits, always being on your toes, improvising"—traits that would serve him well in his stewardship of the New York City Marathon. He eventually settled in Ireland, coming to Brooklyn on a Talmudic student scholarship in 1951. After detours to Kansas City and Cleveland, he made his home in New York. Along the way, he shortened his surname to Lebow. The accent falls on the first syllable, but almost everyone places it on the second, as if he had somehow become French.

Lebow found success in assorted garment-industry businesses, dealing chiefly in knock-offs of designer merchandise. He became a decent recreational tennis player, but when he tried running he was instantly smitten and switched his allegiance. Distance running barely existed in New York in the late sixties. In an attempt to enliven the sport, Lebow, along with Vince Chiappetta, ardently lobbied for the first New York City Marathon in Central Park. Lebow ran it in 4:12:09, placing 45th out of fifty-five finishers. He never claimed to be a good runner, though he would improve.

The running bug bit him hard, and at some personal cost. One New Year's Eve, Lebow kept a girlfriend waiting so that he could fit in one last training session to achieve his yearly goal of 2,500 miles. She left him. If he had added correctly, the relationship might have endured; it turns out he had *already* reached his target.

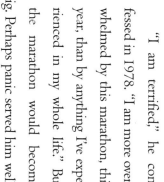

The inestimable and unheralded work of technical director Allan Steinfeld has helped Lebow make the race what it is.

In the early days, serving as race director of the New York City Marathon and president of the New York Road Runners Club was not even a paying gig. Lebow was a bachelor in a sixty-nine-dollar-a-month, rent-controlled apartment. He dug into his own pockets to cover the 1970 marathon's one-thousand-dollar budget; Bill Rodgers's 1976 two-thousand-dollar appearance fee also came out of personal funds.

Lebow understood what a fragile undertaking the New York City Marathon could be. He had a frantic sense of urgency. How could something so mammoth and so intricate go *right*? The unexpected was a virtual certainty; bad weather was an inevitable and frequent snafu. He had a fear that bridges would suddenly break open at inopportune moments. Lebow and the police once negotiated the marathon's precise route in and out of the Bronx while the race was on and the fastest runners were quickly closing in!

"I am terrified," he confessed in 1978. "I am more overwhelmed by this marathon, this year, than by anything I've experienced in my whole life." But the marathon would become more than twice as big. Perhaps panic served him well; Lebow operated brilliantly on the edge. The occasional false start and overpacked finish chute notwithstanding, year after year the New York City Marathon has defied odds and logic to operate smoothly.

With his technical director, Allan Steinfeld, and myriad staff and volunteers, Lebow made New York City the standard, and a slew of international marathons tried to measure up. But what Lebow had wrought came back to haunt him: the America's

Marathon in Chicago, a direct result of New York's urban example, became his fierce competitor for a few Octobers, the only genuine threat to his supremacy, Lebow did not panic, avoiding a bidding war that would have crippled both races. He understood that New York City's special nature came not only from its handful of stars, but also from the innumerable sensations seen, heard, and felt by more than twenty-five thousand entrants and millions of spectators.

Taking a professional approach to the promotion and business of the marathon, Lebow angered a few of the old guard who had no desire to see road running attain mass appeal. Lebow dealt with corporate sponsors and government officials and made friends who could benefit his pet project. In Brooklyn, it was Lebow who yelled in Yiddish to bewildered Hasidim, asking them to bring water. Obligingly, they gave seltzer to the thirsty runners. It was Lebow who pacified street gangs who did not want the marathon on their turf by hiring them as race security, paying them in T-shirts and running jackets.

Striving to create a truly international marathon, Lebow labored to enter Chinese and Russian athletes when such permits to visit the United States were rare. He was anxious to invite Willie Mtolo when sanctions against South African athletes were dropped; Mtolo's 1992 win in a brisk 2:09:29 was a sweet reward. In the nineties, no time was wasted in assuring that the new nations of Slovenia, Croatia, Latvia, and the Ukraine had representatives in the New York City Marathon.

Lebow has never dreamt on a less-than-grandiose scale. During a subway strike in the mid-eighties, he set up a water station on the Brooklyn bridge to address the disgruntled people who were commuting on foot. Bullhorn in hand, Lebow exhorted people to take the inconvenience as an inspiration to walk to work *every* day—that crusade has not yet been won. He helped to create the Fifth Avenue Mile, America's Ekiden, the Trevira Twosome, the Mini Marathon, the Chemical

Bank Corporate Challenge, and the New York Games, and brought the World Cross Country Championships, to the New Jersey Meadowlands. He even wrote a book, *The New York Road Runners Club Complete Book of Running*, with Gloria Averbuch. But the New York City Marathon is his favorite child, and he remains a worried, doting parent.

On and off the job, Steinfeld has seen enough of his colleague to realize he is far from one-dimensional. "A lot of people see Fred as a hard-driving individual. They don't see that he's a caring individual," says Lebow's right-hand man. "He's a very brilliant person. I see him as a Renaissance man. Architecture, culture, and music are important to him. He's not just a running guru."

Lebow's own struggle through 26.2 miles in 1992 was a monumental test of body and will, but as his first-person account of that day in *Runner's World* attests, for every step of the first 8 miles, "I obsessed over the organization of the race."

Lebow need not fret. The New York City Marathon, the fruit of twenty-five years of his toil and vision, is thriving. Seeing Fred Lebow at the finish line in Central Park "was always a welcome sight," three-time winner Alberto

**Opposite: Lebow tearfully celebrated his 1992 finish with Grete Waitz. Below: "Fred, This Run's For You" raised money for Stop Cancer in 1990.**

Salazar proclaimed in 1993. "New York's the greatest marathon in the world," he said. "It's number one and I don't see anyone overtaking it as long as Fred's urging it on."

In Oslo, the Norwegians have created a statue of Grete Waitz. When will New Yorkers put one of Fred Lebow in Central Park?

"Last Sunday, in one of the most cities in the world, 12,000 men, from 40 countries of the world, black, white, and yellow people, Buddhists, and Confucians, suffered during the greatest folk

CURRY BROADSIDE 1939 NEW YORK

violent, trouble-stricken

women, and children

assisted by **2.5 million**

Protestants, Jews, Muslims,

laughed cheered, and

festival the world has ever seen."

# THE COURSE

Race director Fred Lebow is quite certain what makes the New York City Marathon so special: "It's New York. The city is such a magnetic place. It's a major sightseeing tour for foreigners, for people from other states, even for me." Most urban races are simply chases through networks of concrete canyons, but the New York City Marathon takes its runners on a tour of unforgettable topography, architecture, and people. Running through the streets of the five boroughs, glimpsing the city's sights, hearing its sounds, meeting its people, all at a pace of some 10 miles per hour—it can be the experience of a lifetime, which is why so many far-flung visitors strive to duplicate it year after year. If imitation is the sincerest form of flattery, then New York has received its kudos again and again. In the hope of galvanizing the kind of excitement the New York City Marathon has generated in its hometown, many cities in the United States and abroad have added 26.2-mile footraces of their own. None of those marathons, however, can offer what makes the original so special.

Not built purely for speed like Chicago, Rotterdam, or Berlin, the New York course is meant to encompass as much of what is uniquely "New York" as is feasible. Manhattan Borough president Percy Sutton wanted the route to reflect New York's status as the original and ultimate melting pot. With this consideration, New York road-running pioneers Ted Corbitt and Harry Murphy designed the five-borough course, taking it beyond Central Park for its 1976 inauguration. Except for the Manhattan segment, which in 1977 was moved from isolated East River Park paths to the now-famous First Avenue stretch, an invaluable boost to spectatorship, the course has remained essentially the same for the last eighteen years.

The race virtually shuts the city down, but residents universally endorse the event. Over 350 intersections are closed off to all other traffic. Thousands of vigilant police officers set up and guard barricades, and inform New York's seven million residents that going about their usual business on Marathon Sunday will involve detours and delays. The added assistance of staff members and more than thirteen thousand volunteers create the logistical miracle that is the New York City Marathon.

**THE START** Ⓐ
The race begins on the Verrazano-Narrows Bridge. Men and women have long had separate, parallel starts on the span's upper level, but in 1988 a third start for men with slower times was added on the lower tier to accommodate the race's growing field.

**FOURTH AVENUE** Ⓑ
A straight, level 6-mile strip connects multiple ethnic neighborhoods and allows marathoners to hit their strides and sort into packs.

**WILLIAMSBURG** Ⓒ
The world center of Hasidic Judaism, Williamsburg features curvy streets, some paved with cobblestones.

**THE PULASKI BRIDGE** Ⓓ
The link between Brooklyn and Queens is the race's midpoint.

**LONG ISLAND CITY** Ⓔ
After the crowds and tight streets of Brooklyn, Queens feels empty with its warehouses and open spaces. There are many turns before the Queensboro Bridge's on-ramp, but Manhattan is in full view across the river.

**THE QUEENSBORO BRIDGE** Ⓕ
Marathoners run from Queens to Manhattan on a soft, spongy, 3,880-foot carpet that is rolled out to soften the bridge's grating.

**FIRST AVENUE** Ⓖ
The pinnacle of crowd enthusiasm and tall buildings, the slightly uphill First Avenue makes it impossible to feel lonesome by presenting a 4-mile gauntlet of the race's most raucous supporters.

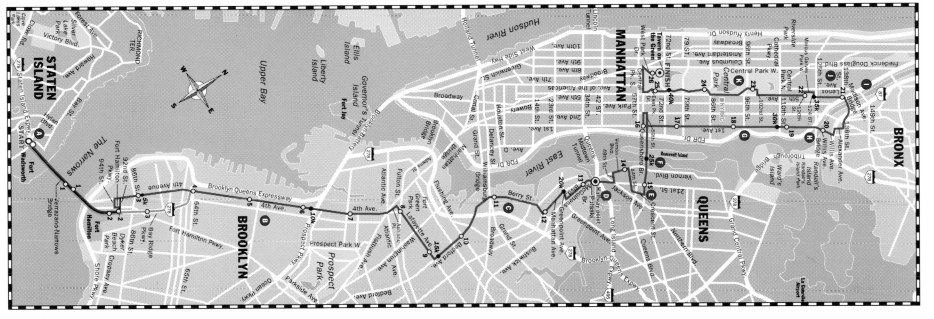

**THE WILLIS AVENUE BRIDGE** Ⓗ
The Willis takes runners into the Bronx—a segment of the race that is less than one mile—at the 20-mile mark, the point at which participants may encounter the fabled "wall."

**THE MADISON AVENUE BRIDGE** Ⓘ
The Madison leads runners from the Bronx back into Manhattan.

**HARLEM** Ⓙ
Harlem is the wellspring of so much African-American culture. Magnificent architecture is intact and visible along the route.

**CENTRAL PARK** Ⓚ
America's foremost urban playground, Central Park provides many curves and three hills. Runners come into the park for the first time at 102nd Street and proceed down East Park Drive. They exit briefly onto Central Park South and reenter at Columbus Circle, passing over a patch of grass. A steep, 400-yard incline challenges the final steps to the finish line.

**THE COURSE**
According to standardized road-race calculation, the marathon course is measured 12 inches from the inside curb on straightaways, and along the tangent of curves. Because the layouts of road races vary according to topography, no two times from different marathons are exactly comparable. The New York route is quite hilly, and therefore is considered a more difficult, slower course.

Whether world-class or amateur, athletes train for long hours all over the world before running the New York City Marathon. Allison Roe runs on a New Zealand beach while her business partner,

...od Dixon, prefers pastoral sheep farms in the countryside. Willie Mtolo hones his talents in the South African twilight, and a top hometown marathoner makes use of Central Park in the off-season.

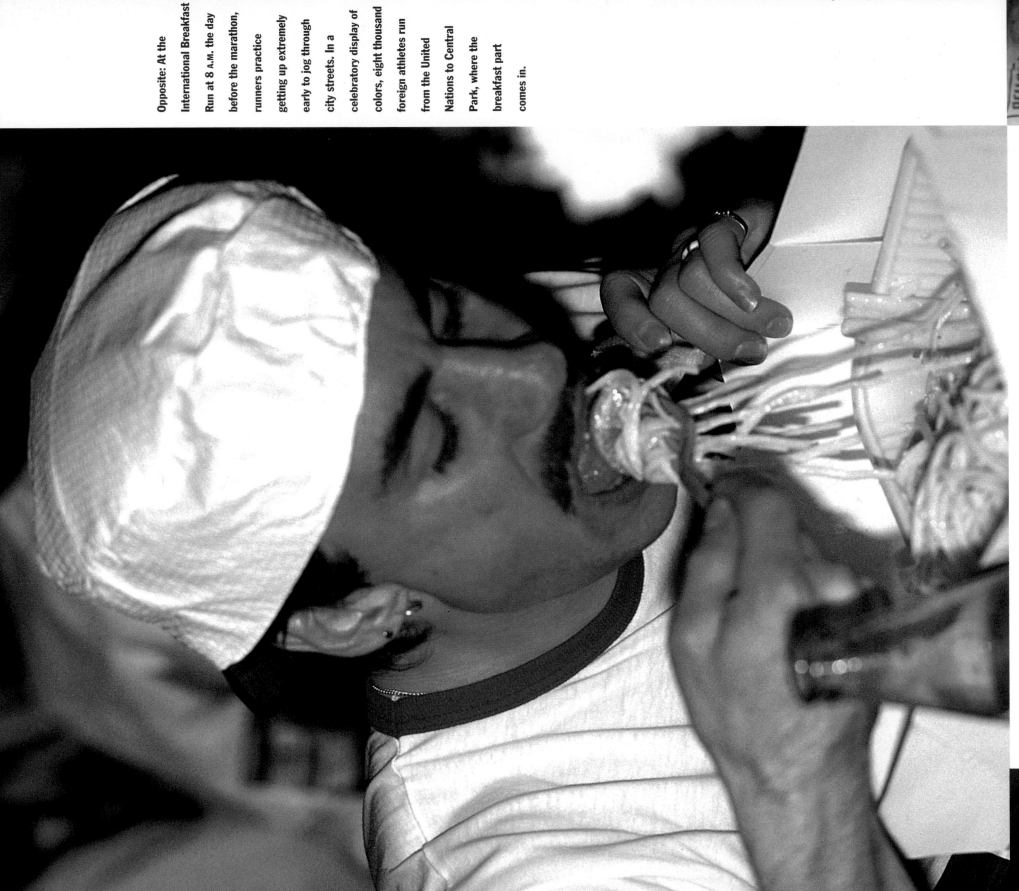

Opposite: At the International Breakfast Run at 8 A.M. the day before the marathon, runners practice getting up extremely early to jog through city streets. In a celebratory display of colors, eight thousand foreign athletes run from the United Nations to Central Park, where the breakfast part comes in.

Above: The secret is out. Marathon training is nothing but an excuse to consume vast quantities of pasta. On the night before the race, fourteen thousand famished runners consume five thousand pounds of carbohydrates at the Marathon Pasta Party, "the world's largest dinner party." Left: Some of it comes in very large boxes.

"It's **not** a very **nice** time, really.

It's just a **waiting** game. You're bored.

You're just **restless**.

The **struggle** is to keep really quiet until **race morning**."

1987 NEW YORK CITY CHAMPION

THE DAY BEFORE THE MARATHON

Opposite: On the morning
of the race, the crush of
humanity on Staten Island
miraculously sorts itself
out and gets to the starting
line on time.

Below: Aerobicists rescue
nervous marathoners who
may be too tense to warm
up as they wait for the start
clock to flash its double
zeros. Below right: These
signs attempt to help visiting
athletes find their fellow
countrypeople, but in the
confusion it might just be
easier to stay lost.

"The starting line of the NYC Marathon is kind of like a giant **time bomb** behind you about to go **off**... It is the most spectacular start in the sport."

BILL RODGERS

TELEVISION COMMENTATOR, 1987

en and women have separate starts on the Verrazano-Narrows Bridge, but it is standing room only as they learn how a sardine must feel. It will take 3.5 minutes for all to cross the starting line.

# the start and brooklyn

The starter's cannon is thunderous enough to be heard by all twenty-seven thousand runners and even in parts of New Jersey. After the boom comes an eerie quiet, as close to silence as the marathoners will experience for the next 26 miles. There are no cheering friends and family on the Verrazano-Narrows Bridge; the most conspicuous sound is the shaking of the structure beneath so many footsteps—the field grew from 2,090 in 1976 to 28,656 in 1992. For 2 miles, runners move from Staten Island to Brooklyn aloft on North America's longest suspension span, so long that volunteer psychologists are on hand to sooth phobias, so long that engineers had to accommodate the curvature of the earth—creating an arc that gives runners the race's first hills.

New York is a city of islands—of the five boroughs, only the Bronx is attached to the North American mainland. The marathon winds through the city via five bridges, affording towering urban vistas. Assuredly the most spectacular is the Verrazano view. In the Narrows below, fireboats spray arcs of colored water skyward, islands that welcomed immigrants at the turn of the century lie to the left, and magnificent Manhattan, with the world's most rightfully fabled skyline, is visible in its entirety. Says Keith Brantly, who placed fifth in 1993, "It's like you've put on glasses after not being able to see for years."

It takes all of a half hour for everybody to get over the bridge, and what an entrance they make. Runners leave the proud hush of the Verrazano into the sudden roar of the Brooklyn crowds, a medley of cheers and yells that will accompany the marathoners without cease until the race's triumphant finish.

Staten Island threatens to secede from the city, but its best reason to *stay* is that the New York City Marathon begins here. If not for the Verrazano, which accommodates a marathon throng that has grown to thirteen times the size it was when the bridge became part of the race in 1976, runners would have to take the ferry to Brooklyn. On the 6-mile Fourth Avenue straightaway, the pack sorts itself out and runners find room for their first full leg strides,

An array of quiet Brooklyn neighborhoods is now used to having thousands of marathoning visitors. At the 8-mile point the men and women will merge and set pace with one another.

Following a "Marathon Blue" line painted in the street along the entirety of the course, runners accept support from well-wishers.

134

It is never too early to involve plenty of hands, and volunteers have become adept at giving over sixty-five thousand gallons of water to a passing pail of marathoners. When their job here

# williamsburg and queens

After Fourth Avenue with its long sequence of ethnic enclaves—Italian, Irish, Hispanic, African American, Chinese, Finnish, Ukrainian, Russian, and Jewish neighborhoods pop up every half mile—runners fly by the warehouses of Williamsburg and Queens. The latest destination for ever-migrating droves of economizing artists, Williamsburg is also home to the world's largest community of Hasidic Jews.

In honor of the large Polish population in Greenpoint, Brooklyn, the last stop before Queens, the Polish Embassy gives its Pulaski Bridge Award to the first runners to reach the race's halfway point. In Queens, the largest borough of the five, marathoners smile for the camera in Long Island City, often called "Hollywood East" for its huge studios. No entry and exit visas are required for this condensed tour.

Organizers worried about how Williamsburg's insular Hasidic community would react to marathoning interlopers in their midst. The response has been surprisingly warm—if somewhat baffled.

Above: New Yorkers discover that the best vantage point is probably their own apartment window. Below: In Williamsburg, a cookie may be just the ticket for depleted runners.

LEE AVE SFORIM CENTER

BOOKS & Religious Articles TAPES & RECORDS

114

TEL 782-7782

ספרים לכל מקצועות היהדות
ספרי קודש מכל הסוגים
טייפס רקורדס וקסטות

# the queensboro and first avenue

The Queensboro Bridge carried Jay Gatsby into storied Manhattan from fictionalized West Egg. After traversing the flat 6-mile stretch of Brooklyn's Fourth Avenue and crossing the halfway point at the Pulaski Bridge into Queens, marathoners make that same mythical journey. Also known as the 59th Street Bridge, the span finds Simon and Garfunkel "feelin' groovy."

In a celebrity-studded ceremony the day before the race, a carpet is rolled over a portion of the exposed metal grating on the Queensboro's surface. Running atop the rug is an odd sensation, but it becomes pedestrian, if you will, when compared to the reception that awaits marathoners coming off the bridge.

While still on the other side of the East River among the warehouses of Queens, ears catch an inkling of what lies ahead in Manhattan, where crowds will be the deepest, most deafening, and most physically proximate to the runners. "I couldn't even see the crowd—we were running toward this roar," remembers 1993 runner-up Bob Kempainen. For Keith Brantly, coming off the Queensboro was "the most unbelievable feeling I've ever had. You feel like you're being sucked down this long vacuum tube of people."

Flying downhill off the bridge and onto First Avenue, the runners make a bravura entrance into the Emerald City that is Manhattan, the true urban segment of the race. This is the part of New York that never sleeps, land of fabled skyscrapers and endless activity. Manhattanites are not shy, nor are they restrained. The entire First Avenue experience, stretching 4 miles to the Bronx border, pumps the adrenaline; though they may be inspired by the cheers of the crowd, most marathoners should heed the warning of that Simon and Garfunkel song: "Slow down, you move too fast."

Above: Perhaps "J" was so frightened of being embarrassed by "Larry" that she had already fled the scene. Marathoners appreciate it when their admirers show up in person, and most have the good grace to do so.

The most ardent fans on First Avenue are often rooting for someone they know, but the result is collective cacophony. After the runners go by, the supporters can adjourn to nearby Central Park to watch loved ones finish.

"Twice a year," says Sergeant Tony Giorgio of the police department, "they all get what's called 'disorderly control training.'" On First Avenue, it certainly comes in handy.

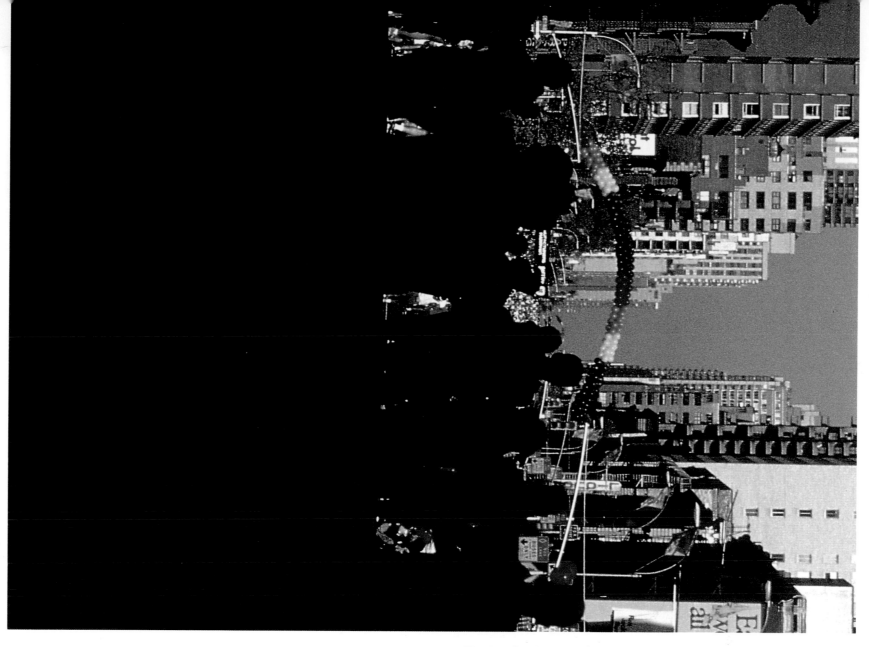

Emerging from under the shadows of the Queensboro Bridge overpass on First Avenue, a few of these marathoners undoubtedly planned to sneak a break from the pack and steal the race. Though the gamble occasionally pays off, the odds are not in the runners' favor; most seasoned racers will not attempt to assume command for a few more miles—the Bronx and Harlem are yet to come.

"It didn't matter who you were, where you were from, they were rooting for you."

Left: For some souls, conventionally running through the five boroughs is not enough. Committed waiters have gone the distance, others have juggled throughout five boroughs, while still more have run in silly costumes. Right: Loyal canine fans can be easily distracted—or tempted to join the race.

Right: Thomas Young promised Pamela Kezios "to tolerate her love of running forever" in wedding vows exchanged on the steps of the Brooklyn Academy of Music after 8 miles of the 1993 marathon. The ceremony was short and the honeymoon began immediately as the two continued their journey through Brooklyn, Queens, the Bronx, and Manhattan on foot.

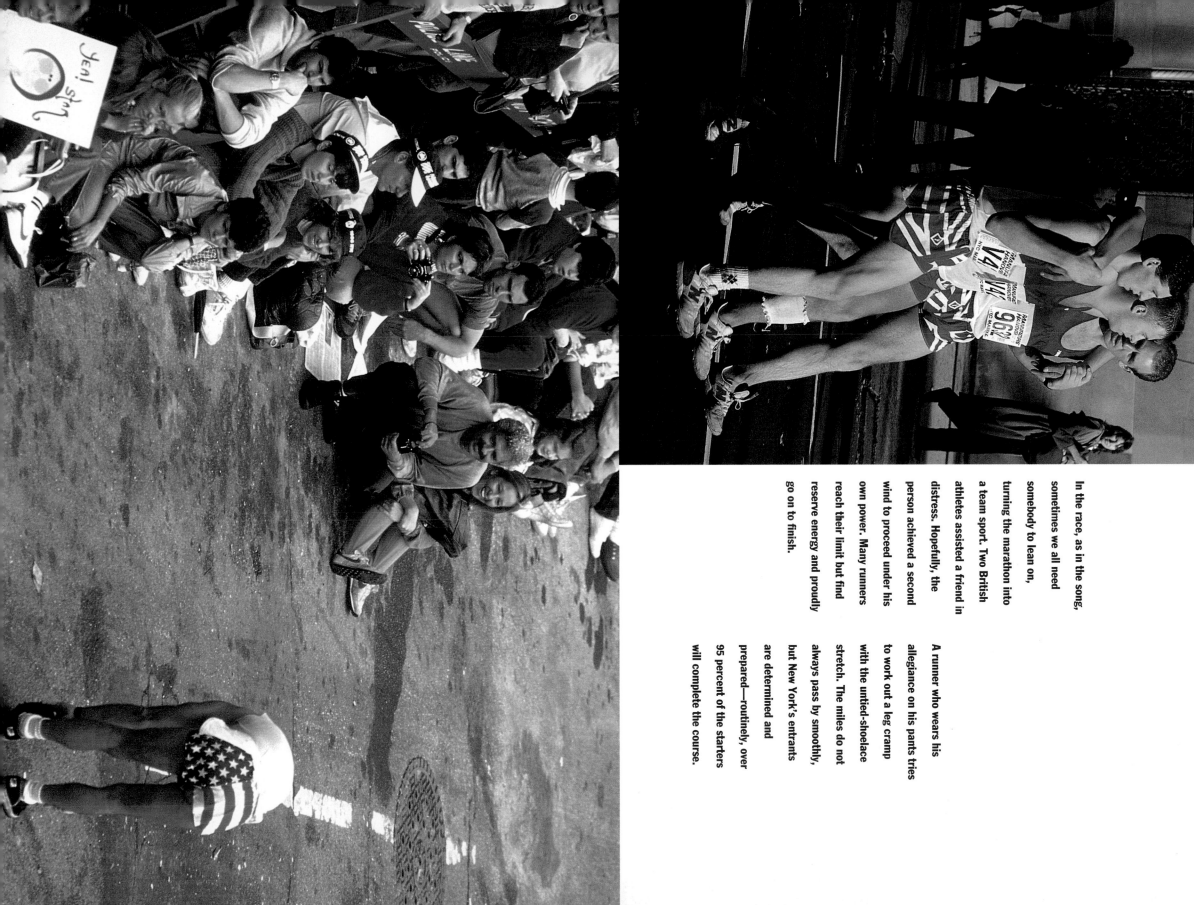

In the race, as in the song,
sometimes we all need
somebody to lean on,
turning the marathon into
a team sport. Two British
athletes assisted a friend in
distress. Hopefully, the
person achieved a second
wind to proceed under his
own power. Many runners
reach their limit but find
reserve energy and proudly
go on to finish.

A runner who wears his
allegiance on his pants tries
to work out a leg cramp
with the untied-shoelace
stretch. The miles do not
always pass by smoothly,
but New York's entrants
are determined and
prepared—routinely, over
95 percent of the starters
will complete the course.

"The **best** sporting **event** in the country is the **New York City** Marathon because people **embrace** the event."

PETER UEBERROTH

CHAIRMAN, 1984 LOS ANGELES

OLYMPICS

# the bronx and harlem

The Willis Avenue Bridge lies at the race's 20-mile mark and carries runners into the Bronx, where the serious competition—and hardship—begins. It is here that many marathoners encounter "the wall," that legendary point when the body has given all it has to give and runners struggle through on guts and a prayer. Bob Kempainen says, "The first 20 miles go by really quickly. The last 10 kilometers take just as long, mentally. Up to that point, it's fun." The Willis has a seemingly innocuous upgrade, but at this late stage the effect can be devastating. The Madison Avenue Bridge leads marathoners into the final Manhattan miles.

Each neighborhood is as distinct as a small country, yet all are linked for one day by the activity of the marathon; along the course, marvels Keith Brantly, "There is never a break between people." Olympian Kenny Moore, an Oregonian now living in Hawaii, comments, "I *hate* New York, every day except Marathon Sunday. The kids slapping hands with you, saying, 'Way to go, honky.' I *love* that!" At select points, the crowd din diminishes enough that runners can actually hear the eclectic musical acts booked to serenade them along the route.

Some champions have been oblivious to the activity, so completely were they focused on their athletic task. But Keith Brantly says, "It's too long of a race to be bolted into concentration the whole time. I was able to savor the moment. One of the perks is that you do get to enjoy the environment."

Along with miles of blacktop and towering concrete, the New York course boasts acres of greenery. Several leafy enclaves, like Marcus Garvey Park, in a landmarked area of Harlem, line the route, whetting runners' appetites for the ultimate—as they navigate around Garvey, Central Park is visible up ahead, and marathoners begin to sense they are closing in on the prize.

The Bronx bridges loom in the fateful 20th and 21st miles. Marathoners who surmount "the wall" encounter landmarked Harlem homes as residents emphatically point the way to the finish line.

When physically and emotionally depleted, it can be difficult to accept that there are still a few miles to go—and that the sweet reward of finishing will make up for all the pain.

''I never felt as bad as
I did over those last 2
miles. It was like running
with a hangover, like
having gone out and
partied yourself to death
and trying to get up the
next morning.''

AFTER PLACING SECOND TO

ROD DIXON IN 1983

# central park
# and the finish

Central Park—it is a magnificent urban oasis, at its most beautiful in full autumn foliage. On race day, the park belongs to the marathoners, the only day they do not compete with taxi drivers, bicyclists, roller bladers, sun worshippers, bird watchers, Shakespeare buffs, or a half million concert-goers. Marathoners enter at the park's northern end after a steady half-mile climb on Fifth Avenue. Further undulations in the landscape lie ahead. Winding down the East Park Drive, runners know the end is near and relish the shaded beauty of their final steps.

Before they reach the finish, the participants exit at the bottom of the park, stepping onto Central Park South, a posh strip of real estate known for its hotels—especially the Plaza Hotel—and horse-drawn carriages. Memorable marathon duels have remained unresolved as late as the 26th mile, when runners reenter the park at Columbus Circle.

"The last 300 yards are my favorite part of the course," says Grete Waitz, not only because the last little tease of a hill has been surmounted. From that point, runners can finally glimpse the classic finish line at Tavern on the Green, where boosters greet the 5-hour folks with the same enthusiasm showered on leaders like Waitz. Eminently proud of their accomplishment, runners reunite with friends and family and let the experience sink in.

"New York has that character of what it is," concludes Bob Kempainen. The sea of humanity has stretched throughout the entire course. Through five bridges, countless neighborhoods, and endless activity and gala good cheer, it is New York that makes the long, strange trip so memorable. Whether it lasts 2:11 or 5:11, the journey is its own reward.

**157**

**Above: By the time runners enter Central Park, they have only 3 miles to go. Hopefully, they have something in reserve. They have yet to encounter the deceptive, seemingly mild rises, which park regulars call "the insidious hills." They are fast approaching their prize, however—while first-timers may think it is a miracle they made it to the end, repeaters relish the rousing Central Park welcome more and more each time.**

**Below: The fans who bear witness in Central Park include regulars in the park's busy year-round road-race schedule.**

**Next year, inspired by what they have seen, the spectators themselves may step up to the marathon test. In 1993, 8,052 entrants—30 percent of the field—had never run a marathon before.**

ometimes, if you have a brain in your head, you should drop out," said New York City Marathon cofounder Ted Corbitt, but five boroughs and 26.2 miles later, *these runners have made it*

They may have thought it would never come, but racers can *hear* the finish line before seeing its banner. The field will stream in for hours, and latecomers get as stirring a reception as champions.

"A volunteer hands me a foil wrap and

I resemble a baked **potato**."

ERELONGMAN
NOVEMBER 15, 1993
THE NEW YORK TIMES

© 1993 Andy Lyons, Agence Shot.

Over thirteen thousand volunteers assist in staging the world's greatest "road show." Some began working months before the race while others remain on the job long after the last marathoner has clocked in, cleaning up the debris— including 1.6 million paper cups—to create a clean slate for the next year. Were it not for the volunteers, the race could never be staged in its grand scale.

They may have been up all night, but the volunteers' esprit de corps and enthusiastic boosterism never flags. Many devote as much time to serving gratis as they do to their paid careers. And some aspire to future positions at quite a tender age.

Left: © 1988 Photo News, Kathryn Dudek. Center: © 1993 Michael P. Voudouris.

**Far left:** Two-year-old David Cavazos of Monterrey, Mexico, proudly watches over his marathoning dad, José. Father and son roles are reversed—it is José who needs a nap.

**Left:** At the postrace Family Reunion Festival on the Great Lawn, marathoners receive medical help, live musical entertainment, congratulations from friends and kin, and a free call home to anywhere in the United States. The impact of their unforgettable experience is slowly sinking in. Who wants to leave?

# MARATHON RECORDS

**World Records**

2:06:50
Belayneh Densimo, Ethiopia
The Rotterdam Marathon
April 17, 1988

2:21:06
Ingrid Kristiansen, Norway
The London Marathon
April 21, 1985

**American Records**

2:08:13
Alberto Salazar,
Eugene, Oregon
The New York City Marathon
October 25, 1981

2:21:21
Joan Benoit Samuelson,
Freeport, Maine
America's Marathon, Chicago
October 20, 1985

**Fastest New York City Marathons**

2:08:01
Juma Ikangaa, Tanzania
November 5, 1989

2:24:40
Lisa Ondieki, Australia
November 3, 1992

**Fastest New York City Marathons by Americans**

2:08:13
Alberto Salazar,
Eugene, Oregon
(first place)
October 25, 1981

2:27:54
Kim Jones,
Spokane, Washington
(second place)
November 5, 1989

## September 13, 1970

Weather: 58–80°, 45% humidity, cloudy
Starters: 127 (126 men, 1 woman)
Finishers: 55 (43.3%) (all men)

### MEN
| | | | |
|---|---|---|---|
| 1 | Gary Muhrcke, 30 | Millrose AA | 2:31:38 CR |
| 2 | Tom Fleming, 19 | Will. Paterson Coll. | 2:35:44 |
| 3 | Ed Ayres | Washington, DC | 2:39:17 |
| 4 | Pat Bastick, 29 | Millrose AA | 2:44:09 |
| 5 | Ted Corbitt, 50 | NY Pioneer Club | 2:44:15 |
| 6 | Eric Walther | St. Anthony BC | 2:45:38 |
| 7 | Tom Hollander | Hamden G. | 2:48:35 |
| 8 | Moses Mayfield, 25 | Penn AC | 2:49:50 |
| 9 | Glenn Ayres | Washington, DC | 2:51:04 |
| 10 | William Kinsella, 26 | New Jersey | 2:52:48 |

### WOMEN
Nina Kuscsik was the only female starter. She did not finish due to illness.

Stats: 6
Foreign Countries: 0

Facts: From 1970 to 1975, the race was held in Central Park and consisted of four 6-mile laps and one 2.2-mile lap. Marathoners soon learned why the Algonquins selected the name "Manhattan," which means "island of hills." The chief of the New York City Fire Department, Dudley Glasse, ran and placed 48th in 4:24:27. Before the race, Gary Muhrcke had considered his teammate Pat Bastick "a contender" and himself merely "a participant." *The New York Times* identified Fred Lebow as "an executive with Taylor Knits." The race began at 11:00 A.M. and the last finisher arrived at 4:10:34 P.M. Al Harvin of the *New York Times* covered the event, and in 1989 he recalled to interviewer John Hanc that the people in Central Park "were doing their thing, throwing frisbees, hanging out, whatever. Nobody was paying much attention [to the marathon]. It was just another off-the-wall event in the park."

Records: Gary Muhrcke set the first course record for the New York City Marathon. Caroline Walker set American and world records, 3:02:53, in Seaside, Oregon. Eamon O'Reilly set an American record, 2:11:12, in Boston.

## September 19, 1971

Weather: 64–69°, 84% humidity, cloudy
Starters: 245 (240 men, 5 women)
Finishers: 164 (66.9%) (161 men, 3 women)

### MEN
| | | | |
|---|---|---|---|
| 1 | Norm Higgins, 34 | New London, CT | 2:22:54 |
| 2 | Chuck Ceronsky, 23 | Twin Cities TC | 2:33:21 |
| 3 | Max White, 20 | Boston AA | 2:33:52 |
| 4 | Tom Derderian | No. Medford Club | 2:37:13 |
| 5 | Hugh Sweeney, 25 | Millrose AA | 2:37:42 |
| 6 | John Garlepp, 33 | Millrose AA | 2:38:53 |
| 7 | Jim Johnsides | New York AC | 2:38:58 |
| 8 | William Kinsella, 27 | Central Jersey TC | 2:40:11 |
| 9 | Augie Calle, 32 | United AA | 2:40:33 |
| 10 | Bill Gordon, 37 | St. Anthony BC | 2:40:36 |

### WOMEN
| | | | |
|---|---|---|---|
| 1 | Beth Bonner, 19 | So. J. Chargers | 2:55:22 AR |
| 2 | Nina Kuscsik, 32 | Suffolk AC | 2:56:04 |
| 3 | Sara Berman, 35 | Cambridge SU | 3:08:46 |

Overall placement of women's winner: 34
Stats: 8
Foreign Countries: 1

Facts: The 1971 race served as the National AAU Junior Marathon Championship. The counterculture met the old guard—Joe Kleinerman described "runners with long hair and runners with long foreheads." The ten fastest runners received wristwatches, while those who placed 11th to 35th left with trophies. Running guru Jim Fixx took a tour of New York, placing 119th in 3:47:40.

Records: Norm Higgins set a course record. On May 9, Beth Bonner set American and world records, 3:01:42, in Philadelphia. On May 30, Sara Mae Berman set American and world records, 3:00:35, in Brockton, MA. In August, Adrienne Beames set an unofficial world record and broke the 3:00 barrier in Australia, 2:46:30. In September, Beth Bonner set course and American records, 2:49:40, in Culver City, CA. In December, Cheryl Bridges set an American record, 2:49:40, in Culver City, CA.

## September 28, 1975

Weather: 61–80°, 62% humidity, sunny
Starters: 534 (490 men, 44 women)
Finishers: 339 (63.5%) (303 men, 36 women)

### MEN
| | | | |
|---|---|---|---|
| 1 | Tom Fleming, 24 | New York AC | 2:19:27 CR |
| 2 | William Bragg, 26 | New York AC | 2:25:20 |
| 3 | Tim Smith, 27 | Mohegan Striders | 2:26:03 |
| 4 | Max White, 24 | Charlottesville TC | 2:28:38 |
| 5 | Michael Baxter, 31 | Boston AA | 2:28:40 |
| 6 | Art Hall, 28 | Oakwood TC | 2:28:52 |
| 7 | Larry Fredrick, 26 | New York AC | 2:29:46 |
| 8 | Mike Konig, 29 | Central Park TC | 2:30:24 |
| 9 | Rory Suomi, 19 | Mohegan Striders | 2:33:06 |
| 10 | Sheldon Karlin, 25 | Washington SC | 2:33:27 |

### WOMEN
| | | | |
|---|---|---|---|
| 1 | Kim Merritt, 20 | Parkside AC | 2:46:14 CR |
| 2 | Miki Gorman, 40 | SF Valley TC | 2:53:02 |
| 3 | Gayle Barron, 30 | Atlanta TC | 2:57:22 |
| 4 | Joan Ullyot, 35 | West Valley TC | 2:58:30 |
| 5 | Marilyn Bevans, 25 | Baltimore Suns | 2:59:19 |
| 6 | Diane Barrett, 14 | Arizona TC | 3:01:41 |
| 7 | Kathrine Switzer, 28 | Central Park TC | 3:02:57 |
| 8 | Nancy Linday, 26 | New York, NY | 3:06:53 |
| 9 | Sue Mallery, 21 | Ohio TC | 3:07:27 |
| 10 | Marion May, 21 | Fairbanks, AK | 3:12:01 |

Overall placement of women's winner: 9
Stats: 26
Foreign Countries: 0

Records: Fleming and Merritt set course records. In April, Liane Winter of Germany set world record, 2:42:24, in Boston; in May, Christa Vahlensieck of Germany broke that record in 2:40:16 in Dulmen; in October, Jacqueline Hansen set American and world records, 2:38:19, in Eugene. Bill Rodgers set an American record, 2:09:55, in Boston.

## October 21, 1979

Weather: 64–80°, 55% humidity, sunny
Starters: 11,533 (10,207 men, 1,326 women)
Finishers: 10,477 (90.8%) (9,274 men, 1,203 women)

### MEN
| | | | |
|---|---|---|---|
| 1 | Bill Rodgers, 31 | Melrose, MA | 2:11:42 |
| 2 | Kirk Pfeffer, 23 | Boulder, CO | 2:13:09 |
| 3 | Steve Kenyon, 28 | Great Britain | 2:13:30 |
| 4 | Ian Thompson, 30 | Great Britain | 2:13:43 |
| 5 | Benji Durden, 28 | Atlanta, GA | 2:13:49 |
| 6 | Jukka Toivola, 30 | Finland | 2:14:00 |
| 7 | Frank Shorter, 31 | Boulder, CO | 2:16:15 |
| 8 | Ron Tabb, 25 | Houston, TX | 2:16:38 |
| 9 | Jon Anderson, 30 | Eugene, OR | 2:16:38 |
| 10 | Oyvind Dahl, 28 | Norway | 2:16:41 |

### WOMEN
| | | | |
|---|---|---|---|
| 1 | Grete Waitz, 26 | Norway | 2:27:33 WR |
| 2 | Gillian Adams, 24 | Great Britain | 2:38:33 |
| 3 | Jacqueline Gareau, 26 | Canada | 2:39:06 |
| 4 | Patri Lyons, 26 | Boston, MA | 2:40:19 |
| 5 | Carol Gould, 35 | Great Britain | 2:42:21 |
| 6 | Vreni Foster, 25 | Switzerland | 2:43:14 |
| 7 | Sue Petersen, 35 | Laguna Beach, CA | 2:47:37 |
| 8 | Sissel Grottenberg, 23 | Norway | 2:47:50 |
| 9 | Doren Ennis, 23 | Nutley, NJ | 2:48:09 |
| 10 | V. Soderholm-Di Fatte | West Valley, CA | 2:49:05 |

Overall placement of women's winner: 69
Stats: 51*
Foreign Countries: 56

*The number of states includes Washington, D.C.

Facts: 296 (32%) runners had never run a marathon before.

Records: Grete Waitz set course and world records. Bill Rodgers set an American record, 2:09:27, in Boston, as did Joan Benoit Samuelson, 2:35:16.

## October 26, 1980

Weather: 43–50°, 39% humidity, fair
Starters: 14,012 (12,050 men, 1,962 women)
Finishers: 12,512 (89.3%) (10,891 men, 1,621 women)

### MEN
| | | | |
|---|---|---|---|
| 1 | Alberto Salazar, 22 | Wayland, MA | 2:09:41 CR |
| 2 | Rodolfo Gomez, 29 | Mexico | 2:10:13 |
| 3 | John Graham, 24 | Great Britain | 2:11:46 |
| 4 | Jeff Wells, 26 | Dallas, TX | 2:11:59 |
| 5 | Bill Rodgers, 32 | Sherborn, MA | 2:13:20 |
| 6 | Inge Simonsen, 27 | Norway | 2:13:28 |
| 7 | Trevor Wright, 34 | Great Britain | 2:13:30 |
| 8 | Ryszard Marczak, 28 | Poland | 2:13:45 |
| 9 | Dick Beardsley, 24 | Excelsior, MN | 2:13:55 |
| 10 | Frank Richardson, 25 | Ames, IA | 2:14:13 |

### WOMEN
| | | | |
|---|---|---|---|
| 1 | Grete Waitz, 27 | Norway | 2:25:42 WR |
| 2 | Patti Lyons Catalano, 27 | Boston, MA | 2:29:33 AR |
| 3 | Ingrid Kristiansen, 24 | Norway | 2:34:24 |
| 4 | Carol Gould, 36 | Great Britain | 2:35:05 |
| 5 | Gillian Adams, 25 | Great Britain | 2:37:55 |
| 6 | Laurie Binder, 33 | San Diego, CA | 2:38:09 |
| 7 | Kiki Sweigart, 29 | Darien, CT | 2:40:34 |
| 8 | Oddrun Mosling, 27 | Norway | 2:41:00 |
| 9 | Gayle Olinek, 27 | Canada | 2:41:32 |
| 10 | Jean Chodnicki, 21 | Saddle Brook, NJ | 2:43:33 |

Overall placement of women's winner: 40
Stats: 49
Foreign Countries: 74

Facts: Classified ads in the *Village Voice* offered $100 for marathon numbers.

Records: Salazar set a course record. Waitz set course and world records. Joan Benoit Samuelson set an American record, 2:31:23, in New Zealand; Patti Lyons Catalano broke that record in 2:30:58 in Montreal, taking it even lower in New York.

> "I've witnessed some astonishing New York showings in my time, but the most impressive performance I have ever seen was when Fritz Niederhauser, who started jogging when he was sixty-seven, crossed the New York City finish line at the age of seventy-three."
>
> — MARKUS RYFFEL, 1984 OLYMPIC SILVER MEDALIST AT 5000 METERS

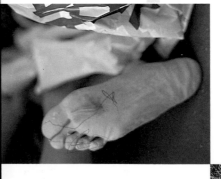

**October 1, 1972**

**Weather:** 45–63°, 63% humidity, fair
**Starters:** 284 (278 men, 6 women)
**Finishers:** 187 (65.9%) (185 men, 2 women)

| | | | |
|---|---|---|---|
| **MEN** | | | |
| 1 | Sheldon Karlin, 22 | College Park, MD | 2:27:52 |
| 2 | Glenn Appell, 22 | New York AC | 2:32:51 |
| 3 | Pat Bastick, 37 | Millrose AA | 2:33:42 |
| 4 | William Bragg, 23 | NJ Striders | 2:33:55 |
| 5 | Arthur Hall, 25 | Staten Island, NY | 2:37:22 |
| 6 | Augie Calle, 33 | United AA | 2:39:17 |
| 7 | Jim McDonagh, 48 | Millrose AA | 2:42:34 |
| 8 | Orlando Martinez, 25 | United AA | 2:42:38 |
| 9 | Dave Faherty, 27 | NJ Striders | 2:43:36 |
| 10 | Charles Collier, 25 | Staten Island AC | 2:43:38 |
| **WOMEN** | | | |
| 1 | Nina Kuscsik, 33 | Suffolk AC | 3:08:41 |
| 2 | Pat Barrett | Shore AC | 3:19:33 |

*Overall placement of women's winner:* 63
*States:* 7 *Foreign Countries:* 0

**Facts:** In 1972, Fred Lebow ran thirteen marathons, all within a 500-mile radius of New York. Sheldon Karlin's coach at the University of Maryland ordered him to cut his hair and would not let him live in a coed dormitory; Karlin quit the team and came to run New York. From 1970 to 1975, the primarily local runners were identified by their club or team memberships. Entrants who did not belong to teams were described solely as "unattached." By 1976, the first five-borough year, the race was drawing increasing numbers of unaffiliated national and international entrants, and runners came to be identified by their hometowns or countries. Just in case, the marathon had an ambulance on standby, but it was not until 1980 that Dr. Andres Rodriguez, his wife, Yolanda, and their daughter, Gloria, would begin to assemble and organize what has become the largest medical staff ever to serve a sporting event.
**Records:** Frank Shorter set an American record, 2:10:30, in Fukuoka, Japan.

**September 30, 1973**

**Weather:** 56–68°, 49% humidity, fair
**Starters:** 406 (394 men, 12 women)
**Finishers:** 282 (69.5%) (277 men, 5 women)

| | | | |
|---|---|---|---|
| **MEN** | | | |
| 1 | Tom Fleming, 22 | New York AC | 2:21:54[CR] |
| 2 | Norb Sander, 31 | Millrose AA | 2:23:38 |
| 3 | William Bragg, 24 | NJ Striders | 2:26:33 |
| 4 | Arthur Hall, 26 | Lakwood TC | 2:27:26 |
| 5 | Hector Ortiz, 22 | Long Island AC | 2:29:02 |
| 6 | Art Moore, 22 | Englewood, NJ | 2:31:08 |
| 7 | Calvin Hansey, 36 | Bermuda | 2:32:01 |
| 8 | Michael W. Baxter, 29 | Boston AA | 2:32:06 |
| 9 | Pat Bastick, 39 | Millrose AA | 2:32:31 |
| 10 | Gary Muhrcke, 33 | Millrose AA | 2:34:10 |
| **WOMEN** | | | |
| 1 | Nina Kuscsik, 33 | Suffolk AC | 2:57:07 |
| 2 | Kathrine Switzer, 26 | Central Park TC | 3:16:02 |
| 3 | Lynn Blackstone, 33 | Central Park TC | 3:55:43 |
| 4 | Toby Lenner, 30 | McBurney YMCA | 4:23:37 |
| 5 | Lila Mukamal, 32 | 92nd St. YMHA | 4:33:43 |

*Overall placement of women's winner:* 53
*States:* 9 *Foreign Countries:* 2

**Facts:** The finish line was located at the same Columbus Circle spot where the first marathon in the United States, stretching from Stamford to New York City, ended in 1896. The runners ranged in age from twelve to eighty years old, but the youngest finisher in New York City Marathon history was nine years old (1978) while the oldest was ninety-three (1991). In response to information about the deleterious physical effects of marathon running for young people, however, the New York City Marathon set a minimum age of sixteen in 1981, raising it to eighteen in 1989.
**Records:** Tom Fleming set a course record. Miki Gorman set an American record, 2:46:36, in Culver City, CA.

**September 29, 1974**

**Weather:** 68–76°, 93% humidity, thunderstorms
**Starters:** 527 (501 men, 26 women)
**Finishers:** 259 (49.2%) (250 men, 9 women)

| | | | |
|---|---|---|---|
| **MEN** | | | |
| 1 | Norb Sander, 33 | Millrose AA | 2:26:30 |
| 2 | Art McAndrews, 30 | Boston AA | 2:28:16 |
| 3 | Larry Frederick, 25 | New York AC | 2:32:18 |
| 4 | Arthur Hall, 27 | Oakwood TC | 2:35:01 |
| 5 | Bill Rodgers, 26 | Greater Boston TC | 2:35:59 |
| 6 | Hugh Sweeney, 28 | East Orange, NJ | 2:37:26 |
| 7 | Michael Baxter, 30 | Boston AA | 2:37:31 |
| 8 | Mike Scarbrough, 19 | East Coast AC | 2:41:00 |
| 9 | Kevin McDonald, 24 | NJ Striders | 2:44:29 |
| 10 | Colin Beer, 41 | Shore AC | 2:45:10 |
| **WOMEN** | | | |
| 1 | Kathrine Switzer, 27 | Central Park TC | 3:07:29 |
| 2 | Liz Franceschini, 31 | New York, NY | 3:34:43 |
| 3 | Faith Berriman, 19 | Dix Hills, NY | 3:55:06 |
| 4 | Ann DeGroff, 39 | New York, NY | 3:55:49 |
| 5 | Durhane Rieger, 24 | Flushing, NY | 4:03:17 |
| 6 | Mary Ann Pepan, 16 | Tyrone, PA | 4:21:00 |
| 7 | Betty Phillips, 36 | Vanderbilt YMCA | 4:27:48 |
| 8 | Cheryl L. Weill, 29 | New York, NY | 4:29:37 |
| 9 | Mary Hart, 16 | New York, NY | 5:18:17 |

*Overall placement of women's winner:* 59
*States:* 13 *Foreign Countries:* 3

**Facts:** For the first time, the winners of the race were invited to do television interviews, and Norb Sander and Kathrine Switzer appeared on the *Today* show.
**Records:** In October, Chantal Langlace of France set a world record, 2:46:24, in Neuf Brisach, France. In December, Jacqueline Hansen broke Langlace's record, also setting an American record, 2:43:55, in Culver City, CA.

**October 24, 1976**

**Weather:** 46–52°, 60% humidity, rain
**Starters:** 2,090 (2,002 men, 88 women)
**Finishers:** 1,549 (74.1%) (1,486 men, 63 women)

| | | | |
|---|---|---|---|
| **MEN** | | | |
| 1 | Bill Rodgers, 28 | Melrose, MA | 2:10:10[CR] |
| 2 | Frank Shorter, 29 | Gainesville, FL | 2:13:12 |
| 3 | Chris Stewart, 30 | Great Britain | 2:13:21 |
| 4 | Richard Hughson, 27 | Canada | 2:16:10 |
| 5 | Pekka Paivarinta, 27 | Finland | 2:16:17 |
| 6 | Tom Fleming, 25 | Bloomfield, NJ | 2:16:52 |
| 7 | Carl Hatfield, 29 | Philippi, WV | 2:17:26 |
| 8 | Daniel McDaid, 35 | Ireland | 2:17:48 |
| 9 | Guenther Mielke, 29 | Germany | 2:18:16 |
| 10 | Ron Hill, 38 | Great Britain | 2:19:43 |
| **WOMEN** | | | |
| 1 | Miki Gorman, 41 | Los Angeles, CA | 2:39:11[CR] |
| 2 | Doris H. Brown, 34 | Seattle, WA | 2:53:02 |
| 3 | Toshiko D'Elia, 46 | Ridgewood, NJ | 3:08:17 |
| 4 | Lauri Pedrinan, 23 | New York, NY | 3:15:50 |
| 5 | Cheryl Norton, 27 | New York, NY | 3:18:50 |
| 6 | Louise Wechsler, 28 | Matawan, NJ | 3:19:11 |
| 7 | Nina Kuscsik, 37 | Huntington St., NY | 3:20:08 |
| 8 | Elizabeth Curtin, 30 | California | 3:22:26 |
| 9 | Toni Plantamura, 23 | New Jersey | 3:22:29 |
| 10 | Jane Killion, 27 | New York, NY | 3:25:01 |

*Overall placement of women's winner:* 70
*States:* 31 *Foreign Countries:* 13

**Facts:** Bill Rodgers called the inaugural five-borough race "the birth of a new kind of marathon." According to his father, Rodgers began running as a boy to catch butterflies; as an adult, his marathon routine included eating breakfast at 3 A.M.
**Records:** Miki Gorman and Bill Rodgers set course records.

**October 23, 1977**

**Weather:** 45–56°, 50% humidity, sunny
**Starters:** 4,823 (4,595 men, 228 women)
**Finishers:** 3,885 (80.6%) (3,701 men, 184 women)

| | | | |
|---|---|---|---|
| **MEN** | | | |
| 1 | Bill Rodgers, 29 | Melrose, MA | 2:11:28 |
| 2 | Jerome Drayton, 32 | Canada | 2:13:52 |
| 3 | Chris Stewart, 31 | Great Britain | 2:13:56 |
| 4 | Esa Tikkanen, 24 | Finland | 2:14:32 |
| 5 | Garry Bjorklund, 26 | Minneapolis, MN | 2:15:16 |
| 6 | Randy Thomas, 24 | Brookline, MA | 2:15:51 |
| 7 | Fernand Kolbeck, 33 | France | 2:16:20 |
| 8 | Kenny Moore, 33 | Eugene, OR | 2:16:28 |
| 9 | Kazimierz Orzell, 24 | Poland | 2:16:48 |
| 10 | Lionel Ortega, 23 | Albuquerque, NM | 2:17:07 |
| **WOMEN** | | | |
| 1 | Miki Gorman, 42 | Los Angeles, CA | 2:43:10 |
| 2 | Kim Merritt, 22 | Racine, WI | 2:46:03 |
| 3 | Gayle Barron, 32 | Atlanta, GA | 2:52:19 |
| 4 | Lauri Pedrinan, 24 | New York, NY | 2:52:32 |
| 5 | Lisa Matovcik, 22 | Pittsburgh, PA | 2:55:03 |
| 6 | Wilma Rudolf, 32 | Germany | 2:56:08 |
| 7 | Jane Killion, 28 | New York, NY | 2:56:22 |
| 8 | Carolyn Billington, 32 | Great Britain | 2:58:43 |
| 9 | Nicki Hobson, 46 | San Diego, CA | 3:00:12 |
| 10 | Gale Jones, 24 | Unionville, CT | 3:02:46 |

*Overall placement of women's winner:* 190
*States:* 42 *Foreign Countries:* 24

**Facts:** With 4,823 racers, this was the largest marathon in history.
**Records:** In May, Chantal Langlace of France set a world record, 2:35:16, in Oyarzun, Spain. In September, Christa Vahlensieck of Germany broke that record in 2:34:48 in West Berlin. Kim Merritt set an American record, 2:37:57, in Eugene, OR.

**October 22, 1978**

**Weather:** 51–75°, 49% humidity, partly sunny
**Starters:** 9,875 (8,937 men, 938 women)
**Finishers:** 8,588 (87.0%) (7,819 men, 769 women)

| | | | |
|---|---|---|---|
| **MEN** | | | |
| 1 | Bill Rodgers, 30 | Melrose, MA | 2:12:12 |
| 2 | Ian Thompson, 29 | Great Britain | 2:14:12 |
| 3 | Trevor Wright, 32 | Great Britain | 2:14:35 |
| 4 | Marco Marchei, 24 | Italy | 2:16:54 |
| 5 | Tom Antczak, 27 | La Crosse, WI | 2:17:11 |
| 6 | Jack Foster, 46 | New Zealand | 2:17:28 |
| 7 | Chris Stewart, 32 | Great Britain | 2:17:47 |
| 8 | Bill Haviland, 28 | Athens, OH | 2:18:39 |
| 9 | Franco Ambrosioni, 27 | Italy | 2:19:08 |
| 10 | Bill Sieben, 26 | Wayne, NJ | 2:19:11 |
| **WOMEN** | | | |
| 1 | Grete Waitz, 25 | Norway | 2:32:30[WR] |
| 2 | Martha Cooksey, 24 | Orange, CA | 2:41:49 |
| 3 | Sue Petersen, 34 | Laguna Beach, CA | 2:44:43 |
| 4 | Doreen Ennis, 22 | Nutley, NJ | 2:46:38 |
| 5 | Eleonara Mendonca | Brazil | 2:48:45 |
| 6 | Margaret Lockley, 31 | Great Britain | 2:50:58 |
| 7 | Nancy Shafer, 27 | Gainesville, FL | 2:52:20 |
| 8 | Carol Young, 28 | Berkeley, CA | 2:52:28 |
| 9 | Glynnis Penny, 27 | Great Britain | 2:53:35 |
| 10 | Deborah Butterfield, 26 | Bermuda | 2:53:42 |

*Overall placement of women's winner:* 105
*States:* 50 *Foreign Countries:* 28

**Facts:** The marathon was by this time so established that Fred Lebow had to turn down thirty-five potential corporate sponsors.
**Records:** Grete Waitz set course and world records. Julie Brown set an American record, 2:36:23, in Eugene, OR.

**October 25, 1981**

**Weather:** 40–55°, 69% humidity, cloudy
**Starters:** 14,496 (12,467 men, 2,029 women)
**Finishers:** 13,223 (91.2%) (11,466 men, 1,757 women)

| | | | |
|---|---|---|---|
| **MEN** | | | |
| 1 | Alberto Salazar, 23 | Eugene, OR | 2:08:13[WR] |
| 2 | Jukka Toivola, 32 | Finland | 2:10:52 |
| 3 | Hugh Jones, 25 | Great Britain | 2:10:59 |
| 4 | Nick Brawn, 24 | Great Britain | 2:11:09 |
| 5 | Ryszard Marczak, 35 | Poland | 2:11:36 |
| 6 | Tony Sandoval, 27 | Denver, CO | 2:12:12 |
| 7 | Rodolfo Gomez, 30 | Mexico | 2:12:47 |
| 8 | Demetrio Cabanillas, 26 | Mexico | 2:13:10 |
| 9 | Alex Kasich, 26 | Eugene, OR | 2:13:19 |
| 10 | Tommy Persson, 26 | Sweden | 2:13:23 |
| **WOMEN** | | | |
| 1 | Allison Roe, 25 | New Zealand | 2:25:29[WR] |
| 2 | Ingrid Kristiansen, 25 | Norway | 2:30:08 |
| 3 | Julie Shea, 22 | Raleigh, NC | 2:30:12 |
| 4 | Laura Fogli, 22 | Italy | 2:34:47 |
| 5 | Jan Yerkes, 24 | Buckingham, PA | 2:35:39 |
| 6 | Karoline Nemetz, 23 | Sweden | 2:37:05 |
| 7 | Carol Gould, 37 | Great Britain | 2:37:25 |
| 8 | Birgit Bringslid, 35 | Sweden | 2:40:16 |
| 9 | Julie Brown, 25 | San Diego, CA | 2:40:48 |
| 10 | Sarah Quinn, 23 | New York, NY | 2:42:50 |

*Overall placement of women's winner:* 113
*States:* 51 *Foreign Countries:* 57

**Facts:** 11,777 (81%) New York runners had completed college or graduate school.
**Records:** Alberto Salazar set course and American records and broke Derek Clayton's 1969 world record. Allison Roe set course and world records. Patti Lyons Catalano set an American record, 2:27:52, in Boston.

**October 24, 1982**

**Weather:** 42–52°, 43% humidity, cloudy
**Starters:** 14,308 (12,233 men, 2,075 women)
**Finishers:** 13,599 (95.1%) (11,700 men, 1,899 women)

| | | | |
|---|---|---|---|
| **MEN** | | | |
| 1 | Alberto Salazar, 24 | Eugene, OR | 2:09:29 |
| 2 | Rodolfo Gomez, 31 | Mexico | 2:09:33 |
| 3 | Daniel Schlesinger | Raleigh, NC | 2:11:54 |
| 4 | Ryszard Marczak, 36 | Poland | 2:12:44 |
| 5 | David Murphy, 25 | Great Britain | 2:12:48 |
| 6 | Thomas Raunig, 23 | Great Falls, MT | 2:13:22 |
| 7 | George Malley, 27 | Wellesley, MA | 2:13:29 |
| 8 | Jose Gomez, 26 | Mexico | 2:13:43 |
| 9 | Marti Kiilholma, 20 | Finland | 2:13:51 |
| 10 | Dean Matthews, 27 | Atlanta, GA | 2:14:00 |
| **WOMEN** | | | |
| 1 | Grete Waitz, 29 | Norway | 2:27:14 |
| 2 | Julie Brown, 26 | San Diego, CA | 2:28:33 |
| 3 | Charlotte Teske, 32 | Germany | 2:31:53 |
| 4 | Laura Fogli, 23 | Italy | 2:33:01 |
| 5 | Ingrid Kristiansen, 26 | Norway | 2:33:36 |
| 6 | Julie Isphording, 20 | Cincinnati, OH | 2:34:24 |
| 7 | Laurie Binder, 35 | Oakland, CA | 2:35:18 |
| 8 | Nadezhda Gumerova | USSR | 2:35:28 |
| 9 | Carla Beurskens, 30 | Netherlands | 2:35:37 |
| 10 | Nancy Ditz, 28 | Santa Clara, CA | 2:38:08 |

*Overall placement of women's winner:* 117
*States:* 50 *Foreign Countries:* 71

**Facts:** There were 5,458 New York Road Runners Club members, 40 filmmakers, 90 economists, 56 editors, and 907 lawyers in the race. Finisher Dave Horning swam 3 miles across the New York Harbor before running his 26.2 miles in 2:54.
**Records:** Joan Benoit Samuelson set an American record, 2:26:11, in Eugene, OR.

**October 23, 1983**

**Weather:** 48–59°, 70% humidity, rain
**Starters:** 15,193 (12,838 men, 2,355 women)
**Finishers:** 14,546 (95.7%) (12,341 men, 2,205 women)

| | | | |
|---|---|---|---|
| **MEN** | | | |
| 1 | Rod Dixon, 33 | New Zealand | 2:08:59 |
| 2 | Geoff Smith, 29 | Great Britain | 2:09:08 |
| 3 | Ron Tabb, 29 | Eugene, OR | 2:10:46 |
| 4 | John Tuttle, 26 | Auburn, AL | 2:10:51 |
| 5 | John Graham, 27 | Great Britain | 2:10:57 |
| 6 | Gidamis Shahanga, 22 | Tanzania | 2:11:05 |
| 7 | Rudy Chapa, 25 | Bloomington, IN | 2:11:13 |
| 8 | Domingo Tibaduiza, 33 | Colombia | 2:11:21 |
| 9 | Derek Froude, 24 | New Zealand | 2:11:25 |
| 10 | Jukka Toivola, 34 | Finland | 2:11:35 |
| **WOMEN** | | | |
| 1 | Grete Waitz, 30 | Norway | 2:27:00 |
| 2 | Laura Fogli, 24 | Italy | 2:31:49 |
| 3 | Priscilla Welch, 38 | Great Britain | 2:32:31 |
| 4 | Alba Milana, 24 | Italy | 2:34:57 |
| 5 | Nancy Ditz, 29 | Menlo Park, CA | 2:35:31 |
| 6 | Christa Vahlensieck | Germany | 2:35:59 |
| 7 | Veronique Marot, 28 | Great Britain | 2:36:24 |
| 8 | Paolo Moro, 31 | Italy | 2:37:46 |
| 9 | Isabel Carmichael, 33 | New York, NY | 2:38:15 |
| 10 | Ann Peisch, 27 | Newtonville, MA | 2:38:19 |

*Overall placement of women's winner:* 141
*States:* 51 *Foreign Countries:* 69

**Facts:** In 1970, Gary Muhrcke won the first New York City Marathon in 2:31:38. In 1983, 43-year-old Muhrcke beat that time by 38 seconds, but now placed 197th.
**Records:** On April 17, Grete Waitz set a world record, 2:25:29, in London. On April 18, Joan Benoit Samuelson broke Waitz's record in 2:22:43 in Boston.

## October 28, 1984

**Weather:** 62–79°, 98% humidity, mostly sunny
**Starters:** 16,315 (13,705 men, 2,610 women)
**Finishers:** 14,590 (89.4%) (12,195 men, 2,395 women)

### MEN

| | | | |
|---|---|---|---|
| 1 | Orlando Pizzolato, 26 | Italy | 2:14:53 |
| 2 | David Murphy, 27 | Great Britain | 2:15:36 |
| 3 | Herbert Steffny, 31 | Germany | 2:16:22 |
| 4 | Pat Petersen, 24 | Ronkonkoma, NY | 2:16:35 |
| 5 | Gianni DeMadonna, 30 | Italy | 2:17:05 |
| 6 | Michael Spoettel, 28 | Germany | 2:17:11 |
| 7 | Antoni Niemczak, 28 | Poland | 2:17:34 |
| 8 | Nick Brawn, 27 | Great Britain | 2:17:42 |
| 9 | Ahmed Ismail, 20 | Somalia | 2:18:16 |
| 10 | Zakaria Barie, 25 | Tanzania | 2:18:27 |

### WOMEN

| | | | |
|---|---|---|---|
| 1 | Grete Waitz, 31 | Norway | 2:29:30 |
| 2 | Veronique Marot, 29 | Great Britain | 2:33:58 |
| 3 | Laura Fogli, 25 | Italy | 2:37:25 |
| 4 | Lizanne Bussieres, 23 | Canada | 2:37:34 |
| 5 | Judi St. Hilaire, 25 | Brighton, MA | 2:37:49 |
| 6 | Carey May, 25 | Ireland | 2:38:11 |
| 7 | Renata Walendziak, 34 | Poland | 2:40:48 |
| 8 | Charlotte Teske, 34 | Germany | 2:41:16 |
| 9 | Rita Marchisio, 34 | Italy | 2:41:18 |
| 10 | Laura Albers, 27 | Grand Rapids, MI | 2:42:12 |

*Overall placement of women's winner:* 51

**Stats:** 51
**Facts:** In the running were 2 Pakistanis, 18 Austrians, 1 Jamaican, 163 civil servants, 109 artists, 77 psychologists, 167 nurses, and 83 mechanics. Mike Lupica of the *New York Daily News* called the marathon "the St. Patrick's Day parade, only faster."
**Records:** Steve Jones set a world record, 2:08:05, in Chicago.

*Foreign Countries: 72*

## October 27, 1985

**Weather:** 54–72°, 30% humidity, sunny
**Starters:** 16,705 (14,099 men, 2,606 women)
**Finishers:** 15,881 (95.1%) (13,403 men, 2,478 women)

### MEN

| | | | |
|---|---|---|---|
| 1 | Orlando Pizzolato, 27 | Italy | 2:11:34 |
| 2 | Ahmed Saleh, 27 | Djibouti | 2:12:29 |
| 3 | Pat Petersen, 25 | Brooklyn, NY | 2:12:59 |
| 4 | Don Norman, 27 | Republic, PA | 2:14:08 |
| 5 | Gerard Nijboer, 30 | Netherlands | 2:14:27 |
| 6 | Allan Zachariassen, 29 | Denmark | 2:15:18 |
| 7 | Bill Rodgers, 37 | Sherborn, MA | 2:15:33 |
| 8 | Guiseppe Pambianchi | Italy | 2:15:40 |
| 9 | Ibrahim Hussein, 26 | Kenya | 2:15:55 |
| 10 | Jorge Gonzalez, 32 | Puerto Rico | 2:16:51 |

### WOMEN

| | | | |
|---|---|---|---|
| 1 | Grete Waitz, 32 | Norway | 2:28:34 |
| 2 | Lisa Ondieki, 25 | Australia | 2:29:48 |
| 3 | Laura Fogli, 26 | Italy | 2:31:36 |
| 4 | Lorraine Moller, 30 | New Zealand | 2:34:55 |
| 5 | Priscilla Welch, 40 | Great Britain | 2:35:30 |
| 6 | Ngaire Drake, 36 | New Zealand | 2:36:53 |
| 7 | Sue King, 27 | Mobile, AL | 2:37:38 |
| 8 | Julie Brown, 30 | San Diego, CA | 2:37:53 |
| 9 | Jacqueline Gareau, 32 | Canada | 2:38:31 |
| 10 | Agnes Sipka, 31 | Hungary | 2:40:22 |

*Overall placement of women's winner:* 73

**Stats:** 73
**Facts:** Grete Waitz was that rare runner who openly confessed, "I don't like the pasta."
**Records:** Carlos Lopes of Portugal set a world record, 2:07:12, in Rotterdam. Ingrid Kristiansen of Norway set a world record, 2:21:06, in London. Joan Benoit Samuelson set an American record, 2:21:21, in Chicago.

*Foreign Countries: 79*

## November 4, 1990

**Weather:** 58–73°, 60% humidity, sunny
**Starters:** 25,012 (20,285 men, 4,727 women)
**Finishers:** 23,774 (95.1%) (19,274 men, 4,500 women)

### MEN

| | | | |
|---|---|---|---|
| 1 | Douglas Wakiihuri, 27 | Kenya | 2:12:39 |
| 2 | Salvador Garcia, 30 | Mexico | 2:13:19 |
| 3 | Steve Brace, 29 | Great Britain | 2:13:32 |
| 4 | Juma Ikangaa, 30 | Tanzania | 2:14:32 |
| 5 | John Campbell, 41 | New Zealand | 2:14:34 |
| 6 | Peter Maher, 30 | Canada | 2:15:05 |
| 7 | Filemon Lopez, 32 | Mexico | 2:16:33 |
| 8 | Yakov Tolstikov, 31 | USSR | 2:16:38 |
| 9 | Herbert Steffny, 37 | Germany | 2:16:47 |
| 10 | Pedro Ortiz, 34 | Colombia | 2:16:57 |

### WOMEN

| | | | |
|---|---|---|---|
| 1 | Wanda Panfil, 31 | Poland | 2:30:45 |
| 2 | Kim Jones, 32 | Spokane, WA | 2:30:50 |
| 3 | Katrin Dorre, 29 | Germany | 2:33:21 |
| 4 | Grete Waitz, 37 | Norway | 2:34:34 |
| 5 | Tatyana Zsuyeva, 31 | USSR | 2:35:48 |
| 6 | Jocelyne Villeton, 36 | France | 2:36:12 |
| 7 | Zoya Ivanova, 38 | USSR | 2:36:29 |
| 8 | Nancy Ditz, 36 | Woodside, CA | 2:37:15 |
| 9 | Evy Palm, 48 | Sweden | 2:38:00 |
| 10 | Lisa Vaill, 27 | Pine Plains, NY | 2:38:05 |

*Overall placement of women's winner:* 50

**Stats:** 50
**Facts:** Marathon organizers used 1.35 million paper cups in quenching runners' thirst, 2,700 police officers made certain that no one crossed the 18,000 yards of barricade tape, 10,215 volunteers were kept awake by 25,000 cups of coffee, and 642 tubes of K-Y jelly ensured that no thighs were chaffed.

*Foreign Countries: 84*

## November 5, 1989

**Weather:** 40–56°, 60% humidity, partly cloudy
**Starters:** 24,996 (20,247 men, 4,749 women)
**Finishers:** 24,659 (98.7%) (19,971 men, 4,688 women)

### MEN

| | | | |
|---|---|---|---|
| 1 | Juma Ikangaa, 29 | Tanzania | 2:08:01* |
| 2 | Ken Martin, 31 | Santa Fe, NM | 2:09:38 |
| 3 | Gelindo Bordin, 30 | Italy | 2:09:40 |
| 4 | Salvatore Bettiol, 27 | Italy | 2:10:08 |
| 5 | Jesus Herrera, 27 | Mexico | 2:11:15 |
| 6 | Nivaldo Filho, 29 | Brazil | 2:12:23 |
| 7 | Osmiro Silva, 34 | Brazil | 2:12:50 |
| 8 | Steve Jones, 34 | Great Britain | 2:12:58 |
| 9 | Belaynch Densimo, 24 | Ethiopia | 2:13:42 |
| 10 | Pat Petersen, 29 | Bay Shore, NY | 2:14:02 |

### WOMEN

| | | | |
|---|---|---|---|
| 1 | Ingrid Kristiansen, 33 | Norway | 2:25:30 |
| 2 | Kim Jones, 31 | Spokane, WA | 2:27:54 |
| 3 | Laura Fogli, 30 | Italy | 2:28:43 |
| 4 | Kumi Araki, 24 | Japan | 2:30:00 |
| 5 | Dorthe Rasmussen, 29 | Denmark | 2:32:18 |
| 6 | Zoya Ivanova, 37 | USSR | 2:32:21 |
| 7 | Emma Scaunich, 35 | Italy | 2:32:25 |
| 8 | Gordon Bloch, 28 | New York, NY | 2:33:01 |
| 9 | Ritva Lemittinen, 29 | Finland | 2:34:00 |
| 10 | Alena Peterkova, 28 | Czechoslowkia | 2:34:22 |

*Overall placement of women's winner:* 51

**Stats:** 51
**Facts:** Tomasz Chmurzynski, a 19-year-old blind runner with the Achilles Track Club, clocked 2:57:00. Had she won in New York, Los Angeles–champion Zoya Ivanova would have received a $300,000 bonus for winning both races in the same year.
**Records:** Juma Ikangaa set a course record.

*Foreign Countries: 89*

Above: © *Runner's World* SA, Tertius Picard.
Right: © 1991 Mike Voudouris.

## CELEBRITIES

| Name | Profession | Year | Time |
|---|---|---|---|
| Kim Alexis | Model | 1991 | 3:52:00* |
| Herman Badillo | Bronx Borough President | 1981 | 3:53:21* |
| Billy Baldwin | Actor | 1992 | 3:24:29 |
| Meredith Baxter | Actor | 1982 | 4:08:30 |
| Robby Benson | Actor | 1989 | 3:59:56 |
| David Birney | Actor | 1982 | 3:44:52 |
| Jacques D'Amboise | Ballet Dancer | 1976 | 4:05:09 |
| Alexander Ferdinand | Prince of the Netherlands | 1992 | 4:33:04 |
| Ray Flynn | Boston Mayor | 1984 | 3:55:00* |
| Kenneth Gibson | Newark Mayor | 1983 | 4:32:37 |
| Mariel Hemingway | Actor | 1988 | Achilles Escort |
| Ingemar Johansson | Boxer | 1980 | 3:16:02 |
| Jean-Claude Killy | Olympic Skier | 1983 | 3:58:33 |
| Ernie Koy | Olympic 10k Champion | 1993 | 5:26:30 |
| Billy Mills | Olympic 10k Champion | 1986 | 4:10:40 |
| Bobby Murcer | New York Yankee | 1988 | 5:00:20 |
| Bobby Nystrom | New York Islander | 1991 | 3:40:22* |
| Floyd Patterson | Boxer | 1983 | 3:35:27 |
| David Lee Roth | Musician | 1980 | 6:04:43 |
| Erich Segal | Writer | 1971 | 3:36:48 |
| Lynn Swann* | Pittsburgh Steeler | 1993 | 4:26:40 |
| Peter Weller | Actor | 1988 | 3:51:26* |

*\*Personal best, in cases where celebrities have run more than one New York City Marathon.*

## THE ACHILLES TRACK CLUB

Founded in 1983 in New York City, the Achilles Track Club encourages people with all types of severe disabilities to participate in short- and long-distance running. The club has thirty-five chapters in twenty-one other countries. Achilles athletes usually start before the rest of the field and are often escorted by volunteers. Club president and founder Dick Traum, himself a longtime marathoner, describes the Achilles philosophy: "Reveling in the pleasure of doing it yourself, with your own body, appreciating the marvelous things the body *can* do rather than focusing on what it *can't* do—in short, just being intensely glad to be alive."

### New York City Marathon Number of Achilles Participants

| Year | Number |
|---|---|
| 1983 | 6 |
| 1984 | 11 |
| 1985 | 23 |
| 1986 | 42 |
| 1987 | 74 |
| 1988 | 73 |
| 1989 | 72 |
| 1990 | 91 |
| 1991 | 102 |
| 1992 | 126 |
| 1993 | 123 |

### New York City Marathon Achilles Winners

| | Time | Name | Location | Disability |
|---|---|---|---|---|
| **1993** | 2:27:26 | Robert Neumayer, 46 | New York | Wheelchair |
| | 3:43:10 | Jakor-Tickona Vshutsev, 35 | Russia | Blind |
| **1992** | 2:10:46 | Angelo Pregonlato, 41 | Italy | Wheelchair |
| | 4:09:57 | Rianna Brycelland, 40 | New York | Polio |
| **1991** | 2:47:15 | Anton Sluka, 30 | Czech Rep. | Wheelchair |
| | 3:54:06 | Olga Nazarenko, 37 | USSR | Blind |
| **1990** | 2:53:00 | Robert Neumayer, 43 | New York | Wheelchair |
| | 4:13:32 | Helene Hines, 42 | New York | Multiple Sclerosis |

**Facts:** Bronx borough president Herman Badillo has run the New York City Marathon thirteen times. Kim Alexis is a five-time veteran, while Peter Weller has traversed the 26.2 miles four times. Ray Flynn, mayor of Boston, has checked out his town's marathon competition six times. Prince Alex ran to raise money for Memorial Sloan-Kettering and cancer-stricken children in the Netherlands.

## November 2, 1986

**Weather:** 46–65°, 75% humidity, cloudy, windy
**Starters:** 20,502 (17,016 men, 3,486 women)
**Finishers:** 19,689 (96.0%) (16,366 men, 3,323 women)

### MEN
| | | | |
|---|---|---|---|
| 1 | Gianni Poli, 28 | Italy | 2:11:06 |
| 2 | Rob de Castella, 29 | Australia | 2:11:43 |
| 3 | Orlando Pizzolato, 28 | Italy | 2:12:13 |
| 4 | Ibrahim Hussein, 27 | Kenya | 2:12:51 |
| 5 | Peter Maher, 31 | Germany | 2:13:21 |
| 6 | Ralf Salzman, 31 | Germany | 2:13:27 |
| 7 | Isidro Rico, 30 | Mexico | 2:13:39 |
| 8 | Rex Wilson, 31 | New Zealand | 2:14:03 |
| 9 | Agapus Masong, 26 | Tanzania | 2:14:09 |
| 10 | Osvaldo Faustini, 30 | Italy | 2:14:09 |
| | Daniel Boltz, 29 | Switzerland | |
| | Peter Pfitzinger, 29 | | |
| | Eddy Hellebuyck, 33 | Belgium | 2:14:30 |

### WOMEN
| | | | |
|---|---|---|---|
| 1 | Grete Waitz, 33 | Norway | 2:28:06 |
| 2 | Lisa Ondieki, 26 | Australia | 2:29:12 |
| 3 | Laura Fogli, 27 | Italy | 2:29:44 |
| 4 | Jocelyne Villeton, 32 | France | 2:32:51 |
| 5 | Karolina Szabo, 24 | Hungary | 2:34:51 |
| 6 | Odette Lapierre, 31 | Canada | 2:35:33 |
| 7 | Emma Scaunich, 32 | Italy | 2:37:50 |
| 8 | Rita Marchisio, 36 | Italy | 2:38:12 |
| 9 | Christa Vahlensieck, 36 | Germany | 2:38:24 |
| 10 | Sharlet Gilbert, 35 | Richmond, CA | |

**Foreign Countries:** 80
**States:** 51
**Overall placement of women's winner:** 51

**Facts:** The five best-represented states were New York (6,260 runners), New Jersey (1,678), California (791), Connecticut (527), and Texas (464). One million cups of water were consumed against 400 portable toilets, while 1,900 New York City police officers made certain that none of the 20,000 marathon medals were stolen.

---

## November 3, 1991

**Weather:** 44–57°, 50% humidity, partly cloudy
**Starters:** 26,900 (23,520 men, 5,380 women)
**Finishers:** 25,797 (95.9%) (20,593 men, 5,204 women)

### MEN
| | | | |
|---|---|---|---|
| 1 | Salvador Garcia, 31 | Mexico | 2:09:28 |
| 2 | Andres Espinosa, 28 | Mexico | 2:10:00 |
| 3 | Ibrahim Hussein, 33 | Kenya | 2:11:07 |
| 4 | Peter Maher, 31 | Canada | 2:11:55 |
| 5 | Isidro Rico, 30 | Mexico | 2:11:58 |
| 6 | Rex Wilson, 31 | New Zealand | 2:12:04 |
| 7 | Daniel Boltz, 29 | Switzerland | 2:14:36 |
| 8 | Jean Baptiste Protais, 31 | France | 2:14:54 |
| 9 | John Treacy, 34 | Ireland | 2:15:09 |
| 10 | Peter Renner, 32 | New Zealand | 2:15:45 |

### WOMEN
| | | | |
|---|---|---|---|
| 1 | Liz McColgan, 27 | Great Britain | 2:27:32 |
| 2 | Olga Markova, 23 | USSR | 2:28:27 |
| 3 | Lisa Ondieki, 31 | Australia | 2:29:02 |
| 4 | Alena Peterkova, 30 | Czechoslovakia | 2:29:32 |
| 5 | Ramila Burangulova, 30 | USSR | 2:31:55 |
| 6 | Joan Samuelson, 34 | Freeport, ME | 2:33:40 |
| 7 | Elena Semanova, 27 | USSR | 2:36:54 |
| 8 | Elena Murgoci, 27 | Romania | 2:39:49 |
| 9 | Grazella Struik, 42 | Italy | 2:40:13 |
| 10 | Carmen de Oliveira, 26 | Brazil | 2:40:57 |

**Foreign Countries:** 92
**States:** 51
**Overall placement of women's winner:** 54

**Facts:** After running New York in 1989 and 1990, Josef Galia, at the age of ninety-three, was the oldest finisher in New York history with his 7:59:34. The Japanese contingent numbered 212, and 266 homemakers ran along de 152 social workers, 18 gamekeepers, 24 mathematicians, and 151 postal employees.

---

## November 1, 1987

**Weather:** 45–64°, 50% humidity, sunny
**Starters:** 22,523 (18,604 men, 3,919 women)
**Finishers:** 21,244 (94.3%) (17,555 men, 3,689 women)

### MEN
| | | | |
|---|---|---|---|
| 1 | Ibrahim Hussein, 28 | Kenya | 2:11:01 |
| 2 | Gianni DeMadonna, 33 | Italy | 2:11:53 |
| 3 | Peter Pfitzinger, 29 | Wellesley, MA | 2:12:03 |
| 4 | Pat Petersen, 30 | Ronkonkoma, NY | 2:12:31 |
| 5 | Tommy Ekblom, 31 | Finland | 2:12:50 |
| 6 | Orlando Pizzolato, 29 | Italy | 2:13:38 |
| 7 | Boguslaw Psujek, 30 | Poland | 2:13:50 |

### WOMEN
| | | | |
|---|---|---|---|
| 1 | Priscilla Welch, 42 | Great Britain | 2:30:17 |
| 2 | Francoise Bonnet, 30 | France | 2:31:22 |
| 3 | Jocelyne Villeton, 33 | France | 2:32:03 |
| 4 | Ria Van Landeghem, 25 | Belgium | 2:32:38 |
| 5 | Karolina Szabo, 25 | Hungary | 2:34:58 |
| 6 | Agnes Sipka, 33 | Hungary | 2:35:26 |
| 7 | Laurie Crisp, 26 | El Cajon, CA | 2:36:01 |
| 8 | Monika Schaefer, 28 | Germany | 2:37:40 |
| 9 | Robyn Root, 27 | Davis, CA | 2:37:57 |
| 10 | Nellie Aerts, 25 | Belgium | 2:38:18 |

**Foreign Countries:** 68
**States:** 51
**Overall placement of women's winner:** 51

**Facts:** Mayor Ed Koch told Hasidic Jews that two things were holy in New York City, "the Talmud and the marathon." Despite innovations to accommodate more runners, marathon officials have had to reject applications since 1979. Between 1987 and 1993 an average of 22,919 applicants have been turned away each year.

---

## November 1, 1992

**Weather:** 40–51°, 45% humidity, partly cloudy, breezy
**Starters:** 28,656 (23,047 men, 5,609 women)
**Finishers:** 27,797 (97.0%) (22,356 men, 5,441 women)

### MEN
| | | | |
|---|---|---|---|
| 1 | Willie Mtolo, 28 | South Africa | 2:09:29 |
| 2 | Andres Espinosa, 29 | Mexico | 2:10:53 |
| 3 | Wan-Ki Kim, 24 | South Korea | 2:10:54 |
| 4 | Osmiro Silva, 31 | Brazil | 2:12:50 |
| 5 | Antoni Niemczak, 36 | Poland | 2:13:00 |
| 6 | Walter Durbano, 29 | Italy | 2:13:24 |
| 7 | Luca Barzaghi, 24 | Italy | 2:13:35 |
| 8 | Driss Dacha, 29 | Morocco | 2:13:35 |
| 9 | David Lewis, 31 | Great Britain | 2:13:49 |
| 10 | Steve Brace, 31 | Great Britain | 2:14:10 |

### WOMEN
| | | | |
|---|---|---|---|
| 1 | Lisa Ondieki, 32 | Australia | 2:24:40* |
| 2 | Olga Markova, 24 | Russia | 2:26:38 |
| 3 | Yoshiko Yamamoto, 22 | Japan | 2:29:58 |
| 4 | Kamila Gradus, 25 | Poland | 2:30:09 |
| 5 | Bertina Sabatini, 26 | Italy | 2:31:30 |
| 6 | Suzana Ciric, 23 | Yugoslavia | 2:33:58 |
| 7 | Silly Eastall, 29 | Great Britain | 2:34:05 |
| 8 | Irina Bogacheva, 31 | Kyrghizstan | 2:34:31 |
| 9 | Kersin Pressler, 30 | Germany | 2:34:52 |
| 10 | Maria Lelut-Rebelo, 36 | France | 2:36:40 |

**Foreign Countries:** 100
**States:** 51
**Overall placement of women's winner:** 40

**Facts:** Lisa Ondieki predicted that the first woman to break 2:20 in New York would "probably be my daughter, Emma." With Fred Lebow running the race himself, his spot in the pace car was taken by technical director Allan Steinfeld.

**Records:** Lisa Ondieki set a course record.

---

## November 6, 1988

**Weather:** 43–65°, 48% humidity, clear
**Starters:** 23,463 (19,330 men, 4,155 women)
**Finishers:** 22,405 (95.5%) (18,431 men, 3,974 women)

### MEN
| | | | |
|---|---|---|---|
| 1 | Steve Jones, 33 | Great Britain | 2:08:20 |
| 2 | Salvatore Bettiol, 26 | Italy | 2:11:41 |
| 3 | John Treacy, 31 | Ireland | 2:13:18 |
| 4 | Gidamis Shahanga, 27 | Tanzania | 2:13:50 |
| 5 | Nikolai Tabak, 30 | USSR | 2:14:00 |
| 6 | Juan Montero, 27 | Spain | 2:14:06 |
| 7 | Kazuyoshi Kudoh, 27 | Japan | 2:14:14 |
| 8 | Mark Nenow, 30 | Sacramento, CA | 2:14:21 |
| 9 | Derje Nedi, 33 | Ethiopia | 2:14:27 |
| 10 | Rustam Shagiev, 25 | USSR | 2:14:34 |

### WOMEN
| | | | |
|---|---|---|---|
| 1 | Grete Waitz, 35 | Norway | 2:28:07 |
| 2 | Laura Fogli, 29 | Italy | 2:31:26 |
| 3 | Joan Samuelson, 31 | Freeport, ME | 2:32:40 |
| 4 | Karolina Szabo, 26 | Hungary | 2:36:40 |
| 5 | Kerstin Pressler, 26 | Germany | 2:37:35 |
| 6 | Alevtina Chasova, 27 | USSR | 2:37:59 |
| 7 | Grazella Struik, 39 | New Zealand | 2:39:32 |
| 8 | Hazel Stewart, 34 | Italy | 2:40:26 |
| 9 | Bente Moe, 27 | Norway | 2:40:41 |
| 10 | Tovel Lorentzen, 28 | Denmark | 2:41:07 |

**Foreign Countries:** 90
**States:** 51
**Overall placement of women's winner:** 59

**Fact:** Though a Soviet woman, Nadezhda Gumerova, had placed eighth in 1982, Nikolai Tabak and Rustam Shagiev were the first two men from the USSR to place in the top ten. Ready to assist were 1,760 medical volunteers and 1,200 stretchers.

**Records:** Belayneh Densimo of Ethiopia set a world record, 2:06:50, in Rotterdam.

---

## November 14, 1993

**Weather:** 54–72° degrees, 61% humidity, clear
**Starters:** 28,340 (21,989 men, 6,151 women)
**Finishers:** 26,597 (94.5%) (20,781 men, 5,816 women)

### MEN
| | | | |
|---|---|---|---|
| 1 | Andres Espinosa, 30 | Mexico | 2:10:04 |
| 2 | Bob Kempainen, 27 | Minnesota | 2:11:03 |
| 3 | Arturo Barrios, 30 | Mexico | 2:12:21 |
| 4 | Joaquim Pinheiro, 32 | Portugal | 2:12:40 |
| 5 | Keith Brantly, 31 | Florida | 2:12:49 |
| 6 | Inocencio Miranda, 32 | Mexico | 2:12:52 |
| 7 | Paul Evans, 32 | Great Britain | 2:13:36 |
| 8 | Sammy Lelei, 29 | Kenya | 2:13:36 |
| 9 | Grzegorz Gajdus, 26 | Poland | 2:15:34 |
| 10 | Moses Tanui, 28 | Kenya | 2:15:36 |

### WOMEN
| | | | |
|---|---|---|---|
| 1 | Uta Pippig, 28 | Germany | 2:26:24 |
| 2 | Olga Appell, 30 | Mexico | 2:28:56 |
| 3 | Nadia Prasad, 24 | France | 2:30:16 |
| 4 | Marcia Narloch, 24 | Brazil | 2:32:23 |
| 5 | Alena Polerkova, 33 | Czech Rep. | 2:33:43 |
| 6 | Emma Scaunich, 39 | Italy | 2:33:02 |
| 7 | R. Burangulova, 30 | Russia | 2:36:13 |
| 8 | Nadezhda Ilyina, 29 | Russia | 2:37:58 |
| 9 | Crystal Roglars, 30 | Belgium | 2:38:41 |
| 10 | Lybov Klochko, 34 | Ukraine | 2:41:44 |

**Foreign Countries:** 105
**States:** 51
**Overall placement of women's winner:** 41

**Facts:** If any of the 7,142 runners from New York State drove to the marathon, they probably encountered some of the 13,700 "No Parking" signs. Marathoners, New Yorkers, volunteers, and race officials looked forward to a celebration—the following year, 1994, would be the 25th edition of the New York City Marathon.

---

## RECORD-SETTING PACES

### New York City Marathon Records

| Mile | Elapsed Time (Juma Ikangaa) | Elapsed Time (Lisa Ondieki) |
|---|---|---|
| | 5:11 | 6:10 |
| | 9:49 | 11:16 |
| | 14:45 | 16:34 |
| | 19:36 | 14:30 |
| | 24:20 | 19:20 |
| | 28:59 | 27:33* |
| | 33:47 | 32:40 |
| | 38:39 | 37:59 |
| | 43:36 | 43:31 |
| | 48:27 | 48:57 |
| | 53:24 | 53:12 |
| | 58:13 | 58:02 |
| | 1:03:12 | 1:04:34 |
| | 1:08:24 | 1:10:59 |
| | 1:12:49 | 1:15:43 |
| | 1:17:39 | 1:21:14 |
| | 1:22:28 | 1:27:04 |
| | 1:27:23 | 1:32:22 |
| | 1:32:07 | 1:38:53 |
| | 1:36:51 | 1:44:31 |
| | 1:41:36 | 1:44:14 |
| | | 2:14:14 |
| | 2:08:01* | 2:24:40* |

### World Records

| Elapsed Time (Belayneh Dinsamo) | Elapsed Time (Ingrid Kristiansen) |
|---|---|
| 4:50 | 5:22 |
| 10:45 | |
| 14:30 | 16:08 |
| 19:20 | 21:31 |
| 24:11 | 26:54 |
| | |
| 2:06:50 | 2:21:06 |

*times estimated by extrapolation*

---

---

> "At 21 miles it hit me like a bolt of lightning. The wall. My love-hate relationship with the marathon developed over the last 5 miles. All I know is the enormous emotion with the marathon was as great as winning seven Wanamaker Miles back-to-back."
>
> — EAMONN COGHLAN
> AFTER RUNNING NEW YORK IN 1991, HIS FIRST AND LAST MARATHON

**AVANT-PROPOS** Le marathon de New York City ne cesse de me surprendre. Chaque année c'est la même chose : je n'en crois pas mes yeux. C'est une manifestation extraordinairement inspirante. Les coureurs de New York et d'ailleurs ont créé un marathon épique qui est l'un des plus beaux témoignages qui soient du produit de la coopération fraternelle. C'est vraiment un jour de magie urbaine.

Le pape Jean-Paul II a dit que le marathon de New York City était « un évènement fantastique » lorsque je l'ai rencontré en 1982. Et cet évènement fantastique ne serait pas réel sans son exceptionnel directeur technique, Allan Steinfeld, l'équipe infatigable du club, les mille trois cent bénévoles qui nous aident et divers services municipaux. Ce travail d'équipe réalisé littéralement par des millions de gens qui ne se connaissent pas est le miracle derrière chacun des vingt-cinq marathons de New York. En tant que directeur de course, j'ai eu la chance d'arriver au bon endroit – New York – au bon moment, lorsque la popularité de la course à pied a atteint son sommet.

Le marathon de New York City est un tremplin pour les athlètes de classe internationale, mais des coureurs de tout âge y participent, quels que soient leur ambition et leurs niveau. Nous avons reçu la participation de coureurs de chaque état des Etats-Unis et de plus de cent pays du monde, une preuve de plus, s'il en fallait, de la camaraderie qui règne dans ce sport.

Le nombre de demandes de participation est tel qu'on pourrait facilement faire deux marathons par an ! Lorsque j'ai couru moi-même en 1992, l'expérience était exactement comme on me l'avait décrite. Le marathon à travers les cinq « boroughs » de New York City est une épreuve tout simplement inoubliable. **– Fred Lebow**

**PRÉFACE** S'il me fallait choisir l'évènement qui a le plus changé ma vie, ce serait certainement le marathon de New York City. Malgré mes records du monde en course de fond, j'étais pratiquement inconnue hors de Norvège avant de remporter le marathon de New York City en 1978. Au lieu de prendre ma retraite de la compétition comme prévu, je me suis retrouvée avec un titre de championne du monde, une médaille olympique, six classements de numéro un dans des marathons du monde entier, une autobiographie, des visites à la Maison Blanche, des milliers de nouveaux amis et neuf couronnes de laurier du marathon de New York City.

Tout le monde est gagnant au marathon. On a tous la même sensation sur la ligne de départ: on est nerveux, angoissé, excité. C'est une expérience bien plus vaste, bien plus riche et, malgré les vingt-sept mille concurrents, bien plus intime que les épreuves de course en stade. New York est le marathon que tous les grands noms de la course de fond veulent gagner. Mais ça a aussi été le cadre de beaucoup d'histoires exceptionnelles sur le plan humain, bien plus que n'importe quelle autre manifestation sportive. On n'a pas besoin d'avoir remporté le marathon neuf fois pour ressentir cette chaleur bien particulière du marathon de New York City. Tant d'autres courses se sont inspirées de ce sentiment ; et pourtant aucune autre manifestation ne produit le type d'enthousiasme ou d'excitation qui caractérisent le marathon de New York City. C'est ça qu'on ne pourra jamais copier.

Je suis très reconnaissante qu'on m'ait invitée à faire partie de cette fête, et je reviendrai toujours encourager les coureurs dans cette ville qui m'a tant encouragée. Le marathon de New York City a tellement à offrir : c'est une lumière qui brillera toujours. **– Grete Waitz**

**INTRODUCTION** Trois amis de l'université et moi-même occupions un petit bungalow au bord d'un lac isolé du New Hampshire. Nous étions en septembre et nous faisions de la voile - assez mal je dois dire. L'après-midi de ce jour-là, au grand dam de mes amis, je suis rentré m'asseoir devant un poste de télé aux images granuleuses. Sur l'écran brumeux, j'arrivai à peine à distinguer Frank Shorter qui venait de remporter le marathon des Jeux Olympiques de Munich en 1972. Les américains se passionnaient plutôt pour le football américain, mais j'avais suivi la carrière de Shorter, cet ancien de Yale, et je pensais qu'il était capable de décrocher l'or sur les 26,2 miles. Les répercussions, à mon avis, seraient immenses.

Elles le furent en effet, bien qu'il fallut encore quelques progrès avant qu'on parle de boom de la course à pied aux Etats-Unis, un boom causé aussi par la prise de conscience collective que la course d'endurance était bonne pour la forme physique. Le premier pas fut fait en 1975 par Bill Rodgers, un coureur aux manières les plus simples qui remporta le marathon de Boston avec le temps record en Amérique de 2 h 09 mn et 55 s.

En 1976 à Montréal, Shorter ajouta à sa médaille d'or de 1972 une médaille d'argent. Les américains virent le finlandais Lasse Viren gagner le 5 000 et le 10 000 m, les courses les plus dramatiques des épreuves d'athlétisme. Le succès « double distance » de Viren fit sensation dans le monde de la course.

L'histoire d'un boxeur filmée par Sylvester Stallone, *Rocky*, un film au succès immédiat qui apparut sur les écrans en 1976, plaça soudain la course à pied, presque par accident d'après moi, dans le domaine du grand public. Dans une des scènes les plus mémorables du film, Rocky court jusqu'au grand escalier du Musée d'art moderne de Philadelphie, finissant en haut des marches en une explosion du triomphe personnel de la volonté. Le public n'avait sans doute aucun désir d'entrer dans l'arène contre Apollo Creed, mais le leitmotiv de Rocky, « tenir le coup jusqu'à la fin » toucha une corde sensible et universelle. Finir, quelles que soient les circonstances, comptait donc pour beaucoup. De 1976 à 1978, la musique de *Rocky* était jouée sur pratiquement toutes les lignes d'arrivée des courses d'endurance.

En 1977, le livre de Jim Fixx, *The Complete Book of Running* (Le grand livre de la course à pied) multiplia les rangs des adeptes du sport, le titre faisant même son apparition parmi les listes de livres qui changèrent le mode de vie américain à la fin des années soixante-dix. Le président Jimmy Carter déclara que la course à pied était son sport préféré et que son idole sportive était Bill Rodgers.

En un court laps de temps, la course devint l'un des principaux exercices physiques des américains. Après tout, peu de temps auparavant, dans les années soixante, on pensait généralement que seul le sprint avait une valeur athlétique. Un entraîneur de Nouvelle-Zélande, Arthur Lydiard, se mit à vanter les mérites de la course de fond et les athlètes qu'il entraînait en tirèrent bientôt de grands avantages. Les coureurs du monde entier se mirent à adopter les techniques de Lydiard. Le message parvint même à des coureurs amateurs et le jogging (ou « footing » comme on l'appelait en France) fut bientôt pratiqué dans les rues des grandes villes.

Je fut donc tenté de retourner à la course, mon obsession à l'école, en 1976. Lors d'un vol d'affaire entre Los Angeles et Cleveland, j'ai lu un article par Kenny Moore dans le magazine *Sports Illustrated* sur deux coureurs de fond rivaux, Filbert Bayi de Tanzanie et John Walker de Nouvelle-Zélande. Moore a merveilleusement bien rendu cette lutte où chacun se mesure tout autant à un adversaire qu'il respecte qu'à soi-même, et il a également décrit cette état de sérénité qu'ont les coureurs lorsqu'ils se savent bien préparés. La rivalité Bayi-Walker était d'autant plus passionnante qu'elle montrait comment des athlètes d'origine diverse pouvait se mesurer en course à armes égales. J'ai eu envie de me mettre à courir sur le champ, mais dans l'avion qui montait l'allée aurait été une pente trop forte !

Tout était donc en place, bien que le boom ne battit son plein qu'avec l'apparition de l'évènement clé : le marathon de New York City. Après six ans de croissance constante dans l'espace restreint de Central Park, par un coup de génie la course se transforma en 1976 en un parcours traversant les cinq boroughs et plusieurs dizaines de quartiers bien distincts. La symbiose était parfaite : le boom avait besoin de New York pour prendre une nouvelle dimension, et seul un marathon pouvait montrer toute la splendeur de New York.

La course est d'autant plus étonnante sur le plan humain que nous vivons dans un monde si revêche, si cloisonné. Lorsque Chris Brasher, médaille d'or du steeplechase aux Jeux Olympiques de 1956, a assisté au marathon de New York City en 1979, il n'avait jamais été témoin auparavant d'une telle solidarité forgée par des inconnus entre eux. Impressionné, Brasher suivit l'exemple de New York et inaugura le marathon de Londres en 1981. Pratiquement tous les principaux marathons ayant été institués dans les vingt dernières années ont demandé des conseils au directeur de la course du marathon de New York City, Fred Lebow et à son directeur technique, Allan Steinfeld.

Pour Brasher, le marathon de New York City était « un spectacle de la race humaine heureuse et unie ». Janet Maslin, critique cinématographique du *New York Times*, écrivit dans *Lear's* que la longue chaîne de coureurs et de spectateurs s'allongeant dans les cinq boroughs de New York était un « Woodstock étiré ».

Le marathon de New York City est bien plus qu'une course de fond. Aucune autre manifestation dans tous les Etats-Unis, pas même le Mardi Gras de la Nouvelle-Orléans, ne transforme autant une ville pour une journée. Des millions de new-yorkais s'investissent moralement dans l'attente de cette épopée athlétique de milliers d'hommes et de femmes qu'ils ne connaissent même pas. Dans une ville qui rechigne à tout problème de circulation, tout défilé ou autre visite présidentielle, tout le monde semble ravi de voir passer les marathoniens.

Plus qu'à n'importe quelle autre période de l'année, c'est au cours de la semaine du marathon que New York devient la capitale internationale qu'elle a vocation d'être. A quelle autre occasion pourrait-on voir des suédois en uniforme jaune et bleu assister à un concert de Pete Seeger au soleil du South Street Seaport ? Pendant plusieurs jours, les sept pâtés de maison entre l'hôtel qui sert de quartier général de la course et les parcours de Central Park sont un va-et-vient permanent d'athlètes internationaux.

Grâce au marathon de New York City, l'élite des coureurs de fond est entré sur la sellette internationale. La course a permis à Grete Waitz d'ajouter dix années glorieuses à sa carrière. Bill Rodgers a gagné des marathons dans des pays lointains parce que, dit-il, « il y avait beaucoup plus d'occasions pour moi que pour Frank Shorter. L'univers du marathon est en expansion grâce à New York. Des marathons sont lancés un peu partout. »

Il n'est pas nécessaire d'être un coureur de classe internationale pour absorber l'atmosphère magique de New York qui est, comme Maslin elle-même en a fait l'expérience, « l'un des marathons les plus joviaux et qui accepte tout particulièrement ceux qui sont, comme moi, à vitesse réduite ». Les coureurs se rendent bien compte que les marathoniens, quels que soient leur âge et leur niveau, ont des buts personnels à atteindre : tous les efforts ont droit au respect. Au contraire du basketball, où un tir de pénalité manqué est une honte, les coureurs ne portent aucun jugement entre eux. Miki Gorman, Priscilla Welch, John Campbell, Rae Baymiller et Fritz Mueller – des gens sur qui vous en saurez plus en lisant ce livre – sont tous des athlètes de grande classe ayant brillé à New York passé la quarantaine, alors que dans presque tous les autres sports à cet âge les athlètes ont pris leur retraite depuis longtemps.

Depuis l'avènement récent de la course de fond, les coureurs dame ont pratiquement le même statut que les les hommes, le marathon de New York City ayant été à la pointe des progrès de la course de fond pour dames. C'est à New York que les deux premiers temps officiels en dessous des trois heures, le premier temps en-dessous de deux heures et demi ainsi que quatre records du monde ont été enregistrés. Lorsque le comité olympique international a vu ce que des coureurs comme Grete Waitz, Allison Roe et Patti Lyons Catalano pouvaient faire à New York, un marathon dame fut ajouté au programme olympique grâce aux efforts de plusieurs personnes telles que Nina Kuscsik.

De nombreuses personnes ont joué un rôle clé dans la croissance de cette manifestation incomparable, mais une large part du succès incombe à Fred Lebow, l'ingénieux directeur de course. Il refuse l'épithète de « visionnaire », disant plutôt, « je suis simplement quelqu'un qui fait des projets à l'avance. Mais tous nos projets n'ont pas nécessairement fonctionné. » Le marathon de New York City marche très bien, cependant, bien mieux qu'il ne l'aurait rêvé en 1970 ou 1976.

New York City est une ville qui regorge d'amour-propre, mais aujourd'hui c'est bel et bien la capitale de la course de fond. Il y a vingt-cinq ans, avant le marathon, New York n'aurait pas fait partie des deux cent premières villes pour la course de fond. Le New York Road Runners Club (Club de course de fond de New York), l'organisateur de la manifestation, compte plus de ving-neuf mille membres et organise plus d'une centaine de courses et de stages chaque année. Le siège du club se trouve à une rue du parcours de 3 km autour du réservoir de Central Park, sur lequel courent aux heures de pointe jusqu'à cinq cent coureurs par heure.

Il fallut attendre plusieurs dizaines d'années pour que les Jeux Olympiques modernes aient l'impact athlétique et social que le marathon de New York City obtînt lors de sa première dans les cinq boroughs. La seule manifestation nouvelle d'après-guerre ayant joué aux Etats-Unis un rôle semblable au marathon de New York City est le Superbowl (la grande final du football américain). Mais le football américain n'est pas pratiqué sur tous les continents, et la participation est limitée à quatre-vingt dix hommes plutôt gigantesques.

Le marathon de la ville de New York est un immense spectacle dont la troupe compte vingt-sept mille marathoniens et des spectateurs si nombreux qu'ils sont tous debout le long des dizaines de kilomètres de trottoir. Et si vous voulez voir un spectacle sur Broadway ayant une telle ampleur, montrant New York sous son meilleur angle, et dont les représentations ne sont pas près de finir, alors... vous pouvez toujours courir ! **– Peter Gambaccini**

**PRÓLOGO** Nunca doy por sentado el New York City Marathon. Todos los años me abre los ojos una vez más y me levanta el espíritu. Los neoyorquinos y los corredores visitantes han creado un maratón épico que es un testimonio asombroso del poder que tiene la cooperación humana. Es un día de magia urbana.

Cuando en 1982 visité al Papa Juan Pablo II, él llamó al New York City Marathon "en evento fantástico". Pero la fantasía no sería una realidad sin Allan Steinfeld, el brillante director técnico, sin el incansable personal del club, los trece mil voluntarios dedicados del evento y varios departamentos de la ciudad. Es un milagro que se haya mantenido durante los veinticinco años de nuestro maratón el "trabajo en equipo" que se requiere de literalmente millones de personas, que son verdaderos desconocidos. Como director de la carrera, siento que llegué al lugar apropiado—Nueva York—en el momento adecuado, cuando el correr estaba llegando a la cima de su popularidad.

El New York City Marathon cuenta con atletas de primera, pero en la carrera participan corredores de todas las edades y de todos los niveles de ambición y habilidad. Le hemos dado la bienvenida a por lo menos un representante de cada estado y a participantes de más de cien países—una afirmación verdadera de la camaradería mundial del deporte.

Son tantas las personas que desean participar que fácilmente podríamos realizar dos maratones al año. En 1992, cuando participé en la carrera todo fue exactamente como me habían dicho—el New York City Marathon de los cinco distritos es realmente una experiencia única. **—Fred Lebow**

**PREFACIO** Si tuviera que elegir el evento que cambió mi vida completamente, sin duda elegiría el New York City Marathon. A pesar de mis marcas mundiales en carreras atléticas, era una desconocida en cualquier otra parte del mundo que no fuera Noruega hasta que gané en Nueva York en 1978. En lugar de retirarme de las carreras de competencia como había planeado, obtuve un Campeonato Mundial, una Medalla Olímpica, seis calificaciones como la maratonista número uno del mundo, una autobiografía, visitas a la Casa Blanca, miles de nuevos amigos—y nueve de esas coronas de hojas de laurel del New York City Marathon.

Todos ganan en el maratón. Todos sentimos lo mismo al inicio de la carrera: nervios, ansiedad, emoción. Es la experiencia más amplia, rica e íntima que he tenido durante mi participación en carreras atléticas, a pesar de que hay veintisiete mil personas. El maratón de Nueva York es el maratón que todas las grandes estrellas desean ganar, pero también ha sido el escenario para una variedad de historias humanas, mucho más vastas que cualquier otro evento deportivo. No se tiene que haber ganado nueve veces para sentirse entusiasmado por el resplandor especial del New York City Marathon. Ha sido la inspiración para muchas otras carreras, pero nunca será posible que logren el alborozo y la emoción del original. Nunca se podrá duplicar Nueva York.

Estoy muy agradecida de que se me invitara a participar y siempre regresaré a alentar a los corredores en la ciudad que también me alentó a mí. El New York City Marathon tiene mucho que ofrecer—siempre brillará. **—Grete Waitz**

**INTRODUCCIÓN** Tres compañeros de la universidad y yo nos habíamos asegurado una cabina frente al prístino lago New Hampshire, donde navegamos, más bien de manera inepta, con el viento del mes de septiembre. Esa tarde, ante la incredulidad de mis amigos, me quedé en la cabina para sentarme frente a un televisor con mala recepción. A través de su borrosa pantalla, a duras penas podía distinguir la imagen de Frank Shorter ganando el maratón en las Olimpiadas de Munich de 1972. Los Estados Unidos se relacionaban mejor con una recepción del pase de un tanto de 25 yardas, pero yo había seguido la carrera de Shorter, el hombre de Yale, y supuse que podría ganar la medalla de oro en las 26,2 millas. Y me imaginé que las repercusiones podrían ser gigantescas.

Y como todos sabemos, fueron inmensas, pero se necesitaron unos cuantos pasos más antes de que los norteamericanos pudieran hablar realmente de un auge del correr—una conciencia popular emergente que incluía el mantenerse en forma a través de la carrera de distancia. El primer paso lo dio Bill Rodgers en 1975, un muchacho larguirucho y cohibido que ganó el Maratón de Boston, estableciendo el récord norteamericano de 2:09:55.

En 1976, Shorter agregó una medalla de plata de las Olimpiadas de Montreal a su medalla de oro de 1972. Los norteamericanos también vieron como Lasse Viren de Finlandia ganó los 5000 y 10,000 metros, las carreras más dramáticas entre los eventos atléticos. La "distancia doble" de Viren fue una publicidad sensacional para la carrera.

*Rocky*, la saga sobre un boxeador que no era el favorito para ganar, con Sylvester Stallone, llegó a las pantallas de cine en 1976 y, de acuerdo con mi propia teoría, impulsó el deporte de correr hacia el reino de la cultura popular de una manera inadvertida. En la secuencia más memorable de la película, Rocky termina su larga carrera con un triunfo extasiado en los peldaños superiores del Museo de Arte de Philadelphia. La audiencia no habrá estado ansiosa de pelear contra Apollo Creed, pero el deseo de Rocky de "llegar al final" conmovió a todo el mundo. Simplemente llegar a la meta, cuando fuera y como fuera, era suficiente. De 1976 a 1978, virtualmente en todas las carreras se escuchaba a toda fuerza al tema de *Rocky* en la línea de meta.

En 1977, *The Complete Book of Running* (El libro completo sobre carreras) por Jim Fixx, aumentó el número de corredores de una manera exponencial, surgiendo en las listas de libros como el que más había alterado de una manera significativa la naturaleza de la vida norteamericana en la década de los setenta. El Presidente Jimmy Carter declaró que correr era su deporte favorito y anunció que su atleta preferido era Bill Rodgers.

En un breve período de tiempo, la carrera de distancia pasó al primer lugar entre los tipos de ejercicios que realizaban los norteamericanos. Después de todo, no hace mucho tiempo, en la década de los sesenta, se creía a nivel internacional que solamente la carrera de velocidad tenía algún mérito atlético. Arthur Lydiard, un entrenador de Nueva Zelandia, empezó a predicar los beneficios de una carrera larga y lenta, y los resultados alcanzados por sus atletas fueron testigos de este valor. Los corredores de todo el mundo adoptaron las técnicas de Lydiard, su mensaje llegó a un mayor número de participantes casuales y las calles residenciales se vieron invadidas de personas normales que salían a correr.

En 1976 me convencieron que regresara a correr, mi antigua obsesión escolástica. En el avión, en un viaje de negocios de Los Angeles a Cleveland, leí en *Sports Illustrated* un artículo de Kenny Moore sobre los corredores de milla rivales, Filbert Bayi de Tanzania y John Walker de Nueva Zelandia. Moore capturó perfectamente lo que significaba probarse uno mismo tanto frente a un adversario venerable como frente a los límites de su propia capacidad, y supo comunicar la equanimidad que los corredores logran cuando saben que están preparados. La rivalidad entre Bayi y Walker cautivó fuertemente la atención de todos debido a que demostró que atletas provenientes de ambientes tan diferentes pueden competir en una carrera por igual. Yo sentí el deseo de correr en ese instante y en el lugar donde me encontraba, pero el ángulo del avión convirtió al pasillo en una cuesta arriba amenazante.

Las piezas habían llegado al lugar apropiado, pero el auge de correr fue sólo repentino hasta que un evento principal se convirtió en su punto crucial—el New York City Marathon. Después de seis años de crecimiento constante por los confines del silvestre Central Park, la carrera dio un marcado cambio en 1976 por una ruta que conectaba los cinco distritos y docenas de vecindarios contrastantes. Nada concretó el auge a tal nivel y nada en la era moderna ha mostrado a la Ciudad de Nueva York de una manera más brillante que su maratón.

La carrera es un experimento humano sorprendente, y aún más asombrante en esta era indiferente y subdividida de manera voluntaria. Cuando Chris Brasher, el ganador de la medalla de oro de Gran Bretaña en la carrera de obstáculos en las Olimpiadas de 1956, vio el New York City Marathon en 1979, se sorprendió de la solidaridad forjada por personas totalmente desconocidas. Inspirado por esto, Brasher inauguró el Maratón de Londres en 1981, tomando como ejemplo New York. Virtualmente todo maratón importante que ha surgido durante las últimas dos décadas ha solicitado el aporte de Fred Lebow, director de la carrera de Nueva York, y de Allan Steinfeld, director técnico.

Para Brasher, el maratón de Nueva York fue "una visión de la raza humana, feliz y unida." Para Janet Maslin, crítica de películas, del *New York Times* que escribe en *Lear's*, la larga fila de corredores y los bienquerientes ubicados a lo largo de los cinco distritos fue como un "Woodstock de las carreras." El New York City Marathon es mucho más que una carrera. Ningún otro evento en los Estados Unidos, ni siquiera el Mardi Gras de New Orleans, transforma de una manera tan completa una ciudad por un día. Millones de neoyorquinos invierten su energía de manera positiva y se ven envueltos en los destinos atléticos de miles de hombres y mujeres a quienes nunca han sido presentados de manera formal. En una ciudad que se queja del tráfico, los desfiles y la caravanas presidenciales, todos los habitantes de Nueva York parecen estar sumamente felices al ver pasar a los maratonistas.

Durante la "Semana del Maratón", Nueva York se convierte más que nunca en la capital internacional que se supone representa. Para dar un ejemplo, ¿en qué otra oportunidad se encuentra uno a visitantes suecos con uniformes de carrera de color amarillo y azul escuchando un concierto de Pete Seeger al aire libre en South Street Seaport? Durante varios días, las siete cuadras entre el hotel sede de la carrera y las pistas para correr de Central Park se convierten en una galería internacional de un ir y venir de atletas.

El New York City Marathon llevó lo mejor de la carrera a la vista del público internacional. El certamen extendió la carrera atlética de Grete Waitz durante una gloriosa década adicional. Bill Rodgers ganó maratones en países remotos porque, como él dijo, "Hubo un mayor número de oportunidades para mí que para Frank Shorter. El mundo de los maratones había florecido gracias a Nueva York. Comenzaron a aparecer en todas partes."

Uno no tiene que ser un corredor de clase mundial para absorber la atmósfera mágica de Nueva York, que es, como la misma Maslin experimentó, "uno de los maratones más divertidos y uno que es especialmente tolerante con nosotras, las corredoras que no tenemos mucha velocidad." Los corredores reconocen que los maratonistas de cualquier edad y nivel de habilidad tienen metas personales y triunfos que alcanzar—se celebran todos los esfuerzos. A diferencia del baloncesto, en el que perder un tiro de falta significa culpa, los corredores son personas que no juzgan y que son clementes. Miki Gorman, Priscilla Welch, John Campbell, Rae Baymiller y Fritz Mueller, personas que usted conocerá a través de este libro, son ganadores de marcas mundiales que han brillado en la Ciudad de Nueva York después de los cuarenta años, una edad a la que muchos atletas de otros deportes ya hace tiempo que se han jubilado.

Desde el inicio de este auge, las corredoras han disfrutado una condición casi igual a la de los hombres, y el New York City Marathon ha llevado la vanguardia en lo referente a la carrera de distancia de mujeres. Nueva York fue testigo de los dos primeros maratones sub-3:00 de mujeres, el primero sub-2:30 y de cuatro marcas mundiales. Cuando el Comité Olímpico Internacional vio lo que personas como Grete Waitz, Allison Roe y Patti Lyons Catalano podían hacer en Nueva York, tuvo que añadirse un maratón de mujeres al programa olímpico—especialmente después de un cabildeo intenso por parte de pioneras como Nina Kuscsik que dio a conocer el New York City Marathon.

Muchas personas merecen que se les dé crédito por el crecimiento del incomparable evento, pero antes que nada tenemos que referirnos a Fred Lebow, el industrioso e ingenioso director de la carrera. El evita la denominación que se le da de "visionario", insistiendo en decir "Soy sólo una persona que planea con anticipación. No todo lo que planeamos funciona." El New York City Marathon funciona muy bien y de una manera mucho más espléndida de lo que Lebow predijera en 1970 ó 1976.

La Ciudad de Nueva York tiende a considerarse de un alto nivel, pero hoy día es en realidad la capital mundial de la carrera. Hace veinticinco años, antes del maratón, Nueva York no hubiera figurado entre las primeras doscientas. El New York Road Runners Club, organizador del evento, ha aumentado su número de miembros a más de veintinueve mil y auspicia más de cien competencias y clínicas al año. La sede del club se encuentra a una cuadra de distancia del circuito de 1,6 millas cerca de Central Park Reservoir—durante este período cumbre, la pista es utilizada por quinientos corredores por hora.

Pasaron varias décadas antes de que las Olimpiadas tuvieran el impacto atlético y social que el New York City Marathon logró con su primera realización que abarcó los cinco distritos. En el período posterior a la Segunda Guerra Mundial, el único evento deportivo nuevo que impactó drásticamente en el público norteamericano de la manera que lo hizo el New York City Marathon fue el Super Bowl. Pero este deporte no tiene imitadores en ningún otro continente y la participación está limitada a aproximadamente noventa hombres robustos.

El New York City Marathon es un espectáculo, con un coro de veintisiete mil maratonistas y con espacio para una audiencia que sólo puede permanecer de pie en las aceras a lo largo de millas y millas. El espectáculo musical que ha permanecido en el escenario por más largo tiempo en Nueva York es *The Fantasticks*, pero estos maratonistas son los verdaderos "fantásticos", y su larga carrera, el evento neoyorquino cuya mayor publicidad se la hace la misma carrera, posiblemente nunca tendrá que colocar un aviso de cierre. **—Peter Gambaccini**

**VORWORT** Der New York City Marathon ist für mich nie eine Selbstverständlichkeit. Er ist jedesmal von neuem ein Quell des Neuentdeckens und der Lebensfreude. New Yorker und Besucher mit Freude am Marathonlaufsport haben geradezu ein Epos geschaffen, ein erstaunliches Zeugnis für die Kraft menschlicher Kooperation. Am Veranstaltungstag ist in der ganzen Stadt ein gewisser Zauber zu spüren.

Als ich Papst Johannes Paul II 1982 traf, nannte er den New York City Marathon "ein phantastisches Ereignis". Doch diese Phantasie wäre keine Wirklichkeit geworden, gäbe es nicht den brillanten technischen Leiter, Allan Steinfeld, sowie die unermüdlichen Mitarbeiter des Clubs, die dreizehntausend engagierten Freiwilligen und verschiedenen Stadtämter. Das erforderliche "Teamwork" von buchstäblich Millionen von Fremden grenzt an ein Wunder, das bereits seit fünfundzwanzig Marathonläufen besteht. Ich als Leiter des Wettbewerbs habe das Gefühl, zur richtigen Zeit am richtigen Ort—New York—gelandet zu sein, nämlich damals, als die Populariät des Laufens ihren Höhepunkt erreichte.

Im New York City Marathon können sich Weltklasse-Athleten profilieren, doch genausogut nehmen Läufer aller Altersgruppen mit mehr oder weniger großen Ambitionen und unterschiedlichster Leistungsfähigkeit teil. Bis jetzt konnten wir mindestens einen Vertreter aus allen US-Staaten und Teilnehmer aus über hundert Ländern begrüßen—eine echte Bestätigung der globalen Kameradschaft, die dieser Sport mit sich bringt.

An der Teilnahme sind so viele Leute interessiert, daß wir jedes Jahr problemlos zwei Marathonläufe veranstalten könnten. Als ich 1992 selbst teilnahm, war es genauso, wie man es mir gesagt hatte: der New York City Marathon durch fünf Stadtbezirke ist wirklich ein Erlebnis, das man nur einmal im Leben geboten bekommt. **—Fred Lebow**

**VORWORT** Wenn ich ein Ereignis auswählen müßte, das mein Leben völlig veränderte, dann wäre dies mit Sicherheit der New York City Marathon. Trotz meines Weltrekords beim Wettlaufen war ich außerhalb von Norwegen unbekannt. Doch das änderte sich, als ich 1978 in New York gewann. Und anstatt mich, wie geplant, aus dem aktiven Wettlauf zurückzuziehen, schaffte ich eine Weltmeisterschaft, eine olympische Medaille, sechsmal den ersten Platz bei Weltmarathonläufen, eine Autobiographie, Einladungen zum Weißen Haus, Tausende neuer Freunde—und neun jener Lorbeerkränze vom New York City Marathon.

Bei diesem Marathon gewinnt jeder. Am Start fühlen wir alle dasselbe: wir sind nervös, voller Lampenfieber und Aufregung. Der New York City Marathon ist umfassender, erlebnisreicher und gibt einem —selbst mit siebenundzwanzigtausend Menschen—eine engere gegenseitige Verbundenheit als alles, was ich sonst bei Wettläufen erlebt habe. New York ist der Marathon, den alle großen Laufstars gern gewinnen würden, gleichzeitig ist er jedoch auch der Hintergrund für unzählige menschliche Begebenheiten, die das, was auf anderen Sportveranstaltungen abläuft, bei weitem überflügeln. Man braucht nicht neunmal zu siegen, um die freundliche Atmosphäre des New York City Marathon genießen zu können. Zahlreiche andere Wettläufe sind von diesem Marathon inspiriert worden, doch herrscht dort nie diese einzigartige Beschwingtheit und erregte Erwartung wie beim Original. Es gibt eben kein zweites New York.

Ich bin dankbar, daß man mich zur Teilnahme eingeladen hat, und ich komme immer wieder gern zum Anfeuern von Läufern in die Stadt, die mich angefeuert hat. Der New York City Marathon hat unheimlich viel zu bieten—er wird immer ein glanzvolles Ereignis bleiben. **—Grete Waitz**

**EINFÜHRUNG** Gemeinsam mit drei College-Freunden hatte ich eine Hütte an einem abgeschiedenen See in New Hampshire gemietet, wo wir, recht unbeholfen, im Septemberwind segelten. An diesem Nachmittag zog ich mich in die Hütte zurück, um—zum Staunen meiner Freunde—vor einem verschwommenen Fernsehschirm zu sitzen. Durch den Schnee auf dem Bildschirm konnte ich kaum Frank Shorter ausmachen, der den Marathon bei der Olympiade 1972 in München gewann. Die US-Zuschauer waren mehr daran interessiert, beim Fangen eines Football aus 25 Yard Entfernung für einen Touchdown zuzusehen, aber ich hatte die Karriere des ehemaligen Yale-Studenten Shorter verfolgt und tippte für ihn bei den 26,2 Meilen auf Gold. Und ich vermutete, die Auswirkungen würden gigantisch sein.

Wie wir wissen, war dies der Fall, doch es sollte noch eine Weile dauern, bis man in Amerika wirklich von einem Lauf-Boom sprechen konnte—bis die Masse allmählich bereit war, Fitneß durch Langlauf anzuerkennen. Der erste Schritt in diese Richtung wurde 1975 von Bill Rodgers unternommen, einem aufgeschossenen Kerl voller Gemütsruhe, der den Bostoner Marathon mit einem amerikanischen Rekord von 2.09.55 gewann.

1976 fügte Shorter seiner Goldmedaille von 1972 in Montreal eine olympische Silbermedaille hinzu. Die Amerikaner saßen auch vor den Bildschirmen, als Lasse Viren von Finnland den 5.000- und den 10.000-Meterlauf gewann, die spannendsten Läufe unter den Wettlaufdisziplinen. Virens "Distanzdoppel" stellte sensationelle Werbung für den Wettlauf dar.

Sylvester Stallones Boxfilm *Rocky* mit dem beliebten Underdog-Helden kam 1976 in die Kinos, und verhalf—meiner Meinung nach—ohne besondere Absicht dem Laufen zur Popularität. In der denkwürdigsten Szene des Films beendet Rocky seinen erschöpfenden Lauf in begeisterndem Triumph auf den Stufen des Kunstmuseums von Philadelphia. Das Publikum mag zwar nicht gerade erpicht darauf gewesen zu sein, sich mit Apollo Creed anzulegen, aber Rockys Verlangen, bis zum Ende durchzuhalten, schlug allgemein an. Einfach das Ziel zu erreichen, wann und wo auch immer, zählte. Von 1976 bis 1978 tönte bei praktisch jedem Straßenrennen die *Rocky*-Titelmelodie an der Ziellinie aus den Lautsprechern.

1977 löste das Buch *The Complete Book of Running* (Das komplette Laufbuch) von Jim Fixx eine bislang ungeahnte Laufbegeisterung aus und wurde Teil der Bücherlisten, die den Lebensstil in Amerika in den Siebzigerjahren bedeutend veränderten. Präsident Jimmy Carter erklärte Laufen als seinen Wahlsport und Bill Rodgers zu seinem Lieblingsathleten.

Für kurze Zeit lag das Laufen weiter Strecken an der Spitze der Fitneßübungen Amerikas. Schließlich herrschte bis in die Sechzigerjahre international die Meinung vor, nur anstrengendes Laufen bringe sportlichen Lohn. Ein Trainer in Neuseeland, Arthur Lydiard, begann die Vorteile von ausdauerndem, langsamem Jogging zu predigen, und die Leistungen seiner Athleten waren Zeugnis für den Wahrheitsgehalt dieser Aussage. Läufer in der ganzen Welt machten sich Lydiards Methoden zu eigen, und ganz allmählich drang die Botschaft bis zu den Gelegenheitssporttreibenden vor: in den Siedlungsstraßen traf man immer häufiger auf ganz normale Leute in Jogging-Kluft.

1976 überredete man mich, wieder der Leidenschaft nachzugehen, der ich in meiner Schulzeit gefrönt hatte, und zu laufen. Bei einer Geschäftsreise von Los Angeles nach Cleveland las ich im Flugzeug in *Sports Illustrated* einen von Kenny Moore verfaßten Artikel über seine Laufkonkurrenz, Filbert Bayi von Tansania und John Walker von Neuseeland. Moore kleidete perfekt in Worte, was es bedeutete, sich sowohl an einem verehrungswürdigen Rivalen als auch an den Grenzen der eigenen Leistungsfähigkeit zu messen, und er brachte die Gleichmut bei Läufern zum Ausdruck, die wissen, daß sie gut vorbereitet sind. Die Rivalität zwischen Bayi und Walker war deshalb so fesselnd, weil sich darin manifestierte, daß Athleten mit unterschiedlichster Vorgeschichte bei einem Wettlauf auf gleicher Ebene miteinander konkurrieren können. Am liebsten hätte ich an Ort und Stelle mit dem Laufen begonnen, doch der Anstieg im Laufgang wäre in diesem Moment aufgrund des Flugwinkels unüberwindlich gewesen.

Die Würfel waren gefallen, doch der Lauf-Boom war lediglich ein "Lauf-Boomchen", bis eine Veranstaltung den Kessel zum Kochen brachte: der New York City Marathon. Nach sechs Jahren steten Wachstums innerhalb der Grenzen des baumbewachsenen Central Parks wurde der Lauf 1976 in einem mutigen Schachzug auf eine Route durch fünf Stadtbezirke und Dutzende von unterschiedlichen Wohngegenden verlegt. Dadurch wurde der wahre Boom entfacht, und mit nichts anderem konnte New York City in neuerer Zeit mehr glänzen als mit dem Marathon.

Der Marathonlauf ist ein erstaunliches menschliches Experiment, umso verwunderlicher angesichts der reizbaren, absichtlich zerrissenen Atmosphäre dieser Ära. Als der Brite Chris Brasher, der bei der Olympiade 1956 die Goldmedaille im Hindernislauf gewann, 1979 dem New York City Marathon zusah, hatte er nie zuvor eine solche Solidarität unter Wildfremden gesehen. Davon inspiriert führte Brasher 1981 den Londoner Marathon nach New Yorker Muster ein. Praktisch jeder große Marathon, der in den letzten zwei Jahrzehnten auf der Bildfläche erschien, orientierte sich umfassend an der Erfahrung des New Yorker Marathonleiters Fred Lebow und technischen Leiters Allan Steinfeld.

Für Brasher war der New York City Marathon "eine Vision der glücklich vereinten Menschheit". Die Filmkritikerin der *New York Times*, Janet Maslin, schrieb in *Lear's*, der sich durch fünf Stadtbezirke erstreckende Faden von Läufern und Fans sei "ein sehniges Woodstock". Der New York City Marathon ist wesentlich mehr als ein Straßenrennen. Kein einziges Ereignis in den USA, nicht einmal der Mardi Gras von New Orleans, verändert eine Stadt für einen Tag so tiefgreifend. Millionen von New Yorkern setzen ihre Energien positiv ein und lassen sich von den Athleten-Schicksalen von Tausenden von Männern und Frauen mitreißen, denen sie nicht einmal vorgestellt wurden. In einer Stadt, die über Verkehr, Umzüge und Präsidentenkolonnen murrt, scheint jeder begeistert zu sein, wenn die Marathonläufer vorbeitraben.

Während der "Marathonwoche" wird New York mehr als zu jedem anderen Zeitpunkt tatsächlich zu der internationalen Metropole, als die es sich gern darstellen läßt. Wann sonst, um ein Beispiel zu geben, trifft man auf Schweden in gelbblauen Lauftrikots, die im South Street Seehafen bei Sonnenschein einem Pete Seeger Konzert beiwohnen? Einige Tage lang bilden die sieben Häuserblocks zwischen dem Hotel, in dem die Laufleitung untergebracht ist, und den Laufwegen des Central Parks eine internationale Arkade ständig hin- und her pendelnder Athleten.

Der New York City Marathon brachte Spitzenläufer ins globale Rampenlicht. Der Lauf verlängerte Grete Waitz' Karriere um ein weiteres glorreiches Jahrzehnt. Bill Rodgers gewann Marathonläufe in fernen Ländern, weil, wie er sagte "dort mehr Möglichkeiten für mich bestanden als für Frank Shorter. Seit New York blüht der Marathonlauf auf. Und zwar überall".

Man braucht kein Läufer der Weltklasse zu sein, um die magische Atmosphäre von New York genießen zu können, die, wie Maslin selbst miterlebte, "eine der beschwingtesten Marathonatmosphären darstellt und die besonders uns Geschwindigkeitsbehinderten gegenüber voller Toleranz ist". Läufer schätzen die persönlichen Ziele und Triumphe von Marathonteilnehmern aller Altersgruppen und Leistungsstufen—Hut ab vor jedem Versuch! Im Gegensatz zu Basketball, wo eine verpaßte Gelegenheit zu Schimpf und Schande führt, sind Läufer ein überaus tolerantes Völkchen. Miki Gorman, Priscilla Welch, John Campbell, Rae Baymiller und Fritz Mueller —Menschen, denen Sie in diesem Buch begegnen—glänzten beispiellos in New York City im Alter von über vierzig, einem Alter, in dem Athleten anderer Sportarten sich schon lange aus dem aktiven Sport zurückgezogen haben.

Seit dem Boom genossen Läuferinnen fast ebenbürtigen Status mit ihren männlichen Kollegen; der New York City Marathon war bahnbrechend für den Frauen-Langlauf. New York war Zeuge bei den ersten offiziellen Marathonläufen, die von Frauen unter 3 Stunden bewältigt wurden, dem ersten Lauf unter 2.5 Stunden und vier Weltrekorden. Als das internationale olympische Komitee sah, was Frauen wie Grete Waitz, Allison Roe und Patti Lyons Catalano in New York erreichten, mußten sie einen Frauenmarathon in die Olympiade einbauen—insbesondere nach intensiven Lobby-Bemühungen seitens Pionieren wie Nina Kuscsik, die den New York City Marathon auf den Plan gerufen hatte.

Vielen gebührt Lob für das Wachstum dieser unvergleichlichen Veranstaltung, doch müssen wir es als erstes dem emsigen und findigen Marathonleiter, Fred Lebow, zugestehen, der das Attribut "Visionär" von sich weist und darauf besteht, nur ein Mensch zu sein, der vorplant. "Nicht alles, was wir planen, funktioniert". Dank des großen Engagements funktioniert der New York City Marathon jedoch recht gut, wesentlich besser als Lebow 1970 oder 1976 hätte vorhersehen können.

New York City tendiert dazu, sich selbst große Achtung zu zollen, doch heute ist es in der Tat die Laufmetropole der Welt. Vor fünfundzwanzig Jahren—vor dem Marathon—zählte New York nicht einmal zu den oberen zweihundert Städten. Die Mitgliederzahl des New York Road Runners Club, Organisator der Veranstaltung, wuchs auf über neunundzwanzigtausend an und sponsert mehr als einhundert Wettläufe und Seminare pro Jahr. Der Hauptsitz des Clubs liegt einen Häuserblock vom 1,6 Meilen langen Ring um den Central Park entfernt, und während der Spitzenzeiten drehen auf diesem Ring fünfhundert Läufer pro Stunde die Runde.

Es dauerte mehrere Jahrzehnte, bis die Olympiade die sportlichen und sozialen Auswirkungen vorweisen konnte, die der New York City Marathon schon bei seiner ersten Durchquerung von fünf Stadtbezirken zuwege brachte. In der Zeit nach dem 2. Weltkrieg hat nur noch der Super Bowl als neues Sportereignis die amerikanische Landschaft so drastisch beeinflußt wie der New York City Marathon. Doch im Gegensatz zum Marathon findet Football nicht auf der ganzen Welt Nachahmung, und die Teilnahme ist auf ca. neunzig Männer von großer Statur beschränkt.

Der New York City Marathon ist eine Show mit siebenundzwanzigtausend "Schauspielern" und einem Stehpublikum, das Meile um Meile auf den Gehwegen entlang der Laufstrecke ausharrt. *The Fantasticks* war das am längsten gespielte Musical in New York, doch die eigentlichen "Fantastischen" sind die Marathonläufer, und für deren Langlauf—die beste Reklame für New York City—fällt wohl kaum je der letzte Vorhang. **—Peter Gambaccini**

**PREMESSA** Per me non c'è nulla di scontato nella Maratona di New York City. Ogni anno mi fa riaprire gli occhi e mi esalta. I newyorchesi e i maratoneti ospiti sono stati capaci di creare una maratona epica, testimonianza straordinaria del potere della cooperazione umana. È una giornata di magia metropolitana.

Durante il nostro incontro del 1982, Papa Giovanni Paolo II ha chiamato la maratona di New York "un evento fantastico". La fantasia non potrebbe avverarsi senza la brillante regia tecnica di Allan Steinfeld, l'instancabile staff del club, i 13.000 volontari e i vari assessorati cittadini. Il lavoro di gruppo da parte di letteralmente milioni di persone che non si conoscono è il miracolo che ha permesso di attuare 25 edizioni della nostra maratona. Quale direttore della corsa, mi sento di essere giunto al posto giusto – New York – al momento giusto, quando la popolarità della corsa era al culmine.

La maratona di New York City mette in mostra atleti di classe mondiale, ed allo stesso tempo accoglie corridori di ogni età, ambizione e capacità. Siamo stati onorati dalla presenza di almeno un rappresentante per ogni stato e da partecipanti di più di cento paesi – un'affermazione concreta del rapporto di fraternità che unisce chi pratica questo sport in tutto il mondo.

Ci sono così tante persone che vogliono partecipare che potremmo facilmente svolgere due maratone ogni anno. Quando io stesso ho preso parte alla gara nel 1992, è stato esattamente come mi avevano detto tutti: la maratona che attraversa cinque quartieri di New York City è una esperienza da ricordare tutta la vita. **– Fred Lebow**

**PREFAZIONE** Se dovessi scegliere un episodio che ha cambiato completamente la mia vita, sceglierei certamente la maratona di New York City. Nonostante i miei record mondiali su pista, ero un perfetto sconosciuto al di fuori della Norvegia fino a quando non vinsi a New York nel 1978. Invece di ritirarmi dalla corsa professionistica, come avevo pianificato, sono finito con un campionato del mondo, una medaglia olimpica, sei volte al primo posto nella classifica di maratone mondiali, un'autobiografia, inviti alla Casa Bianca, migliaia di nuovi amici – e nove corone d'alloro della maratona di New York City.

Alla maratona vincono tutti. Alla linea di partenza proviamo tutti le stesse emozioni – nervosismo, ansia, eccitazione. È un'esperienza più vasta, più ricca e (nonostante le 27.000 persone) più intima che non quella di correre in pista. La maratona di New York City è un evento che tutte le star dello sport vogliono vincere, ma è anche il palcoscenico, incomparabilmente più vasto di qualsiasi altro evento sportivo, di una varietà di esperienze umane. Non è necessario essere nove volte campione per essere toccati dal calore della maratona di New York City. Anche se questa gara ha ispirato tante altre corse, nessuna potrà raggiungere i livelli di appassionata esaltazione di quella originale. New York non ha eguali.

Sono grato di essere stato invitato a farne parte e ritornerò sempre a fare il tifo per i corridori nella città che ha fatto il tifo per me. La maratona di New York City ha così tanto da offrire che brillerà per sempre nell'universo dello sport. **– Grete Waitz**

**INTRODUZIONE** Avevo preso in affitto, insieme a tre colleghi universitari, una baita su un immacolato lago del New Hampshire, su cui andavamo in barca a vela, in maniera piuttosto dilettantistica, nel vento di settembre. Quel pomeriggio, fra lo stupore dei miei amici, lo passai al chiuso, seduto davanti allo schermo sfocato del televisore. Attraverso le ombre opache, si vedeva a stento l'immagine di Frank Shorter che vinceva la maratona delle Olimpiadi di Monaco del 1972. Per un americano è certo più facile capire un passaggio di 25 metri nel football; io, però, avevo seguito la carriera di Shorter, laureato di Yale, e avevo immaginato che avrebbe potuto strappare la medaglia d'oro al miglio 26,2. E pensavo che le conseguenze sarebbero state di portata colossale.

E lo sono state, come ora sappiamo, ma sarebbero stati ancora necessari altri passi prima che gli americani potessero parlare onestamente di un boom della corsa – una coscienza di massa emergente, che avrebbe abbracciato il perseguimento della forma fisica attraverso la corsa di resistenza. Il primo passo venne fatto nel 1975 da Bill Rodgers, un tipo smilzo, per il quale tutto era "oh, un'inezia", che vinse la maratona di Boston, stabilendo un record statunitense in 2:09:55.

Nel 1976, alle Olimpiadi di Montreal, Shorter aggiunse senza sforzo una medaglia d'argento alla medaglia d'oro del 1972. Gli americani seguirono con attenzione anche le corse vittoriose del finlandese Lasse Viren, nei 5.000 e nei 10.000 metri, le più spettacolari fra tutte le gare su pista. Il doppio distacco di Viren valse come pubblicità sensazionale per la corsa.

La saga di un campione di pugilato in cerca di rimonta, interpretata da Sylvester Stallone in *Rocky*, arrivò nelle sale cinematografiche nel 1976 e, a mio parere, senza volere proiettò la corsa nel regno della cultura di massa. Nella sequenza più memorabile del film, Rocky conclude la lunga corsa, in un trionfo estatico, sui gradini del Museum of Art di Boston. Il pubblico non era necessariamente ansioso di battere Apollo Creed, ma il desiderio di Rocky di "andare fino in fondo" colpì nel segno. Il semplice arrivare fino alla fine, in qualsiasi situazione e a qualsiasi costo, diventò importante. Dal 1976 al 1978 in quasi ogni corsa, al traguardo veniva trasmesso il motivo conduttore di *Rocky*.

Nel 1977 il libro di Jim Fixx *The Complete Book of Running* valse ad espandere le schiere dei corridori in modo esponenziale, entrando di diritto nell'elenco dei libri che nel modo più significativo hanno modificato lo stile di vita americano negli anni settanta. Il presidente Jimmy Carter dichiarò che la corsa era il suo sport preferito e che il suo atleta preferito era Bill Rodgers.

In breve tempo, la corsa di resistenza arrivò alla ribalta dell'esercizio fisico negli Stati Uniti. Fino agli anni sessanta, dopo tutto, si credeva a livello internazionale che solo la velocità avesse meriti atletici. Un allenatore in Nuova Zelanda Arthur Lydiard, cominciò a predicare i benefici del footing, lento e su lunghi percorsi, e i suoi atleti ottennero risultati che provarono la fondatezza della sua teoria. Corridori di tutto il mondo adottarono le tecniche di Lydiard; gradualmente il suo messaggio filtrò negli strati dei partecipanti dilettanti e le strade delle città si affollarono di gente comune in tenuta da corsa.

Nel 1976 mi persuasi a ritornare alla corsa, la mia ossessione degli anni di scuola. Durante un viaggio d'affari da Los Angeles a Cleveland, lessi su "Sports Illustrated" un articolo di Kenny Moore su due maratoneti rivali, Filbert Bayi della Tanzania e John Walker della Nuova Zelanda. Moore espresse perfettamente il significato che ha il misurarsi sia con un avversario di valore, sia contro i limiti delle proprie possibilità, e riuscì a comunicare la serenità che raggiungono i corridori quando sanno di essere pronti. La rivalità fra Bayi e Walker era così affascinante perché mostrava che atleti provenienti da esperienze diverse potevano competere in una gara su basi di uguaglianza. In quel momento pensai di mettermi a correre lì per lì, ma l'inclinazione dell'aereo rendeva il corridoio una salita proibitiva.

Tutti i pezzi del mosaico erano a posto, ma il boom della corsa era ancora un fenomeno minore fino a quando un evento chiave lo fece esplodere: la maratona di New York City. Dopo sei anni di crescita regolare all'interno del Central Park, nel 1976 si decise di spostare la corsa su un percorso che collegava cinque quartieri e decine di aree diverse. Nulla ha dato impulso al boom in tale maniera e nulla, nell'epoca moderna, ha messo in mostra New York City in maniera così brillante come la maratona.

La corsa è un tale stupefacente esperimento umano, ancor più stupefacente in questa epoca di divisioni e volontari frazionamenti. Nel 1979, quando fu spettatore della maratona di New York City, Chris Brasher, medaglia d'oro olimpica del Regno Unito nella corsa campestre, non aveva mai visto tanta solidarietà messa in atto fra perfetti sconosciuti. Inspirato da questa esperienza, Brasher inaugurò la maratona di Londra nel 1981, rifacendosi a quella di New York. Praticamente tutte le altre maratone sbocciate qua e là negli ultimi due decenni hanno ottenuto un qualche contributo dal direttore di gara Fred Lebow e dal direttore tecnico Allan Steinfeld.

Per Brasher la maratona di New York City era una "visione del genere umano, felice e unito". Per il critico cinematografico del "New York Times", Janet Maslin, che scriveva sul "Lear's", la lunga fila di corridori e tifosi, che si snodava per cinque quartieri, era una "vigorosa Woodstock". La maratona di New York City è molto di più di una corsa su strada. Non c'è evento negli Stati Uniti (neppure il Martedì grasso di New Orleans) che riesca a trasformare così radicalmente, per tutto un giorno, l'intera città. Milioni di newyorchesi si appassionano ai destini di migliaia di uomini e donne a cui non sono stati presentati prima. In una città che mugugna per il traffico, le sfilate e i cortei presidenziali, tutti sembrano entusiasti e felici di vedere passare la maratona.

Più che in ogni altra occasione, è proprio durante la settimana della maratona che New York diventa la capitale internazionale che sostiene di essere. Quando mai, per fare un esempio, si possono vedere degli svedesi con le loro tute gialle e blu, che sotto il sole guardano un concerto di Pete Seeger a South Street Seaport? Per diversi giorni, nei sette isolati fra l'albergo quartier generale della corsa e le piste di Central Park non si vede che l'andirivieni di atleti di tutti i paesi.

La maratona di New York City ha messo l'élite dei corridori sotto i riflettori di tutto il mondo. La gara ha allungato la carriera di Grete Waitz di un'altra gloriosa decina d'anni. Bill Rodgers ha vinto maratone in paesi lontani perché, ha detto, "a me si sono presentate più occasioni che non a Frank Shorter. Il mondo della maratona è esploso con New York. Sono nate maratone ovunque".

Non è necessario essere uno dei migliori corridori del mondo per assorbire l'atmosfera magica di New York che, come ha potuto sperimentare Maslin stessa "ha più di molte altre maratone un carattere amabile e riesce a tollerare anche chi, come noi, non va molto veloce". I corridori apprezzano il fatto che maratoneti di qualsiasi età e grado si pongano degli obiettivi personali da raggiungere – tutti gli sforzi sono lodati. A differenza della pallacanestro, in cui un canestro mancato attira le critiche, il mondo della corsa non giudica e sa perdonare. Miki Gorman, Priscilla Welch, John Campbell, Rae Baymiller e Fritz Mueller – tutti atleti che troverete in questo libro – hanno tutti brillato come campioni mondiali a New York City dopo i quaranta, un'età in cui atleti in altri sport sono da tempo in pensione.

Sin dall'inizio del boom, le donne sono state trattate alla pari degli atleti maschi e la maratona di New York City è stata all'avanguardia delle corse di resistenza femminili. New York è stato il teatro delle prime due maratone ufficiali con donne sotto le 3 ore, della prima sotto le 2:30 e di quattro record mondiali. Quando ha visto di cosa sono state capaci persone come Grete Waitz, Allison Roe e Patti Lyons Catalano in New York, il comitato olimpico internazionale non ha potuto che aggiungere la maratona femminile alle Olimpiadi – specialmente viste le enormi pressioni da parte di pionieri quali Nina Kuscsik, che aveva assicurato alla maratona di New York City un posto nella storia.

A molti va il merito di aver contribuito all'affermazione di questo evento senza pari, ma il primo posto spetta senza dubbio all'attivo e geniale direttore di gara, Fred Lebow, che si rifiuta di essere chiamato "visionario" e dice: " Sono solo una persona che pianifica in anticipo. Non tutto quello che viene pianificato funziona". Invece la maratona di New York City funziona benissimo, non c'è che dire, molto meglio di quanto Lebow avesse previsto nel 1970 o 1976.

New York City tende ad avere una grande opinione di sé. Ma oggi non si può negare che sia veramente la capitale mondiale della corsa. Venticinque anni fa, prima della maratona, New York non sarebbe entrata fra le prime duecento in classifica. Il New York Road Runners Club, organizzatore dell'evento, ha ormai oltre 29.000 soci e sponsorizza più di cento gare e corsi di addestramento ogni anno. La sede centrale del club è situata ad un isolato di distanza dal circuito di 1,6 miglia intorno a Central Park Reservoir, che nelle ore di punta è percorso da cinquecento corridori l'ora.

Ci sono volute diverse decine di anni perché le Olimpiadi avessero sul piano atletico e sociale lo stesso impatto che ha avuto la maratona di New York City nella versione dei cinque quartieri. Dopo la seconda guerra mondiale, il solo altro evento sportivo che abbia lasciato il segno nel panorama degli Stati Uniti, oltre alla maratona di New York City, è il Super Bowl, la finale del campionato nazionale di football americano. Si tratta però di una gara che non ha imitatori in tutti i continenti e alla quale non partecipano più di una novantina di uomini muscolosi.

La maratona di New York City è un vero spettacolo, con una troupe di 27.000 maratoneti e spettatori assiepati per miglia e miglia sui marciapiedi. Il musical più replicato a New York è *The Fantasticks*, ma i veri "fantastici" sono questi maratoneti; la loro lunga corsa, la migliore pubblicità per la stessa New York, non corre alcun rischio di essere messa fuori cartellone.

**– Peter Gambaccini**

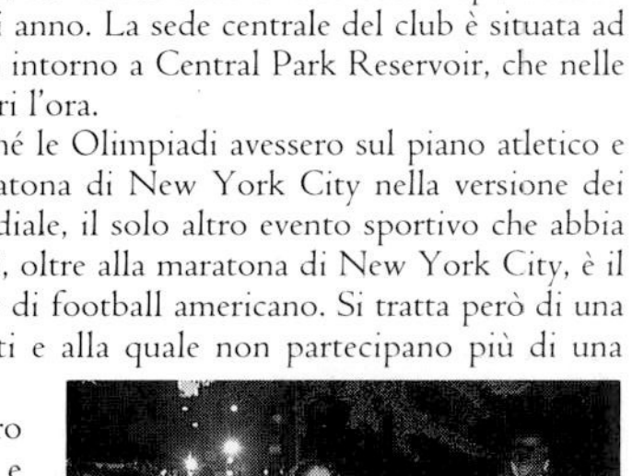

The New York Road Runners Club would like to thank the sponsors of the New York City Marathon, without whom the event would never be possible:

Major sponsors:

Mercedes-Benz

CHEMICAL

John Hancock

asics

BFI Waste Services

The Rudin Family

Runner's World

Supporting sponsors:
Advil
The Gatorade Company
Seiko
Tiffany & Co.
Trevira Carpeting Hoechst Celanese
Vermont Pure Natural Spring Water

Library of Congress Cataloging-in-Publication Data

Gambaccini, Peter
The New York City Marathon: Twenty-Five Years
Foreword by Fred Lebow; Preface by Grete Waitz; Text by Peter Gambaccini; Edited by Charles Miers.
p.    cm.
"Published in association with the New York Road Runners Club, Inc."
ISBN 0-8478-1815-2
1. New York City Marathon, New York, N.Y.—History. I. Miers, Charles. II. Title.
GV1065.22.N49G36        1994        94-10396
796.42'5097471—dc20
CIP

Cover photo © 1993 duomo
Half-title page © 1988 duomo, David Madison
Title page © 1984 Janeart
Table of contents (clockwise from top) © 1986 duomo;
© 1990 David Getlen; © Todd France; © Ken Levinson;
© Scott Halleran; © 1988 Will Cofnuk
Endpapers courtesy of James F. Behr

Edited by Jen Bilik

Distributed by St. Martin's Press

Printed in Japan

4 DEC: 74 JERSEY SHORE Marann. 88/2000
NEW P.R. **Monday** 2:48:31 strong temp in hi
30s to 40s, strong head wind on way out, Pam &
mom & myself, Wind no much. on way ap, ran in
NIKE ELITES & felt OK, took Signidenergysmnt
take G.S. PKmy to Exit 102 (south), went gotta
thru out race, everyone in family had a good
time, Sean is a pisser, le expires me as I do
my warm-ups, i; TOE touching & various
stretching; Roast Buffet w/ Pam & Sean after dinner. last night went

12 FEB 78 NEWARK DIST. Run. 12 Mi.      103/150
NK. NJ. **Tuesday**       1:11:21  Italian food n/s
B/fld egg, sick n dog, still ran here.
take BHW w/ Pam Sean mom are & me
took first new shoes from Pam for Q: day
Burke Vantage (#1 in runners world), Ma
stayed home & cooked Turkey, Sean still
doing my warm up & getting Mummy
comments from Preview.     B+day.

5 MARCH 1978 - Maximum M.A.A. 166 wind cw-Ø.
**Wednesday** cold as hell, 5mm N5.
G.S. to Ex. t 117 to 520 WEST, NICE race, Pam
Sean & J. 2:48:26. cold & icy & snowy conditions
LOST around 7 min due to street. came in 4 ½
lot in age gp, won trophy, got mixed a huge
30, kids who came went to McDonalds by hn
nice day for mc. & a good race. Sean is
up & everyone gets a big Kicle